# THE CHRONICLES OF ELSEWHEN

## MARSHALL MILLER

**BLUE FORGE PRESS**

Port Orchard ⚙ Washington

This collection is dedicated not only to my publisher, Jennifer, my editor, Brianne, my friends, and my furry family, but also to all those readers and writers who know there are other universes out there. Just ask Michio Kaku. And Kitsap Literary Artists and Writers. They *know*!

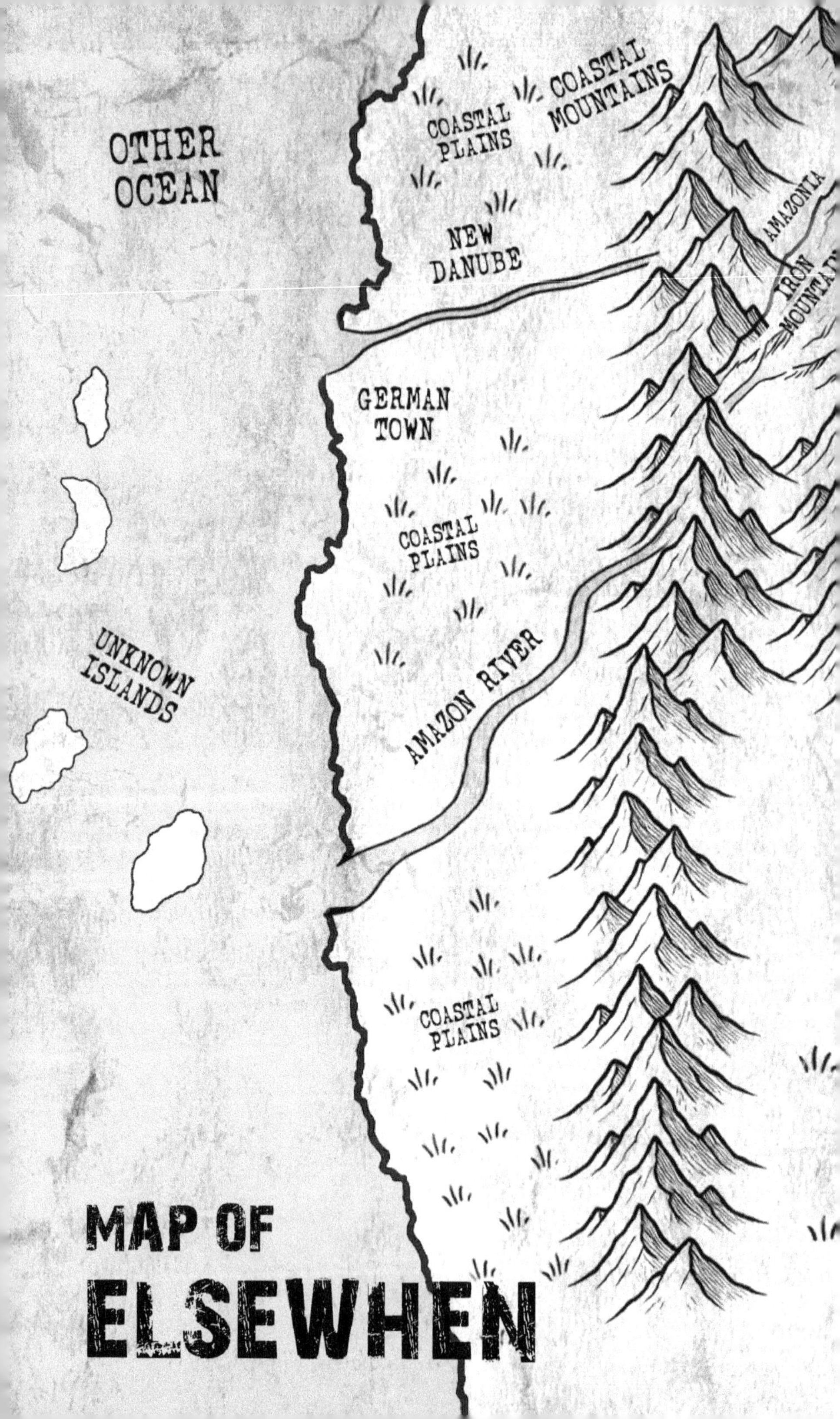

OTHER OCEAN
COASTAL PLAINS
COASTAL MOUNTAINS
NEW DANUBE
AMAZONIA
IRON MOUNTAINS
GERMAN TOWN
COASTAL PLAINS
UNKNOWN ISLANDS
AMAZON RIVER
COASTAL PLAINS
MAP OF
ELSEWHEN

NORTH DESERT
HIGH PLAINS
AMAZONIA
LOW MOUNTAINS
SNAKE RIVER
MOUNTAIN FOREST
GIANT MONITOR LIZARDS
DRAG
DRAGONS
SNAKE LAKE
TRIBUTARIES
FREE TOWN
SCRUB FOREST
SHERWOOD FOREST
SMALL DESERT
DRY PLAINS
GREAT TRASH HEAP
SOUTH DESERT

CHINA RANGE
NORTHERN HIGH PLAINS
YANGSTE RIVER
NEW BEIJING
GREAT ROA
CENTRAL MOUNTAINS
FOREST
DRAGONS
DRAGONS
IRONWOOD FOREST
CENTRAL PLAINS
LOW FOREST BRUSH
NEW MISSISSIPPI
TURTLE MOUNTAIN
SOUTHERN MOUNTAINS
PLAINS
BADLANDS

NEW BRUNSWICK
SKINNY RIVER
FISHING TOWNS
SOUTHERN MOUNTAINS
GREAT OCEAN
CHINA
CHINESE PASS
COASTAL PLAINS
GREAT RIVER
NEW CAMELOT
LESSER BARRIER ISLANDS
COASTAL PLAINS
MAN PASS
GREAT SOUTHERN RIVER
NEW ROME
BARRIER ISLAND
COASTAL PLAINS
SOUTH ISLAND

# MORE BY THE AUTHOR

## SPECIAL AGENT KIM KUPAR NOVELS

Jade Eyes
They
The Why Files

## THE TSCHAAA INFESTATION

Book 1: The Gathering Storm
Book 2: The Tsunami
Book 3: Typhoon of Steel
Free Range Protocol: Tales of the Tschaaa
Beyond the Great Compromise: Tales of the Tschaaa
Survivors: Escaping the Tschaaa

## ANTHOLOGIES

Monstrosity (Unnerving Anthology)
Descent (Unnerving Anthology)
Wicked (Unnerving Anthology)
Phobia (Unnerving Anthology)
The Mighty Pen
Unconditional
Cascadia
Tales of the Slug
Super: Unexpected Heroes Arise

## COLLECTED WORKS & MORE

Inhumanity: A Year of Stories
The Island (The Haunting of Orchard House)
Shane (Angels of Anarchy)

# The Chronicles of Elsewhen

## Marshall Miller

# 1
# THE BEGINNNING

The man trudged ever closer to his once distant goal. It had not been an easy trek. The man started in a low and hot desert, progressed to a more refreshing high desert environment, and was nearing a green patch of foothills attached to an unknown mountain range. At least the name of the mountains was unknown to the traveler. The one fact that Jack Hays knew was that the green he could see bespoke of vegetation. And vegetation needed water to keep that beautiful green color.

Jack had survived on hit and miss supplies of water since he had woke up in this strange land. The Day Sun he saw during the first minutes of consciousness looked like Earth's Sol. With the sunset in the evening and the bright object the traveler called the Night Sun, and two moons appeared, Jack knew he was no longer in Kansas. More importantly, Jack had no magic ruby slippers for a return home.

There was some luck in this new world as a thunderstorm soaked Jack the first day. Still confused, unable to remember his name, and fearing a suffered stroke, the chilly rain did revive him enough that he checked his clothing for usable items. A 12-ounce plastic drink bottle and a sandwich bag allowed him to save some of the rainwater before it sank into the sandy soil. Again, whatever gods or goddesses of Luck existed on the world he had christened, Elsewhen provided him with only a day in full low and hot Arizona-type desert before Jack traveled to a slight incline and into a high desert motif. By then, the man's wits began to return, and he could read the contents of his wallet. However, his memory was still very sketchy.

Jack found some papers in his wallet that said he was retired at age thirty-five from a law enforcement position, and he had memories of wearing a military uniform. But his brain held no specifics. Some survival training came to his forebrain, and he soon began to organize what was on his person.

Jack remembered having a firearm and a vest or jacket, but he had neither when he awoke. He had a money clip with one hundred dollars in bills plus a small folding blade and nail file. Jack recovered a ring of keys with an extended handcuff key and a P-38 military-style can opener attached. His footwear was sneakers, which soon became hot in the sand, less so as the ground became less sand and more soil. A long-sleeved shirt, slacks, and underwear, that was it. The first night was cold, with no fire. Jack was never a smoker, so no lighter nor matches. His cellular phone was still turned on but had no signal once his brain remembered why it was in his pocket. A nice lady named Jane left him a message asking when he would be home and said she loved him. The voicemail and a gold wedding band on his hand informed Jack he was married.

But he had no memory of marriage nor children.

Despite his confusion, Jack's luck held as he stumbled upon the remains of a body and a smashed-up AK-47 rifle. The second day's discovery told him that he was not the only human to fall through the rabbit hole. Previous training enabled him to insert the one bent round into the weapon and achieved functional chambering. Now he at least had some protection, if he even needed it.

After two days of walking towards what looked like mountains on the horizon, Jack found another body's remains. A small rain shower wetted him, but still no signs of anything edible. He had some belly fat, so the man would not starve to death anytime soon. The remains led to the discovery of a source of calories.

Jack discovered what he named crab scorpions. Large and with a round body about a foot across, they looked like land crabs but had a short scorpion tail, stinger, and all. The creatures were feeding off the remains of the corpse when Jack saw them. Jack found a good-sized rock and used it to smash a couple of them while dodging the others. He cracked open the large claws and sucked the raw meat out. Jack knew he needed to find a source for fire or risk being sick from raw meat parasites. At least the protein makeup in this world was digestible, a subject seldom addressed in most science fiction stories.

Using other stones and kicking with his feet, Jack finally cleared them from the remains. A quick search of the corpse revealed a thin leather belt and a broken flint blade knife. Jack used the sharp flint to cut loose a small skin pouch and then scrambled back from the body as the crab scorpions came back to contest him for the desiccated corpse.

"Have it, assholes. I don't eat human flesh."

Using another large rock, Jack smashed a smaller eight-limbed late comer. The man then continued his trek. An hour later, Jack found a local equivalent of a tumbleweed and decided it was time to try out his fire-making abilities. The remains of the flint blade and the steel nail file from his money clip enabled him to create sparks when the file struck the flint. The tumbleweed was so dry it was soon aflame. Within minutes, he was roasting the crab creature.

The crab thing provided a too-small meal, but it was better than nothing. Jack sucked a bit of moisture from his prey and then took a small sip of his dwindling water supply. The late-thirties former resident of the Americas looked up at his goal. The green area higher up on what appeared to be high foothills of a broader mountain range seemed closer, but not enough. If there were no more rain showers or other water sources, Jack would be in serious trouble.

Jack surveyed the area until he saw a clump of low brush and short trees near some boulders. Those would provide some shade until nightfall. Jack needed to conserve his strength and reduce fluid loss. He had not reached the point of drinking his urine, but that was next. Some distant past survival training told him it was possible.

Jack made a rough sleeping spot in some soft dirt under the soft pine and mesquite-like trees. The man soon fell asleep after a check of the area for creepy crawlies. Jack awoke with the rising of the Night Sun and the two moons, which he named Tiny and Squirt, with Tiny being the bigger of the two. They reminded the former Earthman of the moons of Mars, at least of pictures he had seen. He grunted and spoke to himself.

"Too bad this is not Barsoom, and Dejah Thoris is not around. That good-looking woman would help me, even if I am not John Carter."

Jack took a small sip of water and was startled by a flash of lightning and a crash of thunder. Some small animal scurried past him towards a hidden burrow. The man looked towards the sky and saw a rapidly advancing mass of dark clouds. Jack moved away from the trees, lightning magnets, and huddled next to a couple of nearby boulders. Sure enough, a bolt of lightning split a small pine tree and lit it afire. Moments later, the rain came.

The rainfall was heavy and stinging, but Jack stood and suffered the storms furry. He was soon soaked and shivering but was well hydrated for once. He dug a hole and used his sandwich bag to line it so the rainwater would pool. Rivulets coming off the boulders enabled him to fill his plastic bottle and drink some more. Then the thunderstorm was gone.

Jack looked around and saw the pine tree was still smoldering. He looked inside the destroyed trunk and saw there was a tiny flame. Jack retrieved a business card from his useless billfold and held it to the fire. It lit, and Jack added a couple of saved pieces of tumbleweed. He soon had another small flame in the interior of the lightning-struck tree. Now the traveler needed something to roast.

Jack recovered a long splinter from the tree and began to look for any creatures disturbed by the storm. He soon found a good-sized snake exiting its flooded burrow. Jack quickly smashed it with a rock before the animal realized there was an apex predator around. Using the pieces of the flint knife, Jack cut the head off, being mindful of the fangs. He skinned it as if he had done this in the field before, although he had no specific memory. Using the long tree splinter as a spit, he was soon roasting the snake.

An hour later, Jack felt complete with two small pieces of snake meat remaining. The night air was cold, so Jack began walking once again. Less heat meant he sweat less and using less water. As he walked, the American (that was what he remembered as his home) tried to piece together his memory and his reality.

His billfold documents and cellphone said he was an American from someplace named Tacoma, Washington. The name had a vague image attached to it, just out of reach of his conscious memory. Jane's name had an image from the cellphone attached (once he remembered how to view the saved pictures) but not sharp recollections. If this Jane loved him, she would be worried sick. Yet, he had no such attached feelings towards her. Hell, he could not remember anything about her past other than the saved cellphone picture.

Then there was this place he called Elsewhen. One set of recollections his brain provided was some science fiction stories about wormholes and alternate universes. Jack smiled to himself.

"Well, I just proved String Theory and attached universes," he said out loud as his mind provided him the concepts. Now it was a matter of learning the rules of the world to survive. For one thing, the humanoid bodies told him there must be other peoples on Elsewhen. The fact there were corpses bespoke a violent environment. Some of the violence could have come from other humans. Jack would have to be careful of anyone he met.

His stride began to eat up the distance, and it looked like the first patches of green in what could only be foothills of a mountain range seemed within his grasp. Jack then found the next body.

Some buzzard-type birds alerted the man to the death ahead. The birds were the size of what he remembered from school as ancient condors. Birds that size could be dangerous, and Jake had a weapon with just one round in it. He scanned the area and found a couple of good-sized stones for throwing. Predators and scavengers tried to avoid unnecessary injury, so thrown rocks may chase them off their prey. At least, long enough so Jake could examine what looked like a dead human.

Four giant condors were pecking and squabbling when Jake threw the first rock and hit one in the neck more by chance than skill. It let out a screech and stumbled/hopped back. Jake screamed like a Banshee and threw the next rock, waving his arms like a madman. The four birds thought discretion was the better part of valor as they all hopped and then flapped their hung wings to struggle to get airborne. A breeze coming from the mountains helped in their endeavor. Jake hot-footed it towards the body as the condors landed some fifty yards away.

The corpse was female, its long bronze hair braided in an intricate pattern. The dead female wore a light chain mail shirt over a colorful blouse. A flint-headed arrow completely pierced the feminine throat. Next to the body was a large bolt action rifle. Jack grabbed the gun and worked its massive bolt action, which looked like an enlarged version of a German Mauser.

"Where did that bit of knowledge come from?" Jake mumbled. He realized that he seemed to possess an encyclopedia of martial and survival knowledge from a previous life buried in his memory. A quick pat-down revealed three live .50 caliber shells, which reminded him of the Old West Sharps rifle rounds favored by Buffalo Hunters. The rifle contained a spent shell which Jack saved and replaced with a live one.

"Now we are cooking with gas," he said in a loud voice. Jack had a weapon with a hefty punch raised above his head as he yelled at the condors.

"Want to try me now, assholes?"

As he continued his search of the recently dead body (deceased less than a day, he somehow knew), Jack realized he had a long history with death and dead bodies. They did not phase him. He assumed it was not because he was a funeral director. Further searching resulted in the find of an over-under two-barrel massive pistol. In historical India on Earth, it would have been called a Howdah pistol, carried as a backup on big game hunts. The pistol pouch held six spare rounds of a long .50 caliber shell but shorter than the rifle's cartridges. He looked at the dead woman warrior and thought she must have been a powerful woman to handle the weapons she carried.

Jack knew men who would have had difficulty shooting such firearms.

Jack recovered a small water flask and a matching one containing wine as one of the Condors suddenly landed some ten yards away. He tossed a rock at the condor with his off-hand, and it cawed as it hopped backward. The big birds were becoming impatient as their hunger persisted. Eventually, they would rush him. With that thought, Jack hurried the scavenge of the body.

A minute later and Jack had taken off a long cloak, a belt with a copper knife, and a bag containing some pieces of jerked meat. The belt also had a small concealed money purse sewn in. The other condors were beginning to approach, so Jack snapped the flint head of the arrow shaft off as a final move and then backpedaled from the corpse. He decided the mail would not fit him and would just be extra weight in a hot climate. Jack looked at the ground and saw the equine hoofprints he expected. The horse was nowhere to be found, possibly taken by the woman's killer. But he or she did not strip the body of weapons and valuables. The spent shell in the rifle told a tale that maybe the attacker was shot. Jack began to follow the hoofprints up the incline of the foothills, ever watchful for the Amazon's attacker.

Jack decided the woman was an Amazon and would understand why he did not hold a funeral service for her. He murmured a short prayer for a quick trip of the Warrior's spirit to whatever afterlife they owned. Another group of people had fallen down the rabbit hole to Elsewhen.

An hour later, Jack found the remains of the Amazon's attacker. He whistled as he saw the body. Despite some scavenging by the local wildlife, it looked similar to photographs he had seen of Commanche warriors. Plains Indian Tribes on this two mooned world? Was there a rhyme or reason to who was transported to Elsewhen?

"Is this Purgatory, maybe?" he asked out loud. Jack then scanned the body and the area. His supposition about a bullet strick was correct. There was an impact wound on the Comanche's left floating rib. The man had bled out and fallen from his captured mount. The Comanche had an excellent steel Bowie knife and a quiver with two flint arrows. Jack found no bow and assumed scavengers had taken it to chew. Comanches also carry lances, but Jack saw none. He did strip the moccasins of the man's feet.

Again Jack mumbled apologetic prayers to whatever Gods ruled this world for no burial. The Comanche had no food nor water, so Jack was still faced with those shortages. Once again, Jack began his trek towards the green.

As he walked, Jack noticed hoofprints in the same direction as his plotted course. His mind finally reminded him that horses had sensitive noses and could smell water miles away. He smiled at the remembered knowledge.

"I'll just follow you, Horsey," said Jack. "You're better at finding water than I am."

Jack adjusted his newfound booty on his body and continued his trek. The fact a horse was headed towards a water source made Jack quicken his pace. The Day Sun rose in the sky until it was at the equivalent of noon, local time. This observation made Jack realize he did not know for sure if the Everwhen day was twenty-four hours. It seemed the same to his internal clock, but he could not be sure. Another mystery to be ferreted out.

The sun was past its zenith in the hot afternoon sky when Jack noticed his goal was within reach. Some mile ahead, a green batch of something reflected the sunlight. The slope seemed to flatten out onto a possible plateau, with the high mountains still miles further. Jack found the wind to start a jog.

A slight breeze brought the familiar feel of the water as Jack tried to run faster. He concentrated on ensuring he did not trip and fall on the horse's trail followed up the incline. As Jack worked his way up a slight rise, he saw what appeared to be watery mist setting low over the top of the increase.

"Water," he said out loud. Then Jack saw it. Bubbling up from the ground was clearly water sufficient to provide a small babbling brook. As Jack reached the source of the critical moisture, he looked beyond the rise and stopped in his tracks, for the bubbling water did form a babbling brook which worked its way down the reverse slope and ended in a lake. A lovely, clear-water lake.

Just beyond the long lake was a smaller pond. And beyond the second body of water was another pond. All three bodies of water sat on a small plateau that interrupted the slope of the foothills of the more distant mountain range. Jack knew he would not be thirsty any time soon.

As Jack slowly surveyed the tableau, he saw the missing horse carefully making its way to the lake's edge. The horse took a quick drink, then moved back. It was a good-sized brown-colored mount with a saddle and bags still on its back. The horse also seemed wary of the lake or something in it as it repeated the short drink then retreat action some three times more as Jack watched.

"What's up, horse?" Jack said out loud as he slowly descended the slope towards the lake; he unslung the beat-up AK-47 with its single live shell as he had a good idea of the ballistics of the assault rifle. That is if the weapon could fire.

The horse made one more approach, began to drink, then dashed away from the water's edge as something broke the surface of the lake. As the creature scrambled up into the shallows, Jack first thought it was a species of 'gator or croc. But as Jack examined the beast more, it looked more like a very oversized Iguana. A memory of Darwin's discovery of ocean-going Iguana in the Galapagos Islands confirmed the observation that the thing was another animal whose ancestor had come through the looking glass.

The horse beat a hasty retreat as the monster scrambled up onto dry land. It moved fast but not as quickly as the horse. Jack brought the AK-47 up to his shoulder and hoped the sights were somewhere near accurate. The lizard was meat and also a threat to the human using the lake. Thus, it was an easy decision for Jack to decide to expend a rifle round on it.

"Here goes nothing," he mumbled moments before he fired.

Under normal circumstances, the range was close to two hundred meters, not far from the AK. But this was not normal. Once again, the Gods of Luck were with Jack as the jacketed thirty caliber bullet struck the monster iguana broadsides. It penetrated the hide, and the creature began to thrash about as it attempted to find the invisible enemy who had just hit it. Jack dropped the empty AK and unslung the massive bolt action. Jack knew the bullet's mass for the late Amazon's long gun more than made up for the lack of jacketed ammunition.

There was no need for a follow-up shot as the lizard thrashed, then collapsed into a heap. Jack supposed his bullet had struck a vital organ. The horse watched as Jack made his way down the slope to the body. Jack poked the monster iguana several times with the rifle barrel before settling it with the dead Comanches Bowie. Jack tossed the guts aside and saved what looked like the liver and a shot heart. He also cut off a large chunk from the tail as Jack remembered 'gator tail was a delicacy to some. He sliced strips of meat from the haunches and ribcage area before his growling stomach told him it was time to cook a meal.

Jack found another tumbleweed and built a fire just up from the sand and rock lake beach. The horse slowly made its way to the human, and Jack was able to grab its bridle. He could ride but was not a prominent horseman. However, the horse allowed him to remove the saddle and saddlebags, then trotted away in search of forage. The Earthman found some rice balls, stale bread chunks, spices, and dried apples in the saddlebags. Jack began to hum to himself as the thought of a flavorful meal brought a smile to his face.

Jack used a small tin plate from the Amazon's saddlebags to warm the rice balls as he dripped blood from the raw meat pieces as a flavor enhancer. He placed pieces of meat on flat stones moved to the edge of his campfire as he threw more wood fuel on the flames. Within half an hour, Jack was chowing down on the first decent meal in over a week. Jack used the Bowie to slice some slips of wood for use as chopsticks and pokers. After he scorched additional slices of meat in the campfire, Jake finally felt satiated. He walked over to the babbling brook that fed the lake and refilled his plastic water bottle. Jack washed the small tin plate and then scooped about an ounce of water into it. A quick return to the campfire, and Jack sat down, leaning against a solid rock. He drank the water from the tin pan and took a swig of wine from the scavenged flask. Jack belched.

"I feel almost human," Jack said. He sat and contemplated his status. Jack had about twenty pounds of butchered meat left, some slow cooking near the campfire. There were a few pieces of jerked beef in the Amazon's bags, as well as the stale bread. Jack had finished off the rice balls. The only things limiting Jack's stay at this oasis were food and shelter with a water source. There was still meat and ribs to be recovered from the monster iguana. Hopefully, the water source would attract other animals which Jack could hunt. Shelter might be obtained from salvaged wood and digging around the larger rocks to create a small den. Mammals had survived the extinction of the dinosaurs by burrowing into the ground and building dens. What was good enough for them was good enough for Jack.

With that thought, Jack grabbed the Bowie and walked back to the dead lizard. As the man neared the head of the oversized Iguana, something came boiling out of the lake. Jack backpedaled as he pulled the large Howdah pistol from his belt. The creature from the lake was a smaller version of the Iguana; ignored Jack, grabbed the remains of the dead specimen, and drug it back into the lake. It soon disappeared under the lake waters.

"Shit," cursed Jack. He could have tried to shoot it, but his ammunition was limited. He shrugged and made his way back to his campfire. Jack had a full stomach and some saved meat, so he was far from starving. He would have to plan to deal with the lake denizens if he remained here until humans arrived. Jack recognized this area as a true oasis used just before the descent into the hot and dry desert. The American was lucky he had come in Elsewhen this close to the water source.

Jack spent the rest of the afternoon using the tin pan and the Amazon's copper blade to dig around the base of nearby boulders. The horse did not return until the Day Sun was setting, and the two moons began to rise, followed by the Night Sun. Jack escorted the horse over to the brook and made sure it understood this was where safe water flowed. He collected some short grasses, fed the horse, used some to wipe the horse down, and then returned to his den. He also picked up the smashed AK-47 as he figured the metal parts might be of some use. Jack covered the entrance with chopped brush and lay down with the saddlebags as his pillows. With the rifle and large pistol close at hand, he was soon asleep.

Some growls and horse whinnying plus a bray woke Jack. He was up with the pistol in one hand and the copper blade in the other. He pushed the concealing brush back from the entranceway of his den. What he saw stopped him in his tracks.

What looked like crosses between coyotes and wild dogs were arguing over the gut remains of the Iguana. Jack had left them some fifty yards from his makeshift den, hoping they may attract a condor or two he could kill. A couple of the canines were taking an interest in the horse and were circling it. Jack had a sudden memory of a pet dog sometime in his life, so dogmeat had not on the menu. Jack stepped forward and bellowed.

"What in the Hell do you think you are doing?"

Six pairs of canine eyes snapped in his direction. The coydogs or whatever they were seemed to be mindful of the human voice as they all stared at him as their noses worked. Then one slowly padded towards Jack. A dirty brown-looking dog, maybe a shepherd mix, looked to Jack as a specimen that could have been someone's pet on Earth. This observation made the man think that maybe dogs and other pets fell through the looking glass into Elsewhen.

The two canines following the horse suddenly took an interest in Jack and began to circle towards him.

Bursting from the lake was the same smaller iguana lizard as yesterday. It lunged and snapped at one of the two circling dogs, narrowly missing a stable bite. The canine yipped and darted away just as Jack strode forward, aimed, and shot the Iguana in its snout. The lake lizard hissed and let out a barking noise before it began clawing at its nose. Blood began to spout from the nose area of the lizard just as the rest of the canine pack started an instinctive coordinated attack.

They snapped at the rear legs to hamstring the

beast, then caught at its blooding snout when it tried to bite one of them. The substantial tail of the Iguana bowled one canine over as the creature attempted to paw at its facial wound. It turned towards the water, and Jack lunged forward to slash at the tail with the copper blade. The Iguana paused for a moment to turn towards the new threat. As it did, two dog animals both latched onto the bloody snout and began to pull it across the lakeshore. The lake monster slashed at the attackers with its front claws, and they danced backward, just as two other canines bit its tail.

Jack stuck the pistol and knife under his belt and glanced around for a large stone. He found a football-sized rock, pulled it from the sandy soil with both hands, and lifted it above his head. The monster iguana lashed its tail around as the canines danced about, barking and growling. Jack could scramble forward with the creature concentrating on the dogs/coyotes and slammed the large rock between the lizard's eyes near the bullet hole. Blood spurt from the bullet hole as an artery had been sliced. The Iguana, stunned by the blow to its skull, staggered about as the canines bit at its extremities. The arterial blood spurted more as the lizard had trouble coordinating its limbs in an escape bid towards the lake. A final stagger and the Iguana collapsed. The lizard shuddered, then lay still as blood kept spurting from around the bullet wound.

Jack watched as the canines feinted and snapped at the lake beast. When it did not respond, each of the four-legged predators began to look for a body part to chew. The apparent Alpha male claimed the tongue and soon ripped it from the lizard's mouth. Jack jogged back to his den under the boulders and recovered both the rifle and the Bowie as the pack chowed down on the new massive source of meat. When he reapproached the carcass, the Alpha showed its teeth and snapped at him. Jack jabbed the gun's heavy barrel into the sensitive canine nose, which elicited a yelp and a retreat.

"Get this straight, dog," Jack yelled, "I am the apex predator, not you. So, I *will* eat from this prey. Got it?" The man then circled to the rear of the Iguana and began slicing steaks off the tail. As he did, he sensed a body near him. He looked up at the dirty brown canine, which seemed unafraid of him. Jack saw it was a 'she' and, as he looked closer, had a pet collar around her neck.

"So you came from Earth, also. What some steak?" Jack cut a chunk from the tail as he asked and tossed it to the bitch. She caught it, chewed on it, then swallowed.

Jack laughed. "Take the dog out of the home, can't take the home out of the dog."

Jack soon had as many bloody hunks as he could carry. He made his way to his den, put the meat on some flat stones he had collected. Jack soon used some harvested dried grass and another business card from his useless billfold to get a flame from the still-warm campfire coals. Jack fed some more wood pieces he carved off a stunted tree branch typical of high desert vegetation. In moments, he had a friendly fire going.

As Jack prepared the older meat for cooking and stashed the new steaks in the saddlebags towards the back of his den, he noticed the brown dog approach. This creature was no coyote mix but an actual dog. The man smiled and dug out the few remaining pieces of jerked meat. He tossed them from where he sat one by one by one, ever closer. The female dog slowly approached, then began a slow wag of the tail. Jack chuckled, a sound the dog recognized as she wagged her tail more. The Earthman slowly presented his left hand, backside up, for the dog to sniff. The she-dog sniffed, then licked drying blood off it.

"Can I scratch your ears?" Jack asked. Then he slowly moved his hand and scratched under her muzzle. With that, the dog stepped forward and sat on his lap as if it were the most natural thing to do. The man laughed as he scratched canine ears. He looked closely at the collar. There were no tags, but the name 'Sheba' could be made out in the leather.

"Hmm. Sheba, is that your name?" Jack asked. The dog answered with a quick lick to the face. Jack scratched some more ear, then gently pushed Sheba off his lap. He recovered the tin pan and poured some water from the Amazon's small flask for Sheba to drink. She quickly lapped it down.

"Well, I guess I need to figure out a water dish for you," said Jack. He scrounged some more flat rocks, lined a small dug hole, and stretched his tattered plastic bag over them as a seal. Next were several trips to the lakeside, ever mindful of the other canine and possible further water denizens. Using his plastic bottle and the small flask, he soon had the water hole filled. If it leaked, it was slow. Jack also stripped some thick hide off of the giant Iguana. He took it back to the campfire and laid the hide bloody side down on some hot rocks. Jack vaguely remembered some tanning techniques, thought he could keep the hide from going bad. Jack shrugged. He had a canine helper who protected the den, as she snarled when a couple of the other pack members tried to approach. Everything else from here on out was a plus.

The rest of the day, Jack spent cooking the meat, hung some in a crude attempt to smoke it after using the short trees near the lake and two ponds to build a simple meat rack. Sheba stayed near his side other than to leave to do her business away from the den. Jack surmised the dog had not been in Elsewhen that long, but long enough that she instinctually attached herself to a pack. He wondered if she was 'fixed' or could still have pups. The man knew he would soon find out if even one of her former pack were gravid.

Former pack. The words had a unique ring and seemed accurate based on Sheba's attitudes since he allowed her into his new world. Sheba had been someone's loyal companion on Earth. She decided to transfer that loyalty to him.

The canine pack Alpha tore a huge leg bone with meat attached from the Iguana and began to carry and drag it off. Jack thought pups nearby in a den or the Alpha went to bury and cache the meat for lean times. Two other wild dogs or coyote mixes followed suit with small amounts. The predators had been stuffing themselves with the newfound bounty all day and would now leave to sleep it off. That told Jack they knew the lake contained remembered historical threats. Only the strong and intelligent survived in Elsewhen.

One canine hung back. It was a young-looking male who slowly made his way towards the campfire. As he neared, Jack saw he was not a coyote and might just be an unkempt stray like Sheba. The female stood and growled a warning, and the young male stopped. Jack stood and petted his new friend.

"Let me try something, Sheba. I'll let you have the final say."

Jack took a hunk of partially cooked meat and used the copper blade to slice pieces off of it. He walked towards the young male. Tossing small amounts of meat to the canine, he approached. The dog ate all that was given, then lay down. Finally, he rolled over, showing he had young dog testicles. Jack bent over and gently scratched his muzzle as Sheba came up at the show of submission. She sniffed the male all over, looked at Jack, then walked back to the campfire. Jack knelt next to the male dog and saw a problem. Wrapped around its throat was a choke chain that was rapidly becoming too small. It was already tangled in fur and seemed to become embedded in the skin.

"Well, boy," Jack whispered. "We found each other just at the right time. That is about to choke you permanently."

Over the next hour, Jack used a piece of flint to cut the tangled fur around the choke chain. His partial memory finally told him to look in the butt of the trashed AK for a cleaning kit. Jack managed to find a weak link in the chain and work at bending next, breaking it using the screwdriver-like piece and the cleaning brush. The dog quietly laid as Sheba watched. Finally, Jack turned a weak link enough to break it. The chain came loose as the dog whimpered a bit from losing some skin and hair. Jack poured some wine from the Amazon flask mixed with hot water to clean the wound as best he could. He tossed the choke chain out towards the lake. Jack would let some vermin insects clean it.

The dog licked Jack's hand then allowed Sheba to lick his wounded neck. The man smiled.

"One minute alone, the next minute instant family," Jack mumbled. He looked at the male dog.

"In the power vested in me, I name you Solomon, Sol for short, as we already have a Sheba." At the sound of Jack's voice, the young male wagged his tail.

Over the following weeks, Jack expanded the den and searched the three bodies of water for valuable items and material. He found a couple of rusty cans that assured his thoughts about this being a traveled pathway to and from the desert areas. Jack also found a larger tree some one mile away, which provided wood for an atlatl and a staff for a spear. The atlatl he tested with the two found arrows and discovered he could launch them with sufficient force for small game hunting. Jack made a spear using the copper blade as the pointy end.

The canine pack came back once more to the Iguana remains, and Jack let them. The survivor used some recovered skin and sinew to make rawhide chords he used in a small bola. Jack found it mysterious that he remembered all these survival skills but only knew his name from the papers in his old billfold. He looked at the photos saved in his cellphone before shutting it down and removing the battery. Maybe later, the Earthman would figure out a way to recharge it. Right then, the photographs were of someone else's life on Earth.

Jack used hot water and the limited cleaning supplies from the saddlebags to clean the Howdah pistol and the large rifle. Again, some arcane knowledge in his brain told him how to keep black powder and the priming material in the rimfire cartridges from corroding the two weapons. The man figured he must have been a weapon aficionado during his previous life, whatever that meant on Earth.

The spear he made came in handy when a lizard snake (snake lizard?), something six feet long with a snake's sinewy body but short legs, tried to attack the horse. The creature moved fast for being so low to the ground, but the horse dodged it as Jack pinned its head to the ground. It took a couple of minutes to die, then Jack cut the head off completely and tossed it aside. It looked to have fangs, and Jack did not want to screw with any toxins just then. The snake thing provided some tasty meat and skin for a belt.

Jack used the horse, which stuck around the water supply and human companionship, to drag the remains of the creatures and trash to the other end of the lake. The giant condors showed up about that time, and Jack wrapped the bola around one's neck. Stunned, Jack used the spear to finish it off. It took a bunch of feather plucking and gutting to prepare the giant turkey for roasting. The carrion-eating bird did not smell good but once cleaned and cooked; it tasted just fine. The condor provided some twenty-five pounds of meat enjoyed by both Jack and the dogs. He kept the bones from Sheba and Solomon as he would chicken bones. The dogs already had a couple of iguana limb bones to chew for entertainment.

The smaller of the two ponds provided some Earthlike cattails that Jack roasted and used when they softened to clean himself. He had no toilet paper, and there were no corncobs around. Jack spent a day scrounging up some more flat stones, then dug a human-sized hole using the two rusty cans and a wooden spade he had fashioned from the short trees located on the slopes above. The Earthman pounded and pressed the flat stones into the makeshift bathtub, then used some sticky clay mud to seal the cracks between the rocks. A day later and Jack was rewarded with a downpour from a thunderstorm. The dogs huddled in the den as Jack used the stinging rain as a shower. He had created a separate rivulet to feed into his tub, which was soon filled. After the storm passed, Jack heated some flat stones in an enlarged campfire, then dumped them into the bathtub. Jack then slid into the water and soaked in his limited clothing. Jack knew he would need furs and hides or some clothes from live humans, not dead ones. Eventually, the two dogs stepped in and allowed Jack to perform cursory washing them using sand as a scrub before they exited and shook.

"You two do not know how nice this feels," Jack told the two dogs as he lay back to soak some more. Jack was lying in his tub, half dozing, when he heard and felt a large object falling through the air near him. Jack jerked up in time to see what appeared to be a helicopter slam into the lake. The massive piece of metal sank quickly, but Jack saw what he identified as the tail rotor of a Viet Nam-era Huey. Jack scrambled out of the tub, put his ragged shoes on. The two dogs were slowly making their way to the lake, noses working a mile a minute. He grabbed the rifle and the pistol, then strode towards the lake. The impact had sloshed water several feet up on the shore, and Jack looked for any lake residents that may have been thrown from their home. He saw two fish that he scooped up and threw further up on the shore.

Some flotsam and jetsam bobbed to the surface, and Jack saw the body. He splashed into the lake, figuring any predators would be stunned by the impact of the flying machine. Jack drug the unresponsive figure to the shore, then rolled it onto its back. It was a man in fatigues.

"Hey, buddy—" Jack stopped speaking when he saw a piece of the skull was missing. "Shit," he swore. One of these days, Jack hoped actually to talk to a live human in Elsewhen. A partial memory bubbled up, and Jack knew he had seen many bodies like this. Death was a part of his past life on Earth. In a businesslike manner, Jack stripped the uniform and boots from the soldier. He saw the rank and insignia denoted a Sergeant. The fatigues had the oversized pockets of the Jungle variety, and Jack found some treasure in them. There was an old .38 caliber Smith and Wesson revolver, probably circa World War Two, that someone had bobbed the barrel back to two inches. It was fully loaded with six tracer rounds, perhaps for signaling. But tracer bullets still killed people.

From the man's belt, he removed a survival knife with a serrated top edge. In another pocket were a Zippo lighter and a soggy packet of cigarettes. Jack did not smoke, but the Zippo worked so he could give his flint shards a rest. In another pocket, he found a flask full of scotch whiskey. A package of chewing gum and a soaked sandwich rounded out the finds.

Jack split the sandwich between the dogs and set the rest of the booty in the sun to dry. He dragged the dead body, now just in its OD underwear, some fifty yards down to a patch of soft and sandy soil. Recovering his wooden spade, Jack began to dig.

An hour later, Jack laid Sergeant Reed to rest. The dog tags gave Jack a name, and he wrapped them around a crude cross he made with two sticks and some dried sinew.

"Wished you had lived, Sergeant," Jack said. "The dogs are great but are not conversationalists."

Jack put several small boulders on the grave to ward off scavengers and then walked back to the lake. The Earthman cautiously fished out a plastic map case and a couple of small pieces of light metal. Examination of the map told him the helicopter had come from 1970 and Viet Nam. So as Jack had surmised, Elsewhen received people and things from all times and places.

Jack went back to the den with the dogs and wiped the recovered items down as best he could. He now had a 'belly' gun with six rounds to add to the Howdah with seven and the rifle with three remaining shells. Not enough to start a war, but something more to fight with should the need arise.

Jack checked his foodstuffs and decided that he would need to go hunting in the next day or two, even with the recovered fish. Jack gutted the fish and then began to slow roast them over the campfire as Sheba and Solomon intently watched. Jack had ground up various seeds and some cattail remains to make a flatbread. He used the tin pan to fry up the poor man's tortillas, then divided a fish and a tortilla between the dogs. Jack ate the rest of the food and soon had a comfortable full stomach. Sheba and Solomon curled up for a late afternoon nap as Jack looked over the somewhat dried map. It looked like the 'copter was headed to the Vietnam/Cambodian border, so it may have been involved in the Cambodian Invasion if Jack's memory on this was correct. He grunted. Funny how he could remember arcane facts but little about his own life.

The man cleaned up the 'dishes' then walked back down to the lake. Jack snared a dead fish that bobbed to the surface. It looked to Jack that there was no other monster iguana in the lake, nor any other predator sign. If the signs remained the same, Jack might risk a swim and a dive to the wreck. The tail rotor looked to be just a foot or two under the surface.

Jack went back to the den and cooked up the recovered trout. He shared it with the dogs as he watched Day Sun set and Night Sun rise with the two moons. Things could be worse, he thought. The survivor had a full stomach and two canine companions to share some newfound booty. Jack called it an early evening and went to sleep.

Jack was up at dawn and relieved himself as Sheba began to growl. Somebody or something was approaching from the mountain range side of the oasis. He zipped up and grabbed the rifle. The recovered 38 revolver was in a pants pocket, as were the two spare shells to the large gun. Jack walked towards the nearer of the ponds and crouched beside a bush. He heard a horse snort as the two dogs lay next to him.

Weaving their way down a small game trail that passed the two ponds were four horsemen. As they neared the lake, one noticed Jack's den and called out, pointing. The Earthman saw they wore copper-colored helmets and chest plates and a form of jodhpur pants. One rider carried a lance with a bit of flag attached.

Jack surmised they must be a small military unit by their uniform appearance. He stood up, holding the rifle at ready, and called out. "How about stopping right there, guys."

The horseman reined in their mounts, and one called out in what sounded like Chinese. The second rider spoke with an air of one who was in command, and the lead horseman slowly spurred his horse towards Jack, some twenty-five yards away. Jack could now make out their Asian countenances as the lead soldier approached. The man reined in his horse some fifteen yards from Jack and spoke.

"England?" The man asked.

"American," Jack replied. "But I speak English, as do you."

The rider nodded his head affirmatively and seemed to be organizing his words in his head. He then saw Sheba and Soloman as they separated and approached the horse patrol from different sides, crouching some distance away.

"Dogs, you have dogs," the Asian rider said.

"They're family," answered Jack. "Now, how about you tell me why you are passing through."

The second Chinese man must be the officer in charge barked out orders at the English speaker.

The subordinate nodded, then spoke once again. "You see machine fall from sky, Yes?"

"Yes, I did. It sank in the middle of the lake."

"Any—people—on it?"

"One dead man. I buried him over yonder."

The English speaker conveyed Jack's answer to the officer in Chinese. The officer barked out more orders as he spurred his horse and approached. Sheba growled as the English speaker spoke to Jack. "You must come with us."

"Why and where? And tell your boss not to draw that pistol."

The officer seemed to be cursing as he looked at the growling Sheba. The man pulled a revolver from a holster as he glared at the dogs. Jack shouldered his rifle as he yelled, "Don't!"

A shot rang out from behind Jack and higher up on the slopes above. The officer's horse screamed, bucked, jerked, and toppled over into the lake shallows. The Chinese officer was pinned beneath his mount as the English speaker tried to draw a similar pistol from his belt. Jack shot the man from his horse automatically, the large bullet punching a hole through the chest plate with ease. Sheba and Solomon charged the other two riders as the lancer tried to impale them and the fourth soldier drew a carbine from a sheath.

An arrow missed the fourth soldier's face by a hair's breadth as Jack would describe as a Native American warcry echoed around the oasis. The lancer's horse reared as the dogs snapped at its front legs and then bucked as the canines switched to the hindquarters. Jack yanked the revolver from his pocket and aimed it at the rider holding the carbine as a second arrow flew and hit home this time. The rider dropped his carbine as an arrow impaled his throat. The Chinese soldier grabbed at his neck and fell from the saddle. The lancer tried to control his mount and turn it around to flee. Another shot was fired, and Jack saw the lance-carrying rider jerk and fall from his horse.

A stereotypical buckskin-wearing frontiersman rode up on a large mount and lept to the ground. A muscular plains Indian closely followed him in buckskin breeches.

"Howdy, Pilgrim," the frontiersman bellowed. "Friends, so don't shoot us."

Jack looked at the dying horse in the shallows and saw the officer free himself from his mount. Screaming and cursing, the officer pulled a short copper-colored blade from his belt. Jack shot him in the chest. The Chinese man fell back into the lake and lay still. The full metal jacket bullet had penetrated the copper cuirass.

"That pistol of yarn has a bite," the frontiersman said. "I'm Blue Baxter. This here Comanche is called Spotted Wolf."

Jack looked at the Native American while still holding the .38 revolver. "I'm Jack Hays. I thought Comanches did not like white men."

Blue laughed. "We have an understanding. Wolf, don't kill me; I don't kill him."

Spotted Wolf dismounted and made his way to the dead horse in the shallows. He pulled a large Bowie from a sheath and began to slaughter the beast.

"We'll eat right tonight if Red Macbeth don't find any more Chinee sneaking around. Sometimes they send out scouts first."

"Your friend is out looking for more people?" asked Jack.

"Chinee claim this oasis. Their traders come through here a couple of times a year. They barter with people in the Central Mountains, people out past the

North Desert. They are riled when we come up here from Freetown."

"Freetown?" asked Jack.

"Yessiree. We chased the Chinee bastards out. Well, not all of them. Just the Emperor's boys."

"There is a Chinese Emperor in Elsewhen," stated Jack.

"You call it Elsewhen?" asked Blue Baxter. "I call it Last Place. For this is the damn Last Place I want to be!" Blue's laughter was loud and long. Sheba and Solomon padded up to each side of Jack and eyed the strange men.

"That's a damn fine bitch. If you can breed her, the pups will be worth a fortune."

Jack looked at Sheba and scratched her ears. Solomon had tried to hump her once, but she had rebuffed him with a snarl. Jack thought he had seen some menstrual blood recently but was no veterinarian.

"We'll see what happens. Right now, I'm just trying to figure things out."

Blue paused for a moment, then spoke. "You don't remember everything, do you?'

"No, I don't."

"Well, Jack. Some people come and remember the past; others don't. Some people can't handle it and kill themselves. We have people from all times and places. God only knows why. Hell, Red and I were aheadin' to the Alamo when *zap!* We're here."

Jack looked at Spotted Wolf, slaughtering

the horse.

"How about Spotted Wolf?" Jack asked.

"Near as I can figure, he was from about 1850 or so," replied Blue Baxter.

"How long have you all been here?"

"Five, six years is my guess. Time seems funny around here."

The Comanche warrior drug the body of the dead Chinese officer from the lake as fresh steaks, the heart, and liver bled from atop the equine ribcage. The Indian pointed to the bullet hole in the cuirass and grunted.

"Is that just copper plate?" Jack asked Blue.

"Yessir. There is tons of copper around. The Chinee control most of the iron ore, coal, and such, make steel. These copper chest plates are more for a show, though they will sometimes deflect a bullet or a blade."

Blue walked over to the man Jack had killed with the rifle.

"Here, have a look." Blue tossed a pistol taken from the dead Chinese at Jack. He caught it and turned it over in his hands.

"Looks like a Colt Navy, but with Chinese writing on it," said Jack.

"Them Colts came after Red and me," Blue answered. "But a bunch of others at Freetown say the same. Chinee are good at copying things."

"This one was made for rimfire ammunition, Blue."

Blue chuckled.

"Yep. After Red and me again. Hell, caps and ball were the newest things when we were heading to the Alamo."

Jack started to toss it back when Blue waved him off.

"Keep it. You killed the Chinee; you get the spoils."

The three men spent the next half hour collecting the spoils from the dead as the two dogs looked on. A few jerked meat were tossed their way by Blue Baxter, who belly-laughed as every bit was caught. All the copper armor was piled together, and the weapons were divided based on who killed who. Jack wound up with a rimfire pistol and a lever-action carbine that was the spitting image of a Volcanic from the 1850s. It had been modified to take the same rimfire .38 caliber ammunition as the Colt pistol clone. The riders' bodies were dragged some fifty yards away and piled high with the dry brush the men could scavenge. The corpses would be cremated in the morning, along with the remains of the horse. As Spotted Wolf took the horse steaks over to Jack's campfire, a third man rode up. Red Macbeth looked like a lither version of Blue.

"Hey, Red. Meet Jack here. From the old U.S.A. also."

"Pleased to meetcha," greeted Red as he shook Jack's hand.

Jack passed around the flask of whiskey from the dead Viet Nam veteran to the great enjoyment of the men, even Spotted Wolf.

"Wolf here can drink with the best of us," said Reed. "He ain't like some of those drunk Injuns you see hanging around trading posts."

Red Macbeth looked at the former Amazon rifle. "You got that off'n a big woman, warrior type?"

"Her dead body, yes," answered Jack. He then saw Wolf looking at the two arrows next to the atlatl.

"I took those off of a dead Comanche," stated Jack. He and the Amazon argued and both lost. Jack walked over, picked the arrows up, and handed them to Big Wolf. "Here. You can use these arrows better than me."

"Thank you," replied the Comanche. The Indian placed the arrows into his quiver, then continued preparing the horse steaks for roasting. The three 'white men' stood watching the warrior as he used copper rods from his saddle pack for roasting spits, arranging them around Jack's campfire. Sheba and Solomon watched with keen eyes, drool forming around their muzzles.

Blue laughed. "Those two will be well fed tonight, and they know it."

"Well, they deserve it," said Jack. "They help keep me alive."

"What next, then?" asked Red. "You wanna stay here, try and scavenge from that flying machine in the lake?"

Jack paused for a moment as he formed an answer. He had been living day to day with the dogs. Maybe his sketchy memory slowed his planning ability as he had not given the future much thought past where to find the following week's meals.

Finally, Jack answered, "I'd like to keep whatever was in the helicopter out of the hands of people who may misuse it. It was a war machine, more advanced than what you and the Chinese have from what I have seen."

The three other men laughed.

"Jack, you have to come to Freetown," said Blue. "We have people there with flying machines, motorcars, better guns. That's why we fought off the Emperor from New Bejing."

"Can you get some of them up here?" Jack asked.

"That's our job. We scout, then report back about stuff like that machine in the lake. The city-state council will send a team up here to get it."

Jack thought for a moment, then replied, "How about I stay here, and you guys go get this help. I have those two Chinese guns and some fifty rounds of rimfire for them. I can hold off another small patrol if need be."

"Whoa, Hoss," said Blue. "Next time, once one of the horses that ran away make it back to their stable at New Bejing, the Chinee will send a dozen or more horsemen. You can't hold them off."

"I'll stay here with him," interjected Red. "You and

Wolf here high tail it to Freetown. You hurry, you can make it in four days."

'If we don't run into Dragons," replied Blue.

"Dragons? You mean these lake iguanas?"

"Two-legged lizards," Spotted Wolf stated as he produced four small steaks on the metal spits for the men. "We can kill them, but they are tough. They are as tall as a man."

Jack stared at the three scouts. Elsewhen was becoming weirder by the moment.

"Okay," said Blue. "Mike stays here and plays cards with you. Big Wolf and I leave at sunrise and haul ass."

Everyone grunted acknowledgment and then began eating their steaks. Jack started to feed Sheba and Solomon some of his meat until Wolf brought two large steaks. Jack laughed when he saw they were more substantial than the men's pieces of meat.

"We must keep these wolf cousins strong, happy," said the Comanche. "Their kind warned us many times of danger."

"Ain't that the truth," added Jack.

There were new steaks, and Red produced two-quart bottles of beer from his saddlebags. The men passed the beer around as they talked, two very full canines now laying near Jack snoozing away.

"Watch this one at cards, Jack," Blue said as he pointed at Red. "He cheats."

"Just 'cause I win, don't mean I cheat."

"I just had a memory," said Jack. "I played some cutthroat Texas Holdem' at a place called Las Vegas. I think I can handle one man."

"Well, if it's a fun game from Texas, I'll play it," stated Red. "But I have a question, Jack."

"Go ahead, Red."

"Some of the newer people talk about moving pictures. They said these were stories about people like us three, Mountain Men and Injuns. Did you see them? Were the people in the stories like us?"

Jack looked at his three new friends in Elsewhen, thought of the dead Chinese soldiers awaiting a cremation bonfire in the morning. He grinned.

"They can't hold a candle to you three. Not a single candle."

The Day Sun set, and the Night Sun rose. The ancient waters of the oasis reflected the lights of another passing day.

The men may come and go. The lakes and ponds remained.

# 2
# LOST AND FOUND

Mark Stone's brain jerked awake, his eyes snapped open, and he felt about to vomit all at once. Luckily, the window of his SUV was open. He was able to jam his head out and puke the contents of his stomach down the side of the vehicle rather than into his lap. He then flopped back into the driver's seat as his vision blurred and the world spun around a bit. He was about to try the old drunk's tactic of putting one foot on the ground or floor when the spinning stopped.

Mark tried to get his mind to work as he kept his eyes closed. There was enough ambient light to tell him the Sun was up as it made its way into his eyelids. He took a full and deep breath, then let it out. His stomach stopped doing flip-flops, so he dared to open his eyes. He saw brush and vegetation in front of his windshield.

"What?" he said out loud as he looked around. He had been lucky to get his head out the window as it looked like his four-wheeler was sitting in the middle of a huge bush. Had he run off the road after passing out, had a stroke? Mark reached for his cell phone attached to the dashboard and tried to dial '911'. He immediately saw he had no cellular signal. Mark cursed and turned off the phone, leaving it in its cradle. His head began to ache, and Mark realized he might be a bit dehydrated after losing everything in his stomach. Mark Stone reached to the cup holder and removed the large coffee he had bought. It was air temperature, which told him it had been sitting in the car for more than a few minutes. He gulped it down, and his stomach did not revolt, so Mark thought it had been the correct action. Mark felt better, so he tried to open his door. After about six inches, he found the brush around his SUV prevented any further movement.

"Where in the Hell am I?" he wondered out loud. He began racking his brain. Had he ran off the road, down into some unfamiliar patch of brush? Mark was in the Pacific Northwest with some thick forests. But he remembered driving down a main road just a couple of miles from his home. Ah, Shit. Home. His wife Cheri would be frantic when he did not return from the trip to the grocery store. It was time for him to get out of the SUV and figure out where he was.

Mark had a decent folding blade knife from his days as a Special Agent. He found it in his jacket pocket, unlocked the blade, and then pushed the driver's door open as far as possible. Mark began to cut the barricading vegetation as best the man could. A half-hour later, he was able to exit the SUV. The former law enforcement officer managed to push thru the blocking brush and branches to the rear hatchback. The automatic opener worked, and the hatch door opened up about one foot. Thus the man knew the SUV still had some juice in its electrical system. The space provided enabled Mark to reach in and grab a tool he kept for just such possible situations.

In a box labeled 'JEEP,' he took out a combination short ax and pick. The bladed object looked more like a weapon than a tool, but at that moment, the stout blade would help Mark clear the vegetation. He set to work. Within another half hour, Mark Stone had removed sufficient brush to the rear that the hatch completely opened up. He sat down on the floor of the cargo area to catch his breath. Mark was retired, so he was no longer a young stud capable of working all day chopping down trees.

"If Dad could only see me now," he mumbled. His father had been a commensurate tree cutter as Mark had grown up. But back then, there was a chain saw or two. Mark reached into one of the two bags of groceries from the store. He took out the half-gallon of chocolate milk his wife had requested. The cold from the store cooler had long since worn off, again telling Mark he had been 'out' for a while. The man shrugged and said, "Well, no use letting it go bad," and began to drink it. It tasted good in the somewhat humid heat.

As he drank the milk, he glanced around. Some of the vegetation seemed to be small fir and evergreen trees, as was typical for much of the Pacific Northwest of the United States. Mixed in were just strange types; some looked more tropical, and one bush had large bluish berries. Mark thought of trying one but stopped. What if it made him sick? There were no doctors out there.

Out here. Out *where?*

"We're not in Kansas anymore, Toto," he said. Mark looked at the ground. It seemed to slope a bit down in the direction the nose of the SUV pointed. Walking downhill meant he might reach a water source as well as some trail, animal, or—what?

Mark pulled his five-shot Ruger .357 Magnum from his inside jacket pocket. A retired cop, he could legally carry a pistol in all fifty states. His revolver was a beefier version of many a five-shot 'belly gun,' and the agent had a six-round stripper clip in his pocket. At least he had something other than the oversized hatchet to defend himself.

Mark put his pistol away and stood up. He finished the chocolate milk, which bulged his stomach a bit and gave him some food, energy, and hydration. He glanced in the grocery bags and took stock of his stores. A couple of single servings of microwaveable creamy tomato soup, a compact case of ramen noodles, a bottle of catsup, a box of snack crackers, a small container of plastic sandwich bags, and a bottle of red wine rounded out his potential supplies. His mind was already working on the reality he was nowhere near his home and would have to travel to find it. His military and first responder training gave Mark survival tools until he worked his way back to civilization.

"Civilization…" he mumbled, "but whose? Am I on Barsoom? If I am, I hope I find a Dejah Thoris."

Mark used a blanket he kept in the back seat in transporting the family dogs to construct a carrier for his supplies. The retired Special Agent decided to work his way down the slope near the front of the SUV. Siting and waiting for 'rescue' when Mark could not even recognize anything about his location was useless. Without a cellular signal calling for help was out of the question. His gut said his survival was up to him.

Mark made his way to the SUV front and set to work, creating a pathway in the odd brush. As he worked at cutting a path, he realized that the exercise would help clear the cobwebs away, if nothing else. Keep it up, and he may work off some of that fat around his middle.

Surprisingly, after a half-hour of work, he discovered a definite thining in the brush further down the grade. Mark stopped for a breather (being late fifties in age did not make him a young pup anymore). He surveyed the area back up to the SUV and further down the increasing slope. It looked like some game trails weaved their way through the odd woods. For a moment, Mark thought about trying to cut a path wide enough to roll the SUV through but decided he needed to figure out the situation before such a project. He walked back up to the vehicle, locked it up, and recovered his crude blanket carrier. The man knew starvation was nowhere near, and he was hydrated enough for the immediate future. Plus, Mark knew how to construct a solar still from the plastic sandwich bags to regain some water in his urine. The retired 'cop' paused for a moment and tried his cell phone one more time.

"Damn, still nothing." Mark turned the phone off and slipped it back into his pocket. He adjusted his small load of food and set out for what looked like the nearest game trail.

Mark weaved his way through the pine and fir trees, finding several animal trails that eventually snaked their way and formed one main one. He looked at the animal sign and thought he recognized some hooved deer type, as well as what he thought was a wild pig or two. Mark also saw some unfamiliar clawed prints of some size. He once again made sure his pistol was handy.

Mark walked for some quarter-hour when he thought he heard a human shout. Damn, maybe he could be rescued after all. Mark Stone increased his speed down the rough trail. A minute later, he heard loud voices speaking in a language other than English. The retired federal agent listened to a male and female voice arguing that his somewhat trained ear sounded Chinese.

"Foreign students on a hike?" Mark mumbled.

The brush suddenly thinned. Mark slowed and looked down at what seemed like a small clearing. He froze in his tracks when he saw the five mounted humans.

On clearly average-sized horses were four males clothed in what could only be archaic uniforms. The riders had metal breastplates that denoted historical heavy calvary, with helmets Mark had seen in a museum room of Asian-style headgear. Now he could tell that one figure was arguing with a lone horse-mounted female figure. They were speaking a dialect of Chinese.

There was a break in the foliage, which allowed Mark a clear view of the man and woman arguing. The Asian-looking male seemed to have some ornate fourragere and cordage denoting an officer on his uniform. He was holding in his left hand a rope that was attached to the woman's throat. In appearance, the early thirties lady was a raven-haired European beauty with substantial curves in all the right places her long dress could not hide. She spoke Chinese in Mark's estimation, like a native-born person.

As Mark watched from his concealment cover, the Chinese officer viciously yanked on the rope, almost unhorsing the woman whose hands were bound in front. The former federal agent had used force during arrests and on uncooperative prisoners. However, the action of the Chinese man seemed so unwarranted, no matter if the woman was a criminal arrestee. Before Mark consciously thought of the ramifications of his actions, he dumped his blanket pack and pulled his pistol. He stepped partially from the cover of the bushes and yelled.

"Hey, asshole! You always jerk women around?"

All eyes were on Mark as he kept the .357 concealed behind his right thigh. The officer yelled and motioned with his chin towards Mark. The nearest Chinese mounted soldier spurred his mount towards Mark, lowering a short lance as he did so. Mark saw the sharp metal blade of the lance pointing directly at his chest, and the rider did not look like he was going to slow his mount. In one smooth motion from years as a firearms instructor, he raised his pistol and shot the advancing soldier in the face. The rider toppled from his mount, dying as he hit the ground. Time seemed to freeze.

The woman exploded into action. She reached up with her bound hands and yanked on the rope around her neck as she slid off her mount. The raven-haired female's movement almost unhorsed the Chinese officer. The officer tried to yell orders, pull at a sidearm on his belt, and not be pulled off his horse by the rope. He had made the tactical mistake of having the line attached to his prisoner wrapped around his arm. Now the woman had as much control over the officer as he had over her.

The two remaining mounted soldiers responded to their officer's command and grabbed at some long guns in saddle scabbards. Mark scrambled to the cover of a large tree as he shifted his pistol to a two-handed grip. He saw the struggle between the officer and the woman, and

Mark made a snap decision. He fired a round at the man's chest plate.

The .357 round hit with sufficient force to de-mount the Chinese officer. Mark ducked back behind the tree a moment before one of the soldiers fired a shot at him. The retired federal agent's brain registered the weapon was loaded with black powder, as evidenced by the cloud of smoke produced. He did a quick- peek from around the tree and saw the two mounted troops yelling as they dismounted with rifles in hand.

"Shit," Mark said as he realized he was outnumbered two to one. His initial actions now seemed much too hasty. The brutality towards the woman had prompted him to act without much forethought. Now, he might be in a trick bag. As Mark searched his brain for the following action, he heard a loud report. Then another. Then a scream, then another. The retired 'cop' slowly cut the pie around the tree to see what had transpired.

He saw the European woman with a massive revolver in her hand as she went from one Chinese individual to another and kicked them with her foot. None of the soldiers moved, so Mark assumed they were all dead or dying. Before he came entirely into the open, he called out.

"Hey, lady. Don't shoot, okay?"

The raven-haired woman swung the huge revolver towards Mark, so he ducked back behind the tree.

"Hey, dammit. I just shot two men because

of you."

"Englander?" the woman yelled.

"American. Now, how about pointing that horse pistol in another direction."

Mark heard a short laugh. "Sorry. *Entschuligen Sie.* I... did not have good luck with men lately."

Mark peeked around the tree and saw the woman had laid down the pistol and used a copper-colored long knife or short sword to see the rawhide bonds from her wrists.

Mark slowly approached her as he looked for any sign of life in the bodies. He looked at the body of the Chinese officer and saw there was a partial bullet penetration of the metal cuirass. As he looked closer, he saw the man's throat had been slashed open.

"You have a name, American?"

"Mark Stone. And you?"

"Susan Von Braun. I am German."

"Yeah, I figured from your accent. How did you learn Chinese?"

"I lived in China as a doctor assigned to a Christian Mission. Before I came—here."

"So, this is not China?"

The woman named Susan looked at Mark as she felt and searched the pockets of the corpses.

"You just—came?" she asked.

"I guess. One minute I'm driving my SUV, the next... I wake up near here."

The fact he had just shot two men suddenly sank in, and Mark began to shake a bit. Susan walked over to him and held her hand out to shake.

"I thank you, Mark Stone. You saved me from a very bad thing. These Emperor's soldiers were about to drag me back to New Beijing." Susan paused for a moment. "You have not killed before, yes?"

"No—Susan, if I may use your first name, Doctor. Some thirty years in law enforcement and the military, I never had to shoot anyone. Lots of training; this is the first time I had to use it."

From far off came the echoes of some bugle. Susan began to curse. "Please, help me collect the horses. We need at least two. You ride, yes?"

"Not in years. This fat older body will need some help getting on a horse."

"You must learn fast, Mark. For other patrols are looking. And they heard the gunshots."

In some ten minutes, Mark and Susan had three mounts in tow. The doctor had stripped the dead soldiers of all metal items, including the breastplates.

"Metal is money—especially iron like in the officer's chest plate. Copper is common. The rest are rarer."

The former agent removed a duplicate of a Colt Navy cap and ball from the officer with a spare loaded cylinder. It was an exact copy of an 1851 Colt like Wild Bill Hickock had once carried but with total Chinese markings.

Mark also grabbed two rifles, which his firearms history fascination told him were breech loaders similar to Snider Conversions of the late 1860s. They had been converted to fire rimfire cartridges of which he and Susan recovered some three dozen.

The massive fifty-caliber rimfire five-shot revolver Susan used was hers.

"That asshole Leutnant Shanghied me and took my pistol," Susan said. "Now, he is dead."

"Locally made?" Mark asked.

"Yes. The Chinese in this place are adept at copying other people's manufactured items. They very occasionally improve on them."

"So, Susan, where is this place?"

The doctor shrugged. "No one knows. It is a different world, place, and time. People come from different years, even centuries. I guess from different universes."

"How long have you been—here?"

"I believe I have been here some five years. The first weeks are blurry. Many who arrive come with limited memories."

"Has anyone come up with a name for this reality?"

"Some call it... Elsewhen."

After loading the third mount with the salvage from the four bodies and the saddlebags, Mark used a nearby log as a step to mount the horse. Susan led the packhorse as they started at a walk and then increased to the trot's gait. Even at a trot, Mark was having a problem keeping a secure seat on the saddle.

After about ten minutes, he called out to Susan. "Hey, stop—I'm just slowing you down."

"No, Mark. We must keep going. Once they find our tracks…."

"They will catch up."

Mark managed to slide off the horse and pulled one of the rifles from its scabbard. "Hand me a water skin. I'll grab some of the rounds for this rifle and convince the Chinese to stop following us. By the way, where are we going?"

"To a place called Freetown. It is about a three days ride from here. That is where I was going when they caught me."

"The so-called Emperor has no control over that place, Freetown?"

"He uses them as a buffer to what lies out West. The Chines know there are bands of dangerous people and animals out there. A few brave traders travel with Chinese goods and come back with precious metals, jewels, and salvaged products from more advanced peoples. At least some are more advanced than my time."

"When was your time?" asked the retired cop.

"1929. China under Chiang Kai-shek. That is why I speak Chinese well, in addition to English. French and German."

"Why was this Emperor so hot on taking you back here in—Elsewhen."

Susan sneered. "I was his slave and doctor to his many concubines and whores. Five years of that function was enough for me, so I fled."

"I can understand that," replied Mark.

Mark took the rifle, a handful of shells, and a water skin. He walked back on the horse trail looking for a good spot to perform some bushwacking. Mark found a clump of rocks up on the slope near where he had left the SUV. Mark used some brush to create a small hidey-hole and waited.

A half-hour later, Mark heard the unmistakable sounds of galloping horses approaching his hideaway. The former agent had set up a rifle rest using his jacket. The sights on the rifle were a bit crude but sufficient to hit what he wanted. He sighted the gun down the path as the sound of the mounted riders grew near.

Mark shot the lead horse when it was almost one hundred yards away. The galloping horse tumbled into the path of the second horse and rider, who flipped end over end as it struck the shot horse. The last two horsemen swerved their mounts to dodge the collision as Mark reloaded and fired once again at the next horse. This shot was high and took the third Chinese soldier off his mount;

the last rider reined in short, yanked his horse around, and galloped back the way he came. Mark reloaded his rifle and slowly approached the three downed riders. One of the cavalrymen lay moaning, his mount trying to rise on a broken leg. Mark shot the horse in its head.

"You're becoming quite the assassin," Mark mumbled. He went to the dead and dying soldiers and horses, checking for weapons. In a saddlebag, he found a Remington rolling block pistol with original U.S. Navy markings. Mark took the handgun and a few loose rounds, plus a lever-action rifle in one sheath. The long gun looked like a replica of an early Volcanic, a pre-Winchester weapon. Mark picked it up, found a flask of some type of rotgut in a saddlebag, turned, and went looking for the one riderless mount.

Ten minutes later, he managed to find the mount and made calming noises as he took its reins. Mark then began to walk in the direction of Susan Von Braun. If the one rider who fled came back, he'd have to shoot him also. Training had taken over, so he was functioning, but Mark had no bloodthirsty desire to kill anyone else. Mark began his walk up the trail.

Finally, Susan Von Braun appeared with all three horses. She smiled, then frowned at Mark as she spoke. "We need no more *pferds*—horses."

"Well, I brought this along in case I could not locate you. Now, if you can aid me in taking the saddle and such off this beast so that it may run free…."

Mark was back on his uncomfortable mount in ten minutes and managed to keep up with Susan in a trot. He finally managed to get his riding rhythm and not bounce off his horse. Somehow, Mark survived an hour of walking and trotting until Susan called a halt. The former agent gratefully slid off his horse and tried to stretch a bit. Susan pulled out a water skin and let the horses drink, so Mark did the same to his mount. As they allowed the horses to cool down a bit, Mark decided it was time to pump Susan for more information.

"Besides the Chinese, who else is in Elsewhen?"

"There are some Romans who set up a New Rome on the Great Central Ocean. Also on that coast is someone with an imagination named Camelot. Some of those people seemed to originate in the time of the Crusades. We have fisher folk scattered up and down the coast in smaller towns and villages."

"So, people were—dumped here from various cultures and apparent times in history, right?"

"Yes, that seems truthful."

"Any alien creatures or beings?"

Susan paused in thought, then answered.

"There be dragons in these forests."

"Dragons?"

"The Chinese call them that, yet they look like dinosaurs. They stand a bit taller than a man on their hind legs. These dragons eat most everything, so most people avoid them."

"The Chinese, what era are they from?"

"The original Emperor and his family seem to come from the sixteen hundreds. Other Asian, Japanese, Koreans, and Tonkin peoples, come from various times and places. Some Chinese soldiers from an era just before mine, I think the Boxer Rebellion, appeared not long after I did. When soldiers with weapons appear, the current Emperor tries to seize them and then copy as many of the weapons as are useful."

"Why hasn't he conquered the whole known area?"

"He is building up his forces as we speak. The lack of decent metal deposits limits the Emperor's ambitions. Thus, instead of iron and steel, the Chinese use many coppers, make brass and bronze when they can amass some tin and zinc."

Mark removed the rifle from the scabbard and looked more closely at it. It was a mixture of brass and iron. "Susan, have you seen this type of rifle before?"

"Yes. The Emperor's technicians are trying to make ones that will take more powerful shells".

Mark worked the lever-action and ejected a shell. He examined it in his palm. "Looks like a 41 caliber, between a short and a long shell from the 1860s on Earth. At least its not those god awful rocket shells of the original Volcanics."

"You know a lot about guns, Mark Stone."

"I was a firearms instructor when I was what you

would call a police officer. I was also a history major."

"Well, my new friend, if the Emperor catches you, you will be locked up with all the others with knowledge he wishes. For he wishes to control all with that knowledge."

"I guess, Susan, I'll just have to make sure he does not catch up with me."

After seeing to their toilet, the two fugitives remounted their steads and continued on their journey. Mark kept looking back to look for any dust from fast-moving groups of horses. He and Susan were moving further and further from his SUV. He hoped the brush the vehicle was concealed in was sufficient to hide it from the Chinese troops. The metal in that car would make someone very wealthy, according to Susan.

The Day Sun was approaching the horizon just as Susan located a small stream running by a cave.

"That trader was correct in his map," the woman said with a smile. "We camp here tonight."

"Thank God," said Mark. "my butt needs a rest."

The Day Sun set as they finished watering, rubbing down, and feeding the horses. Susan used flint and steel to light a fire expertly. Within minutes, the raven-haired woman had some rice balls heating over the fire. As the local sun set, a very bright star rose into the night sky, with two smaller moons chasing it across the horizon.

"Barsoom, I greet you," Mark said with a grin.

Susan looked at him quizzically.

"Barsoom?"

"What Edgar Rice Burroughs called Mars in his John Carter books. His characters, including Tarzan, would fit right into this lost world."

Susan laughed, and it sounded a bit musical to Mark's ears, much like his wife's. Susan must have noticed a dark thought cross his face as she stepped forward and took his hand. "Come. I saw your wedding ring and know you miss your family. There is still a chance…."

"There is little chance of a return if we cannot figure out how we got here."

"Which could happen, my friend."

Mark saw the pretty woman was trying to cheer him. He knew she must have gone through the same angst some five or six years ago when she was yanked into this reality. Thus, he smiled back. No use raining on her parade.

"I will leave the science to you, Doctor. Now, may I try one of those rice balls? They smell interesting."

They ate, and Mark broke out the bottle of wine he had brought. It took a bit of ingenuity to get the cork out, but Susan produced two cups, and they soon toasted each other. The horses concealed in the empty cave became restless, and Susan looked out past the firelight.

"What's up?" Mark asked.

"Mole rats. They come out at night. These are as big as dogs."

"Well, I have a solution for that."

Mark rose, grabbed a lit branch from the campfire, and the lever-action rifle. He stepped to the edge of their camp, let out a Rebel yell, and threw the firey branch. The retired special agent almost hit a dark shape with the makeshift torch, which took off with a loud squeal. Susan began to laugh.

"And thus John Carter fights off the giant rats of Barsoom," Mark said with fake gravitas.

"Come, my hero," Sussan said with a laugh in her throat. "We will build up the fire and make our beds close to the horses. And keep our guns close."

A quarter of an hour later, the two used the bedrolls of the now-dead soldiers to make some decent beds for each of them. Mark poured them each a drink of wine and raised it in a toast.

"To comradeship and friends," he said.

"To heroes who appear at just the right moment," Susan said with a grin.

Mark gazed at her. God, she was beautiful, but the man quickly tamped that thought down. He was not a cheater and would not start now.

Mark threw the wine drink back in his throat. "And now, to sleep. I see the next two days as long and hard, at least on my butt."

There was that laugh again. "Yes. Goodnight, friend Mark Stone."

"Sleep tight, Susan Von Braun."

They were soon both asleep.

Partway through the night, Mark woke to feel a warm body snuggled up to his back. He sighed as he looked up at what Susan called the Night Sun high above.

"Dejah Thoris," he whispered, "you are something else."

He rolled over and cuddled up to Susan. Both were soon sleeping the sleep of the right and innocent.

# 3
# LOST AND FOUND
## PART II

Mark Stone looked through the spyglass taken from the Chinese Emperor's soldiers during the rescue of Suan Von Braun two days prior.

"So that's Freetown," he said. Mark handed the spyglass to Susan, who placed it back in its case.

"Yes. It has been in existence for many years before I—arrived. I was here once before, about a year ago."

"What brought you here?" Mark asked the curvy raven-haired German lady.

"The Emperor sent me when there were rumors of a virulent sickness. I was his most educated doctor, so he was willing to risk losing me if I could make sure it was not a plague."

"What was it?"

"Typhus from poor sanitation. I had riders bring

powdered lye and some crude but effective medicines the other doctors and I had achieved. Some of the developed Chinese drugs were reasonably effective."

"Antibiotics?" Mark asked. Susan smiled at the older man.

"You know some medicine. Antibacterials, sulpha-based drugs, were being developed in Germany and tested in China when practicing medicine. The Chinese knew some very similar treatments. Some of their traditional medicines worked. Some, well—"

"Like Rhino Horn for impotence and sexual inadequacy."

Susan laughed. "I will make a doctor of you yet. Policeman."

The retired federal agent laughed with his new friend. It was funny yet not so odd the two recent strangers could become this close. Yet Mark knew from his experience that surviving death and injury created close bonds between people who had never met. The fact that Susan was so attractive in her body and mind made it easy. Mark had to keep reminding himself that he was married, even if in another universe.

The close to three days of travel on horseback had given the two opportunities to discuss their shared predicament. Where Elsewhen was and how to return to their homeworld and reality. Both knew that the chances were remote but kept hope alive. No matter what happened, the two new friends and companions knew they had to survive if they were ever to hope of returning to their Earth. Plus, they now had a common enemy, a local Chinese Emperor.

"That looks like a crude lookout tower at the town's entrance," said Mark.

"Yes. If you look closer, it is staffed by a youthful male."

"Well, I hope if he does not speak English, that he speaks a language you know, Susan."

The two nudged their mounts into slow walks as they covered the last mile to the edge of Freetown. Approximately one hundred meters from the lookout tower, a young voice called out in German. Susan quickly answered the challenge, and a toe-headed male in his early teen years stepped onto a small porch at the top of the access ladder. Mark saw as they neared the sentry that the young man had a flintlock musket.

"Think he can use that?" asked Mark.

"It is more for warning and signaling than defense. The townspeople are not noted for being violent."

"What if some threats appeared from that, I guess you would say it is west of here? Do they have a defense force, a militia?"

Susan shrugged as she answered, "They have a lawman and a town council made up of the significant business owners in town. Which are primarily Chinese."

"But they are not aligned with the Emperor."

"Yes and no. Freetown is a place to send

malcontents without having to martyr them with an executioner's sword. At the same time, some use the threat of the Emperor's displeasure to get their way. It is complicated."

"And a Yankee round-eyed dog like myself had better watch his Ps and Qs."

Susan laughed once again, a pleasant sound to Mark's ears. "Yes, my friend. Especially since you do not speak Chinese, an armed patrol will probably look for us within days. We will have to find a place where we can stay as well as hide."

Mark grunted. "Silence can be bought," the man said.

"Yes. This is why our first stop will be at a business that deals with metal and money."

With a smile, Susan spoke to the young man in German—Mark believed it was a question about the location of the local moneychanger. The boy, soon to be a man, pointed towards the town as he gave directions. Susan thanked him and flipped a coin in his direction. The sentry took the payment with a grin. The two travelers nudged their horses along and entered the town proper. Within five minutes, Susan halted them in front of a wide storefront with a large sign. Painted on the sign in half a dozen languages was the purpose and ownership of the business.

"Money, Trade, and Metal," Mark read aloud. "Liu Chang, proprietor."

"Please stay outside. Mark. Water the horses while I conduct some business."

"Wheel and deal, I see," answered Mark with a smile. A momentary look of confusion on Susan's face told the former lawman that she was unfamiliar with English expression. Still, the context seemed familiar to her as she finally smiled back.

"I will see what we may get from the metal on that packhorse. The spare rifles we will try and sell at a gunsmith down the road if he is still here."

"I'll keep them hid from the local Chinese populace," said Mark. "They will know the Chinese soldiers just did not give them away."

Susan dismounted from her stead with ease as Mark managed to slide off of his mount. He groaned. "This old body is not conducive to horseback."

Susan laughed as she answered, "Walk a bit while you see to the horses. I won't be long."

"If you are, I am willing to come in guns a-blazing."

Susan shook her head as she laughed some more. Mark knew she saw him as this crazy New American. However, he was serious, even if she did not realize it.

Mark took a wooded bucket next to the communal water trough and began to water the three mounts. He could just hear the beginning of a conversation as Susan displayed samples of the metal objects Mark and she had taken from the dead soldiers. The voices began to rise in timbre and volume as Susan pushed Chang for the best price while the Chinese man tried to bully this upstart woman. Ten minutes later, Mark had his hand on the butt of the Colt Navy Clone and stepped towards the open business door when Susan came striding outside, still arguing over her shoulder. She looked at Mark and grinned.

"I have him where I want him," she said with a lower voice and widening grin. Susan went to the packhorse and grabbed two large bags, which contained the metal armor and a couple of the copper sword knives. Not for the first time was Marc surprised by the strength of the young German lady as Susan carried and dragged the booty bags into the shop. There followed some more arguing, then the sound of counting out loud. The raven-haired lady exited the establishment and tossed a near full leather coin bag at the former lawman.

"Your half in gold, silver, and copper. Don't spend it all at once," Susan said with a satisfied grin.

Mark grinned as he hefted the bag. "Arrrgh. Pieces of eight, my beauty?"

Susan caught the meaning of his joke and laughed at his best pirate imitation. "The equivalent," she answered. "We came at the right time. Trade-in metals have been slow this last month. What I sold Chang, he will have smelted this night to hide its origins in Chinese equipment. We should be safe thanks to his greed for a profit."

Mark slipped the bag into the front pocket of the

hoodie he was wearing, one of his salvaged clothe items from the SUV. Judging by what Susan had told him over the last couple of days, metals such as what they just sold made them moderately wealthy in Elsewhen. "Where to next, Doctor?"

"Down the street to where I remember a gunsmith resides. We can sell the rifles—"

"We can sell *a* rifle. Trust my expertise in this. The repeater and a breechloader will come in handy on the trail."

Susan flashed an attractive smile and nodded her head in his direction. "I will yield to your expertise in all things martial. Now, shall we walk or—"

"We shall walk the horses and give my ass a rest. You are the horse person. I am not."

On the corner of the following city block was a large storefront. The painted sign above in English and Chinese stated, '*Weapons and Gunsmith. If it is broken, we will fix or replace it.*'

"Good," said Susan. "Mister Walken is still in business."

"He came from a modern era?" asked Mark.

"More modern than most. You will enjoy talking with Christopher Walken, I believe."

Mark had to stifle a laugh. Yes, in his world, he would enjoy talking with Christopher Walken. The retired lawman uncovered one of the Snider breechloaders as he glanced around for an audience, saw none, then went into the shop. Inside was the typical long counter of many a gunshop. Behind the shop counter and in front of the back rows of weapons was a large muscular man who resembled a blacksmith more than a gun salesman. The dark bearded man with hints of gray in his hair nodded at the travelers as he spoke.

"Afternoon. You look like you may speak English."

"Guilty as charged. I think you will be interested in this." With that statement, Mark laid the long rifle on the countertop.

The gunshop owner's eyes widened a bit as he recognized the weapon. "Well, I'll be. I heard the Chinese were making some more breechloaders, but not Sniders."

"Here, a shell for you," said Mark.

"Looks like a 50-70 or thereabouts. You have many of these shells?"

"Sorry. I have to keep the rest for the trail."

Chris Walken looked in the bore using a homemade bore light that seemed to operate on a small Triple A battery.

"What year you come from?" Mark asked.

"1939. I got the bore light from a guy who said he came from after the Cold War. Whatever that was."

"How much?" asked the gunsmith.

"We need ammunition for her horse pistol there. Also, any.38 Special laying around, plus cap and ball supplies. Oh, and something like a .41 short or long."

Chris looked at Mark directly. "You have a run-in

with the Chinee assholes?”

"A bit. So, silence is golden.”

Christopher laughed. “Comes with the territory.”

The shop proprietor turned around and rummaged about some boxes and small cubbyholes among his weapons for sale. He turned back around with a section of oiled cloth and laid his treasure on it for Mark and Susan's perusal. “Several .38 Special I have had for a while as most people want the old stuff like the Chinese make. A few large rimfires for her horse pistol. A small box of .41 shells for the lever-action you have stashed. Small tin of percussion caps for your Chinese Colt in your belt, with a bit of powder. I'm short lead for bullets until Sinjin, my trader, comes again.”

"Sounds good to me,” replied the retired Special Agent. He looked at Susan.

"Do not look at me, my friend,” said Susan as an answer to his look. “You are the martial expert.”

"Okay. Deal then.”

"Have any copper I can bum off you? I can make some same shells for the Snider.”

Mark pulled some 20th Century copper and zinc pennies from his pocket. He added a couple of nickels and dimes.

"These should do. These have a crapload of different metals in them.”

"Yeah. Others tell me the metal in money became cheaper and cheaper after World War II. By the way, how long you been here? In Elsewhen?"

"About a week. And you?"

"About eight years near as I can tell," answered the gunsmith. "With everyone bouncing in and out like in a cheap Science Fiction magazine story, I have a hell of a time keeping track."

Mark laughed. "Ain't that the truth."

Just then, another voice joined the conversation. "Gentlemen and lady. How are you this fine day?"

Mark turned slowly, his hand on the Colt under his hoodie. The voice had a twinge of a Southwest Texas drawl in it, and Mark soon saw why. A tall and wiry man sporting a traditional ten-gallon hat and what looked like a Texas Ranger Badge on his linsey-woolsey shirt stood with a hand near a Colt Peacemaker. A couple of steps behind him was a young man with what appeared to be a double-barreled flintlock fowling piece.

"Hey, Ranger. Or should we call you Marshal Dillon?" asked Chris.

Mark tried not to burst out in nervous laughter. Christopher Walken and now Marshal Dillon. It was as if God was testing his sense of humor and the bizarre.

"Well, I was made the town marshal a couple of years back. But I was a Ranger when God or the Devil spits me out here. So, both fits."

Dillon gave both Mark and Susan a once-over as the two travelers met him with a steady gaze. "Can I see that Chinese Colt you have your hand on?" asked the

Marshal/Ranger.

"I only pull a pistol out if I plan to use it."

"Sounds reasonable to me as long as the previous owner is not some Chinese connected to the so-called Emperor. If you bring trouble to my town, I will have to ensure you don't stay."

"We were just passing through," said Mark. Then Susan interrupted.

"I am a doctor. I missed meeting you the last time I was here. If you need a doctor's skill, we may be able to come to an arrangement." The local lawman paused as he examined the two people standing in front of him, then continued, "We can always use some Western Medicine. Some of the Chinese powders and things seem to be a waste of time and money though they swear by them."

"I know both Marshal Dillon. Better than most people if I may be so bold."

This comment elicited a chuckle from the town marshal as his young assistant behind him remained stoic. "You have to be bold to survive in this place people call Elsewhen. You sound like you have been here for a while." Dillon looked at Mark. "You seem to be a newcomer."

"Good observation, Marshal," said Mark. "Was yanked here about a week ago. I hope to be a fast learner. I was in law enforcement in my time."

The Marshal paused again, then offered his hand to shake. "You have the air of a lawman. Matt Dillon is my full name. I was Rangering around Amarillo, Texas, when I was caught in a Northerner. One moment I'm freezing under snow. The next, a flash of lightning, and I'm here, my horse running off with my 45-75 Winchester and all my gear. I had my Colt here; Somewhere there is a saddle and my possibles."

"You made your way here, on foot?" asked Susan.

"Yes, Ma'am. I was only about ten miles west of here. I've been told if I had continued west instead of east, I'd probably be dead."

"True," stated Chris. "Not much out past Freetown in the Low Plains, other than rumors of nasty bands and tribes."

"Well, I showed up, broke up some fights the first day I was here, and hired to keep the peace. Both sides trust me, which is good since half the population is Chinese."

"Any suggestions on a place to stay in Freetown, Marshal?" asked Mark.

"The Empress Hotel is the best. But it and the others are Chinese-owned. Only Ma Bell's Saloon and Bawdy House is a white-owned place. So if any Chinese troops come knocking, don't expect any support."

"How about you. Marshal?"

"I and a few others try to keep the peace and stop people no matter who they are from being drug off. But remember, I work for the so-called Business Council, which is mostly Chinese."

"Thanks for the warning. Now, I think Chris and I

will finish our business, and then we need to find the stable.”

“Follow the horse flies; There are two horse hotels on the edge of town.”

Dillon tipped his hat to Susan. “Ma’am. Have a nice day.”

The Marshall and his apparent deputy turned and walked down the street. Mark looked at Susan. “Well, you’ve been here before. Where do we stay?”

“I stayed at the Empress. They were kind to me. If you have the metal, they give you the service. And you get a hot bath there, plus indoor plumbing.”

Mark grinned. “Well, Doctor, you just sold me. Shall we finish and head to the stables?”

Chris Walken sent them to the stables, which would give them the best deal and not ask too many questions. It was owned by a transplant from 1890s Russia who had learned to speak several languages. And he hated the Chinese.

“You can keep your mounts here. Young Lady. No questions from where they came. I’ll help you swap brands later. The Chinese can go—” and Josef went into a stream of curse words and invectives from several languages. The Russian even offered to buy the extra horse for a reasonable price.

The two travelers thanked him and went to procure their lodgings. The Empress clerks remembered the dark-haired German, meeting her with smiles. They soon had an oversized room up the primary flight of stairs with a bath attached. Susan arranged for a bathtub of hot water as Mark brought their clothes, saddlebags, and concealed weapons to their room.

"I claim the first bath, Mark Stone. Then I will go shopping for some fresh clothes for us."

"I'll need some underwear if you want to buy me some. That is if you are not too shy to buy for a fat older man."

Susan laughed. "I am a doctor, remember? I have seen it all."

Mark went down to the small hotel restaurant and had a cup of hat tea plus some eggrolls. He bought a large bowl of hot and spicy soup with some extra egg rolls plus a bottle of wine and brought them back to the room.

Mark found Susan was still in the tub, with many soap suds covering her naked body. She showed a sly smile at Mark as he tried not to look too closely at her. "Care to join me?"

"Too dirty. I'll wait."

"I think the American expression is party pooper, Mark."

The older man flushed a bit. "I brought you some food and wine."

"Oh, good! I'll be right out…" and began to stand up. The retired lawman beat a hasty retreat.

A few minutes later, a towel wrapped, Susan

exited the bathroom and sat down at the small table in the room. She began to inhale the eggrolls and drank the plum wine. She giggled as she noticed Mark watching her eat. "You like to watch women eat?"

"I am enjoying the smell of a freshly washed young lady. It brings back pleasant memories."

"Your wife?"

"Yes. Cheri will be worried sick. I have been gone for almost a week."

"Remember, my friend. A week here in Elsewhen maybe just minutes on our Earth. A Chinese scientist told me that different worlds and universes might exist at different time rates."

Mark sipped his wine, then answered, "I hope so, Susan. As much as I enjoy your company, I need to get back to my wife and my four-legged family—our dogs."

Susan stood up and almost lost her towel. "The water is still warm. I was not too dirty…."

"Hint taken. Conserve water, shower with a friend."

Mark took his bath in his skivvies to attempt to wash his single pair of underwear simultaneously as he bathed his body. He added the final contents of a kettle on the small room stove and then crawled in. He groaned with pleasure at the near hot water. God, his sore ass (and other muscles) needed the healing warmth.

He began to doze off after making sure his

Ruger.357 Magnum pistol brought by him to Elsewhen was on a within reach small lamp table. Like parts of the American Old West, this was shaping up to be a violent environment. The retired lawman sipped his wine as he waited for Susan to return with clean clothes for them, as well as other odds and ends. The Doctor was also looking for a place to hang her shingle if they could dodge any of the Emperor's toadies. Mark dozed off thinking about what job an older beefy badge and gun carrier could perform in Elsewhen.

Susan woke him up by barging into the bath area, singing some German song in a delightful voice. Mark jerked awake and automatically covered himself as there were no more concealing suds.

Susan laughed. Music to Mark's ears. "I have seen more men's genitalia than there are days in the year."

"Yes, but not mine. And I am old-fashioned, Doctor Von Braun."

"Well, finish your bath unless you wish for me to wash your back. Then try these clean clothes on. I can have them tailored or returned if necessary."

A quarter of an hour later, Mark Stone admired himself in the full-length mirror the hotel provided. The cotton pants and shirt fit nicely over the silk underwear the German Doctor had found him. Mark would heat some more water and hand wash his Home Earth clothes before sleep. He knew they would have to be ready to disappear and hide in the morning if any Chinese soldiers showed up in Freetown.

"You have an accurate eye for measurement, Susan."

"Thank you. And this light suit coat should fit you. Plus, what I think was called a Bolo Tie in your Old West."

"Yes. And may I say your new blue dress matches your eyes quite nicely."

Susan did a quick spin, which allowed Mark to see she had no stockings covering her shapely legs. *Down boy, he thought.*

"Now, we have plenty of money thanks to deceased soldier coin pouches and sold metal objects. Tonight, we go out for a well-cooked meal. If we have to hit the trail, as you would say, a healthy meal in our stomachs will help in our travels."

"I bend to your logic, pretty lady. I will let you pick the establishment since I am new in town." Mark bent and offered his arm in a traditional male escort fashion.

"Shall we, Milady?"

"Why, of course, kind Sir. Just let me conceal my horse pistol in this extra-large purse I found."

"Always the practical one. My Ruger is in my belt."

"Dancing also?" Susan asked with a sly smile.

"Let us not push this tired old body. Not yet, at least."

They had an excellent Chinese meal at a nearby restaurant. With their stomachs full and bodies warm from some plum liquor, they stepped out onto the sidewalk at dusk to walk back to The Empress Hotel. Just then, three men approached from the street and stopped at a respectful distance from the couple, the two buckskin wearing doffing their wide brined hats. Mark slipped his hand onto the butt of his revolver as Susan stepped to the side, her right hand in the oversized handbag.

"Pardon me, Ma'am, Sir," said the nearer of the two, a tall full-bearded man who had Frontiersman written all over him. "I hear tell you might have a horse for sale. Red here, and I need one as our Injun friend went and got his kilt."

"What are your friend's names?" asked Susan with a smile.

"Yeah, Blue," said the red-headed man with a bushy mustache, "Ain't ya got no manners? I'm Red Macbeth, Ma'am. The Injun here is a Comanche called Spotted Wolf in our language. Blue is Blue Baxter."

"Comanche," said Mark. "I heard they are not exactly friendly to so-called white men,"

"Ole Wolf, here is the best Pard now," said Blue. "We came over to Limbo about six years ago. Other people call this place Elsewhen, but I think God sent us to Limbo until we get our heads straight."

"Yessir, Spotted Wolf, and we have been riding together for almost the whole time," added Red. "Which is why we are trying to help him find a horse. He can't hunt with us with no horse. No hunt, no meat to trade for coin or supplies."

"How did he lose his mount?" asked Susan.

"A couple standing dragons ran up on us as we was a making camp. They must have been real hungry to do that in daylight. They killed the horse before...."

"Standing dragons?" asked Mark.

"Those are the dinosaurs I mentioned," explained Susan. "About six feet tall and fairly fast."

Mark nodded understanding, then began to shake hands all around. Spotted Wolf said "Hello" when he shook hands but remained an image of stoicism.

"May we revisit this conversation tomorrow?" asked Mark. "Susan and I may have a better idea as to what we plan to do."

"Well, if ya stay, watch the Chinee," warned Blue. "They are about as trustworthy as a scorpion on a hot rock. Will sting you if it fancies them."

"Yeah. Give a holler if the Chinee try to hurt you and your lady friend," said Red. "We'll a come running."

"Thank you," said Susan with a smile. "You are most kind to strangers."

"Not enough ladies around Freetown," said Red. "Ladies, keep us menfolk in line. Well, sometimes, at least."

The new apparent friends laughed and made plans to meet at the hotel for breakfast in the morning. "We'll buy," said Mark, which caused a slight smile to appear on Spotted Wolf's face. Mark and Susan walked arm in arm back to the Empress Hotel and asked the desk clerk to awaken them at sunrise. They then returned to their room. Mark collapsed into an overstuffed chair as Susan went into the bathroom.

"God," he mumbled. "I could sleep for a month." Mark turned towards the closed bathroom door.

"I'll make a bed for me on the floor," the retired federal agent called out.

"Whatever for?" came the muffled reply.

"I think it would be a good—" Mark never finished the statement as Susan stepped out from the bathroom wearing the sheerest of silk nightgowns.

As Mark sat stunned, Susan strode over to the chair. "Stand up," the Doctor ordered.

"Susan, I don't think this is a good idea," Mark said as he stood up and looked at the gorgeous dark-haired woman. Susan was near as tall as he was, especially as she was wearing some high-heeled shoes.

"You think too much," said Susan as she turned him and shoved him onto the large bed. "The chances we can return to our Earth is remote. Sorry, I must be so blunt, but we must live and love, for now, the present. Not tomorrow."

Susan let her negligee slide off her well-endowed body.

"Oh, Lordy," said Mark as Susan climbed on top of him, and they kissed.

It was well before sunrise, and Mark slipped out of bed. He walked to the back window of the hotel room, which looked over a faux balcony onto the back street. He had not meant to give in to the sexual passion which had been nipping at his heels since helping rescue Susan from the Chinese. However, it was the nine hundred-pound gorilla in the room. And they both sensed it.

He looked at his wedding ring. Someplace was his home reality. Maybe what Blue had said was correct. This place was Limbo as preached by the Roman Catholic Church. If it was, Mark had just committed a mortal sin of adultery.

"Yeah, right," Mark mumbled to himself. He looked out the window into the darkness, lost in thought. Then his peripheral vision caught motion coming from his left. He looked at the cause of movement. Mark saw a Chinese cavalryman leading a group of horses to the back of the hotel.

"Shit," he said as he stepped from the window. He went to the bed and woke Susan up as quietly as possible.

"Time to leave. Emperor's guys outside."

Susan slid out of bed, kissed Mark, and hurried to dress. Mark pulled his pants on and started with his shoes when he heard heavy steps coming up the nearby stairs. The retired lawman grabbed the Chinese Colt pistol and stepped to the room's primary access door. He cracked the door and peered out into the hallway. At the top of the stairs near the railing stood a uniformed soldier holding a lever-action rifle. Shadowy figures were making their way up to the stairway guard. Mark knew he had just moments to act before he and Susan were trapped in the room.

Mark stepped into the darkened hallway, the lights probably extinguished by the guard at the top of the stairs. In one fluid motion, Mark cocked and fired the Colt Clone revolver. The bullet struck the face of the Chinese soldier, and he toppled down onto the other men climbing the stairs. Shouts and cries of surprise filled the air as Mark scrambled in a crouch to the top of the stairs. Someone fired a wild shot as Mark aimed and fired his revolver. He tried to hit faces and extremities as he knew some of the breastplates could deflect the lighter bullets. The pistol hammer clicked on an empty chamber much too soon, and he ducked to the carpet.

Above him came the loud blast of Susan's horse pistol as she jumped into the fray. The half-inch slug would penetrate the lite armor of the Chinese. Mark crawled like a one-year-old back to the open door of the hotel room as Susan fired a second round at the attackers. As she did, Mark somehow sprang to his feet and grabbed the former Chinese military lever-action rifle. The retired federal agent had filled the twelve-round magazine with the ammunition bought from Chris Walken, so he had plenty to use. Mark stepped around Susan, yelling at her to finish packing the essentials for escape.

Mark shot and put a round through the right eye of a man yelling orders. As the Chinese officer collapsed like a cheap suit, other soldiers made a mad scramble to the main street doors of the Empress Hotel. Mark levered another shell into the rifle chamber as he stepped into the shadows at the top of the stairs. From his concealment, the former lawman could see half a dozen bodies lying still or twisting and moaning.

A loud bellow penetrated the night air.

"What in Holy Hell is going on? Who is shooting up my town?"

"Is that you, Marshal Dillon?" Mark called out.

"Who else? You and the young lady want to lay your guns down and come talk to me?"

"We'll talk," called out Susan, "but with our guns handy."

The town lawman laughed and stepped into the hotel lobby. As he did, the proprietor of the Empress Hotel appeared from some hidey-hole and began to yell and scream.

"He says—" began Susan.

"I know what he says. I can speak Chinee with the best of you. I guess Mister Kung here tried to tell the Chinese Lieutenant to wait until you were riding out of town before bracing you. He was overruled."

"How'd they sneak in?" asked Mark Stone.

"Mister Wang, who owns the largest general store here, had his son on duty at the lookout tower. They let the soldiers in between rounds by my deputies.”

Mark began to curse up a storm as he walked down the stairs. He picked up a dropped Chinese Colt pistol as well as a short flintlock musket someone was carrying. Mark laid the long weapon on the checkout counter and checked the cylinder of the revolver. No shots had been fired, so it still had the six loaded chambers. Susan walked up behind him, and he watched as she recovered another lever-action rifle. Kung, the hotel owner, seemed green in the gills as he saw these round-eyed barbarians with all these guns.

“Where is this Wang character?” asked Mark.

“In the street, trying to get the other soldiers to come back in and get you two.”

Mark looked directly at Matt Dillon. “What are you going to do?”

“I want to try and stop any more shooting. Bullets do damage to innocent people and property.”

“You going to let them take us?”

“They lost that right when they snuck in here, did not talk to me, then led to a shoot-out. Hell, the soldiers probably wanted to shoot you in your bed.”

“The Emperor is like that,” said Susan. “Summary execution is standard when he is angry.”

Dillon sighed. “I may work for the Chinese majority here, but most do not want to work with the Emperor and his boys.”

“Except for Wang and company,” added Mark. He

walked by the Marshal and into the street. Matt Dillon had his hand on his Peacemaker as his deputies walked up.

"Marshal," one said, and the local lawman motioned him to stop as he watched Mark walk towards the surviving unwounded soldiers.

The three mounted troops were arguing so intently with a red-faced Wang they did not even notice Mark until he was on top of them. Their eyes widened, and one had a hand on a pistol in his belt. Mark shoved his revolver's barrel into that man's face. "Go ahead. Make my day."

All three Chinese raised their hands. Mark then turned his attention to Wang. He one-handed shoved the rifle barrel into Wang's face, making the senior businessman sputter and protest.

"Marshal—" Wang called out in English.

"I should just shoot you now, asshole. Trying to kill us in our beds—"

"Stone. Don't!" Matt Dillon called out. "Ever hear of Tongs?"

The former special agent knew that they were the Triads and organized crime in his time and place. He knew some Tong members were probably part of the growing street crowd. He would get off a shot or two, and then many dead bodies would be in the street. Mark took a deep breath and then let it out.

"You should feel lucky, punk." With that statement, Mark backed up, his guns still on the Chinese.

"You have screwed with the wrong man, Homeys. I have nothing to lose since I was yanked from my family and wound up here, in Elsewhen. Leave me and mine alone. Susan."

"Yes, Mark," came the answer behind him.

"Time to check out."

As Susan and Mark packed their things and had their horses brought from the stable, Marshall Dillon stood by. Blue, Red, and Spotted Wolf, attracted by the commotion, came to talk to the travelers.

"We can still get breakfast," said Mark. "We'll just have to find another place at which to eat."

At that moment, a tall and zaftig bleached blond, middle-aged woman walked up to the small group. Red and Blue grinned and walked over to hug the apparent close friend.

"Ma Bell. We was a-comin' to see you," said Red.

"Don't lie to Mother. You were coming to see my girls." Ma Bell looked at Susan. "You're that doctor who was here a year or so ago. You helped a lot of sick people, including some of me and mine." With that, the brassy blonde hugged Susan. "I'd say welcome back, but my ladies say you had a run-in with the Chinee horsemen."

"Yes, we did. So I guess we will have to move on—"

"You can come down to my place. Ma Bell's Saloon and Bawdy house welcomes everyone. Chinee,

Jap, Kraut, Nigra, Frenchies, even Injuns, and Englishmen."

Ma Bell looked at a smiling Mark. "You're her, man?"

"After a fashion, I guess," replied Mark.

"He saved me from being yanked back to the Emperor," said Susan. "So, I'm now at the end of the known world. At least in this direction."

Ma Bell clapped Mark on his back with enough force to almost knocking him over. "I heard you're quite the pistol man. Tell you both. I won a cabin at the end of town in a poker game. You, Doctor, come check my girls out for the Grippe and female problems, while this man backs up my Nigra Amos in a fight, you two can have it, rent-free."

"We'll have to get paying jobs also, Ma Bell," said Mark. "We don't have unlimited funds, even after selling Red and Blue one of our horses."

Ma Bell laughed. "A deal maker, I see. Well, maybe we'll have you run for Mayor, Mister—"

"Stone. Mark Stone. And I thought the Chinese business owners have the power."

"You mean toadies like Wang, with his so-called Tongs. Well, even the Chinee who own and work at places like the Empress Hotel are tired of his crap and connections with the Chinese Empire. We all have been independent for years. And the Emperor knows he needs us for a buffer with the West." Ma Bell linked arms with Mark.

"Come on. I'll feed you all on my tab, even Spotted Wolf there. I say my kitchen is better than the hoity-toity places in town. Then we'll start planning on how to run this town."

"We'll vote for ya!" said Blue. "Anyone who can handle a gun like you can make a great Mayor."

Mark laughed. "This ain't your first rodeo, is it, Ma?"

"No, son, it ain't. I was en route to San Francisco to pick up some new talent when—*zap!* I'm here. That was five years ago. Hell, I had to teach everyone in Elsewhen how to run a bawdy house. Now, everyone copies Ma Bell."

"Come on!" commanded the Madam. "I need to eat. How do you think I got this fine figure?"

A couple of hours later and the travelers were checking out the cabin Ma Bell had offered them. It had been well kept and even had a pump connected to a small well.

"We'll have to use a privy, no indoor plumbing," said Mark.

"Not yet. But soon. I'll make good money as a doctor. You can help me with difficult patients when you are not being Mayor."

"You and Ma are serious!"

"Yes. And this is not my first rodeo, as you say. I sense a-change coming. I sensed it when I first fled. It has been getting stronger since I met you."

Susan Von Braun walked over and threw her arms around Mark's neck, and proceeded to kiss him long and deep. As they finally parted, Mark tried to be dangerous.

"Susan, I'm married—"

"Not here. Not now. And I do not think a loving wife would want you to be old and miserable if she thought you still lived. But, I have to be blunt, mean. You and I. We are dead to the people who knew us."

Mark stood frozen for a moment. Then he spoke. "I guess I'll have to accept that possibility. It does not make it easy."

"Nothing is easy in Elsewhen, Mark Stone, But we can strive to make it better. True?"

Mark managed to smile though he felt a pain of loss. "I guess I cannot argue with Dejah Thoris."

"My name is Susan. And now, since there is a bed over there, you can explain the whole story of this— Martian Princess you keep talking about. Then I'll show you what a flesh and blood princess can do."

Mark smiled. He knew she would.

But in the back of his mind, there would always be hope. There would be the hope that someday Elsewhen would be in the rearview mirror of his SUV stuck for now in the hills.

Hell. Mark could at least dream.

# 4
# METAL, MONEY, AND MAYHEM

Mark Stone shifted his butt on the horse saddle for the umpteenth time. As he groaned a bit a voice behind him laughed.

"You were not born on the saddle, were you?" The voice was from Blue Baxter, one of the pair of frontiersmen who had agreed to accompany Mark on this recovery and/or salvage operation. The dark-haired and full-bearded man had the same rough humor as many a person in this world called Elsewhen. However, with the mood came honor and loyalty, human characteristics often needed in this rugged land.

"No, Blue, I was not. I rode a desk chair often, not a horse."

"Ridin' a desk," said Red Macbeth, the other member of the duo. "I'd pay to see that."

"Did ya use spurs on that there wooden mount?" added the red-headed and bearded Macbeth.

Mark laughed at the image. "No, Sir," replied Mark. "Some bosses tried to use spurs on me a couple of times. They did not like it when I bucked them off."

The two buckskinned-clothed men laughed long and hard.

"I can tell you are not one to be beaten on and abused," observed the tall and broad Red. "Especially if you had a pistol handy."

The second day he and Doctor Susan Braun had been in Freetown, Mark had cemented his reputation as a pistolman in the mixed culture community. He and Susan had shot it out with some hired thugs employed as the Chinese Emperor's Soldiers. In this strange world called Elsewhen, a Chinese Emperor, a Roman Warlord, and some people who tried to create New Camelot existed. And that was just out East. Mark had seen the results of the Emperor when he had saved Susan from further imprisonment. The shoot-out had resulted when the Emperor's toadies kept tracking Susan. Losing your number one doctor was not something the ruler of New Bejing and beyond wanted to allow.

Many years as a law enforcement firearms instructor in his previous reality had stood Mark in good stead. And, his actions had shaken up the Freetown establishment so much that Mark was elected the First Mayor and Custome Official of the sprawling and growing community. He and Town Marshall Matt Dillon ran the town for the various citizens and tried to keep the factions from beating, stabbing, or shooting each other.

Thus, Mark was unsure about leaving Freetown to recover the SUV that transported him to this strange land. However, the metal and machinery were equal to untold riches in their area Elsewhen, where only copper was in abundance. Mark had left the vehicle blocked in by thick brush and trees miles from Freetown. Hopefully, it was still undiscovered by the Chinese or other peoples. Frontiersmen Red and Blue volunteered to help tow it back using a team of mules they brought along. The Comanche Spotted Wolf scouted up ahead of the group for the four-wheeled prize. Mark offered to share some of the proceeds from the sale of the SUV and its contents. Upon hearing that, the trio was even more enthusiastic.

Mark once again had a sore behind from horseback. At least, he thought, all the extra exercise was burning fat off of him. Mark was getting back into fighting trim. Elsewhen was not a world that allowed the weak to remain free, not to mention alive.

"Look familiar?" Blue asked.

"We stayed last night at the first campsite Susan and I used once escaping the Chinese patrol," answered Mark. "The clearing where I first saw Susan should be nearby."

An odd bird call rang out from the deep mountain forests. Spotted Wolf was letting them know he was on his way back. Some five minutes later, the Comanche warrior rode up.

"I find where you and woman met," said Spotted Wolf. "It is a mile from here."

"Good," replied Mark. "Then up the hill from there should be the Jeep. Any sign of people dragging something large or cutting trees down?"

"No, Pistolman. Only an old sign of Chinese horse." The Comanche had used the nickname Mark had earned from his handgun use. Most people used Mayor to his face now, but people like the tribal member still used his other moniker.

"So, we'll be rich as kings soon?" asked Red.

Mark laughed. "Well, if we can hook those mules up and pull the Jeep out, you'll be at least be princes."

Blue laughed and pounded Mark on the back, almost unhorsing him. The two frontiersmen had the strength of a professional NFL lineman from Mark's world without the extra weight. Survival living did that to a human.

"Well, daylight's burning," added Red. "Let's get a move on."

Mark managed to keep up during a fast trot. God, he would be glad to have a different mode of transportation. They were soon at the recognizable clearing.

"Yes, this is the place," said Mark. He pointed up the slope from the trail.

"Up there, maybe a half-hour walk should be the Jeep."

Spotted Wolf spoke a couple of sentences in Comanche.

"Wolf says he saw some Dragon sign," translated Blue. "Said we should go up nice and slow on foot."

"Okay, gentlemen," replied Mark. "Grab your Hawken rifles; I have my .50 caliber breechloader, the Chinese Colt, and my Ruger."

"Spotted Wolf stays here, watches the horses and squirrel rifles," stated the Comanche. The American Indian slid effortlessly off his mount as Mark groaned and managed to dismount. Red and Blue both laughed.

"I guess we need to build you that desk to ride," Blue said with a grin.

"No need to hurry," replied the former federal agent as he tried to work the kinks out of his behind and legs. "Maybe I can get my SUV Jeep running again. Then I'll find some fuel and drive all over the place."

Spotted Wolf took the men's mounts as Red and Blue, experienced muleskinners, made sure their pack mules had the necessary harnesses and tow ropes loaded. The Comanche soon had all four mounts unsaddled and relaxing in some shade. He took a lever-action carbine from Mark's mount and sat on a nearby boulder.

"I read somewhere that Comanches were the best

light cavalry in the world," said Mark. "Seeing how Spotted Wolf tends to the horses, I can see why."

"I heared some Texas Rangers were getting as good," said Blue. "I'd have to see it to believe it."

"So, you knew of the Rangers?" asked Mark.

"Yessir. Me and Red met them during the War with Mexico. Saw those big revolvers they had."

"Colt Walkers," said Mark.

"Yep. The Rangers and we traded some shots with the Mexicans. Red and I went to scout around the Mexican camps when *bam!*"

"What happened?"

"Bolt of lightning hit Blue and me," interjected Red. "Then we was in Limbo, or Elsewhen as you call it."

"We're ready if you are," said Blue.

"I'm walking, right?" asked Mark.

"Hell, yeah," replied Red. "These mules are made for haulin', not riding."

Mark led the way, looking for signs of the animal path he had followed. A half an hour later, Mark saw where he had cut some brush over a month prior.

"It's just ahead." Mark pointed as he spoke. Just then, the mules began to pull on their ropes and harnesses. One let out a warning bray. The frontiersmen unslung their Hawkin fifty-four caliber rifles.

"Dragons—real close by," said Red in a low voice. Mark readied his breechloader.

A man tall shape dashed from the brush, and Mark

got a glimpse of a snout full of teeth a moment before both fifty caliber Hawkins rifle spoke as one. A feathery and lizard hide-covered shape slid to a stop a few feet from the mules. Somehow the muleskinners kept them from running moments after killing the dragon.

"Keep watch, pistolman," warned Blue. "There may —"

Another bipedal refugee from the Age of Dinosaurs burst from the brush. Mark fired his rifle from the hip but still managed to hit the creature. The fifty-caliber bullet struck the knee joint of the forward leg, and the beast sprawled to the ground. With practiced ease, Mark transitioned to the Chinese Colt and put a bullet in its head. The lead bullet flattened against the thick skull of the dragon. Before Mark could fire a second shot, Blue was on top of the fallen and stunned beast. His razor-sharp Bowie sliced across the throat and opened the jugular of the reptile, blood spurting up and about as the blade cut deep. Blue scrambled back as the beast thrashed around, then lay still.

"Chariots of fire that were close," said Red as he controlled the pack mules.

"Try to hit them center body next time, Mayor," stated Blue as he wiped the dragon blood off his face with his bandana. "And that small Colt doesn't do much to these beasts other than maybe make them pissy."

"Thanks for pulling my chestnuts out, guys," replied Mark.

"Hell, at least you hit it," answered Blue. "I've seen many a pilgrim feeze when charged by a large beast. I saw a man gutted by a Texas Long Horn during the Mexican war. The fool thought a wild longhorn was like a milk cow."

Blue then used his massive Bowie to cut the heart and livers of the two dinosaurs. As he did, Mark looked closer at them. They looked like a cross between a tiny T-Rex, Utahraptor, and a bit of Gojira. Blue wrapped the fresh meat up in a large piece of tanned hide he carried.

"We'll eat good tonight," a grinning Blue said.

"We won't eat at all if'n you don't get a move on," growled Red.

"Keep your pants on. We're close. The dragons were hanging around Mark's wagon, looking for something to eat."

The two muleskinners got the agitated pack animals moved up the slope. Within moments Mark saw the front end of the SUV and yelled with joy. "There it is! Just like I left it."

"Better hope the dragons didn't shit on it," said Red.

Some of the brush had regrown about the vehicle, so the three men used hatchets and short bronze swords to thin the surrounding vegetation quickly. Mark unlocked the Jeep and climbed into the driver's seat. He had replaced the battery with a new heavy-duty one before he was 'zapped' into Elsewhen. Now the retired federal agent said a prayer and turned the key. He hoped his trip into this world or universe had not fried the vehicle's electrical system.

The engine turned over, and Mark let out a whoop of joy. God of this universe apparently smiled at him. The two frontiersmen stepped back with the mules when Mark started the Jeep and stared at the motor vehicle. The pistolman shut the engine off and climbed out.

"Well?" Mark asked with a broad grin.

"Sounds funny," stated Red. "I thought it would be like a steam engine."

"Smells too," added Blue.

"Gas gauge tells me I have an almost full tank," said Mark. "If I drove slow, I could make a couple of hundred miles. But then no fuel at Freetown."

Blue shrugged. "Well, we brought these mules to pull that thing. Might as well use them."

The three men cleared some more brush and small trees from in front of the SUV, then hooked up the team of mules to the vehicle. Mark put the car in neutral and maneuvered the SUV as the mules pulled. As the trio made the trip down the game trail Mark had used over a month prior, they had to occasionally clear brush or a small tree out of the way. Once they passed the dragon carcasses, they saw no other large animals.

It was slow going, but about an hour later, they neared the first spot where Susan and Mark had met. As they did, they heard some Chinese voices. Someone was coming down the pathway the Chinese patrol had used after catching Susan.

"Shit," said Mark as he readied his rifle.

"Stay here," said Blue. "I'll check on Spotted Wolf." The woodsman disappeared into the foliage. Red kept the mules quiet as Mark found cover behind a more massive tree. Minutes passed. Then Blue reappeared and spoke in hushed tones.

"There is a small group of Chinese on the pathway. They look like bandits, or maybe deserters. Spotted Wolf heard them coming and hid the horses and gear."

"The Emperor has deserters?" asked Mark.

"Yep. He'll order them killed if they are caught. But the Emperor does not treat his people well. So people runoff like runaway darkies down South."

"So, now what?" asked Mark.

"Up to you," answered Red. "It's your doing."

Mark paused in thought, then responded, "If we do nothing, sneak around them, what happens?"

"They go to Freedom Town and raise Hell. That is one reason why we have a Marshall now."

Mark was deep in thought when they heard a definite female scream. "That answers that question," said Mark. "We go."

They secured the mules not to try to run off with their load, then went straight towards the scream. The three men came out of the brush right where Mark had exited when he first saw Susan Von Braun. There were six dismounted men and six horses in a half-circle around two young girls, maybe equivalent to teenagers in Mark's day. As Mark looked closer, their clothes were at least the late 20th Century.

The largest Chinese male, wearing the remains of a soldier's uniform, laughed as he grabbed at both the young women. The thug grabbed one, then the other, as they screamed at him in what sounded to Mark like Russian. Finally, one girl struck and clawed the thug's face as he tried to pull her to him. The man slugged her to the ground.

*"Hey, asshole!"* Mark yelled out as he stepped from behind a tree. Someone yelled in Chinese, and a couple of men, one European looking, yanked rifles from saddle scabbards. They never had a chance to use them as an arrow slammed into the European's throat, and then an arrow struck the other rifleman. It took a moment for the rest of the thugs to realize they were under attack. Red and Blue stepped from the bushes, and each shot a man. Mark used the Colt copy on the Chinese with the scratched face, hitting him in the groin. The last man threw his hands to the sky and received an arrow at the base of the neck. Then all was quiet except the sobbing of the two females. They huddled together as four more strange men approached them. One started to rattle off in Russian. Red managed a word or two the young lady seemed to recognize. The two young women let go of each other, and both walked up to Red.

"You never said you spoke Russian," said Mark.

"I learned a little over the past few years," replied Red.

"American? English?" the taller dark-haired young female, the one who had clawed the thug (now holding his groin on the ground, bleeding out), asked as she looked at Mark.

"Yes, young lady. Mark Stone here. With Red MacBeth and Blue Baxter here. Oh, and Spotted Wolf with his bow."

Both of the almost grown women stared at the Comanche as he walked up.

"You have names?" Mark asked the stunned ladies.

"I'm Ivana," said the taller one. "This is Mariana. Where are we? Who are you?"

A couple of sips from a flask produced by Blue helped to calm the two sisters. They were Ivana and Mariana Klimenko, seventeen and sixteen, respectively. One moment they walked to secondary school in Saint Petersburg, then there was a bright flash. They awoke lying on the forest road, confused and scared. Later the thugs arrived.

Mark tried to explain the realities of Elsewhen as his companions drug the bodies into the brush, where they quickly stripped them of all their weapons, valuable clothes, and anything metal. A few more sips from the flask helped with the explanation.

"So, we are in another universe, another world?" asked Mariana.

"That is the best explanation, young lady. You popped in here just like the rest of us have. Except I brought a car along."

"We were studying to become electrical engineers at the University," said Ivana. "We understand a lot of science and science fiction. So, can we go-home?"

Mark sighed before he answered, "Maybe. Theoretically. But no one has ever come back a second time to tell anyone what one can do with Elsewhen."

The two sisters conversed in Russian. Mark knew how shocking this was for the two young ladies. No radio, television, cars, or even electricity existed here. At least not yet. It would be rough, even on tough Russians.

"So, Mark Stone," asked Mariana. "May we come with you to Freetown? We are used to hard work—"

"No need to ask. All are welcome in Freetown. I'm the Mayor, plus Immigration and Customs Chief. So you are granted entry."

"These youngin's about ready to go with us?" asked Blue.

"Yes, they are. And I was about to ask Ivana and Mariana if they had ever driven a car."

Both sisters nodded yes.

"Well, you two get to go to work then. Right now."

With the two sisters helping, they made good time. The mules pulled the SUV, and the two Russian girls steered. They started the vehicle up a couple of times to make sure the battery was charging, and the sisters listened to a CD for a few minutes. There were intermittent tears as the sisters realized their chances of seeing family members were about nil. The two Russians liked the liver and heart that Red and Blue cooked up the first night. They used bedding taken from the dead thugs to sleep on, Mark making sure no one had any ideas about some nighttime assignation. Ivana and Mariana also talked with Spotted Wolf, thanking him for his timely intervention as well as quizzing him about Comanche's life.

Five of the six thug horses had been recovered and tied to the back of the Jeep. Wolf claimed three, and Mark said the other two could belong to Red and Blue. The one Chinese Mark shot in the groin had a filled leather coin purse, so Mark had claimed that, along with a .44 Chinese Clone Colt. Mark had the other three agree to give the two sisters a share of the liquidated SUV proceeds. The two young ladies had a few coins with them, so they had 'metal' to spend in Freetown.

Three days later, the group entered Freetown. Susan had received word the band was approaching and met them at the city limits. She endeared herself to the Klimenkos when she greeted them in Russian.

"They will stay with us until we can find a place for them in our society."

"We will work——" began Ivana, and Susan cut her off.

"We can arrange that later. I am the Town Doctor, and I say you rest with us. We have a spare room with indoor plumbing coming tomorrow. You can help us figure out how to electrify the town."

Mark chuckled. "You did a lot while I was gone if you have indoor plumbing coming."

"Husband, if we are to live the rest of our lives here, I demand we are comfortable."

Mark always felt a pang when Susan talked that way. He had a wife waiting for him, maybe. However, Susan was the Doctor and made an excellent living. As Mayor, Mark's job paid little, another reason for recovering the SUV. They lived together as husband and wife, so Susan calling him 'husband' was correct.

Susan led the two young ladies towards their new home, which also doubled as a doctor's office.

"Girls getting settled?" asked Blue as he and Red walked up.

"Yes. Susan took them under her wing."

Red chuckled and grinned. "You got yourself one smart and a tough woman there, Mayor. Purty, too."

"Yeah. Gods smiled on me when they dumped me near that roadway."

"Hell, friend," said Blue, "your pistol work made

your good fortune. You could be dead or a slave."

Mark sighed. He just wanted a simple retirement. Then this all happened.

"Well, times a wasting as they say. Let's join Spotted Wolf at the stables and do some horse and Jeep trading."

A week later, Mark, Christopher Walken, Marshall Dillon, and the two frontiersmen watched as Ivana and Mariana put the following touches on the Jeep project. It turned out that the two Russian sisters were trained in theoretical science and practical electrical and mechanical work.

"Our Grandfather was a mechanic in the Great Patriotic War," Mariana had told Mark. "Our Father was an Engineering Officer with the Strategic Rocket Forces of the Union of Soviet Socialist Republics. They both taught us to work hard and not be afraid to have dirty hands."

"And," Ivana added, "we learned to fix almost anything. There were a lot of shortages before the USSR dissolved."

First, the two students had modified the Jeep's fuel system to run on alcohol from Walken's still. That solved the gasoline fuel problem. Next had come to the scrounging from the citizenry of Freetown, some six thousand souls, every odd piece of machinery they had picked up in their travels. Mark soon learned what he thought was an exaggerated myth was a reality. There was large Trash or Salvage Heap about a month's hard ride south of Freetown. Many travelers and refugees have skirted it on their way north, grabbing odds and ends of detritus someone or something had dumped there.

"You say this is a small mountain of metal and plastic?" he asked Christopher.

"It is machines, remains of bodies, parts of vehicles and houses from every time and every place. I saw it through a spyglass on my here with a couple of other new arrivals who were as confused as I was—and as scared."

"Well, Hell, what's to stop us from going there and scavenge what we need? My God, a couple of dozen armed men with wagons—"

"Dragons," said Christopher.

"You mean like we shot getting the Jeep? We could make some giant crossbows like the Romans had, not have to worry about having enough shot and powder—"

Christopher snorted. "Those pissants? For that is what they are compared to these giant dinosaur monitor lizards. I also heard some wild tribes hang around the edges, dodging dragons and bushwacking people."

Mark paused in thought. From the description and what the Russian sisters had gleaned from the other town residents, Mark thought there was a lot of helpful technology just waiting for them.

"I can see the wheels in your head

turning, Mayor."

"Yeah. But that is for another day. Let's see what Ivana and Mariana have for us."

After a short speech to a crowd of onlookers, many of them young men who wanted to leer at the two new single females, they fired up the Jeep machine. For it was no longer just an SUV but also a source of power for many uses. The former Jeep could be a lathe, a small sawmill, a motorized winch, even a small electrical arc welder thanks to added salvaged batteries and an alternator.

All these uses were, of course, for a price.

"Contact us at KMMBW Machine Works," Ivana said. "We will not be undersold."

Mark laughed at the last phrase. Someone had been teaching them good old Madison Avenue marketing. The four men in the salvage trip had arranged to take a small percentage of the proceeds from the Jeep user fees after deciding not to strip it down. Some empty pop cans and coins found in and under the vehicle seats were also divided. The metal and weapons took from the dead bushwhackers were liquidated. All the men had a nice stash to use for future expenses.

"I call dibs first," Christopher called out. "I think I can turn out some nice gun barrels using the lathe and arc welder."

"You may discuss pricing with Mariana. Anyone else?"

It took a few minutes for the new technology to sink into the townspeople, but they soon lined up. Marshall Dillon hung around to make sure no one tried to bully the two young Russians. The lawman saw just how tough the two sisters could be and tipped his hat as he continued his rounds. Mark smiled. He already felt like an adopted Uncle to the two young ladies. He would make sure they had as comfortable a life as possible.

Later that night, at their shared home, the giggling school girls in them came out.

"We will be rich. Everyone wants our services and expertise," Mariana said with a wide grin. Ivana walked up and hugged Mark.

"You are now our uncle if you have not already figured that out. Of course, and a business partner to share in the profits."

"For people who received schooling in Marx, you caught on fast."

"You knew of Putin, yes?" asked Mariana. "He taught us in 2016 there was no shame in making rubles."

"That was your year?" asked Susan.

"Yes. But now we must adapt to—this year, this time."

"Mother and Father would want us to survive, be happy, no matter where we are at." Ivana blinked back tears as she spoke, and Miriana hugged her. Susan walked up and hugged them both.

"I will be honored to be your aunt," said Susan.

"Of course. And we will pay you back for room and board—"

"Hush. The family does not pay for family aid. Someday you will help Mark and me. Then we are—Even Steven is the phrase, Husband?"

"Yes. Now, you young ladies need to rest. You have many contracts to fill starting tomorrow."

"Yes, Uncle."

That night in their bed, Susan and Mark laid and snuggled.

"How does it feel to have an instant family of two grown young ladies?" Susan asked.

"Weird, but nice. I had no children with Cheri. It wasn't in the cards. But I am no young pup—"

"Hush, Mark. You are far from old and feeble. As you have proven to me in many pleasant ways."

"I am still over fifty, and what, some twenty years older than you?"

"Age is often a state of mind. And here in Elsewhen, people who survive the early days seem to be—younger."

"Well, if there is something in the air or water to reverse our aging, a lot of people will not want to go back to their old life?"

"And you, my loving man. Do you wish to return if possible?"

The question was constantly nagging in the back

of his mind. He missed his wife Cheri, still loved her, but he loved Susan in the here and now.

"I wish to live for the rest of my life happily. I want to ensure you live happily ever after also. That is my answer this night."

Susan kissed him, began to caress him. "That answer is good enough. Now, make love to me."

"Yes, my Dejah Thoris. Under the twin moons of Barsoom."

The two Russian Sisters were busier than one-armed paper hangers during the following week. New industrial technology attracted those who rented the power of the Jeep. Others came who just wanted to watch the modern marvel. Christopher created some two dozen rifle barrels and a couple of pistol frames using the lathe and small arc welder. Others came forward to cut wood for housing and furniture.

The unique function was the ability to recharge scrounged batteries. Mark was surprised at the number of people who found all types and sizes of batteries in their travels. Some were due to the discovered lead content, hidden away for use as bullets. Enough had been kept in their original condition to support a robust recharging operation—for a fee. Ivana and Mariana even produced a few crude electric cells using copper, zinc, and saltwater. One could heat water using an attached coil, an astounding feat to humans from hundreds of years in the past.

Unfortunately, with such success came jealously and the greed of others.

At the end of the first week, Mark, in his official capacity as Mayor, walked down Mainstreet to check on the young women. As he neared their booth not far from Christopher Walken's gun store, Mark heard raised voices. He quickened his walk to see what was happening.

Three large Chinese with Tong written all over them were arguing and pushing up against Ivana and Mariana. Mark had learned enough Chinese to understand the three toughs, thought they could muscle in and take charge of the Jeep whenever they felt like it. One shoved Ivana roughly back. She cursed and planted a classic front snap kick to his man parts. The thug folded up with pain and fell to the ground. The second thug wrapped his arms around Ivana. Mariana rewarded him by beaning him with a large wrench. The third Tong member pulled out a copper sword knife and advanced on the two Russians. Mark swore and pulled his Ruger pistol from his inside the belt holster.

A wraith seemed to birth from the shadows before Mark could bring his pistol to bear. Spotted Wolf used his tomahawk to slash open the knife welding Chinese Tong member's throat. The thug Mariana beaned tried to pull an object from beneath his loose-fitting tunic. The Comanche let out a war-whoop and buried his fighting hatchet in the man's skull. The thug collapsed to the dirt street. The last Tong tough tried to rise from the ground but was stopped by a Comanche foot in his face, breaking his Chinese nose.

"Spotted Wolf," Mark called out. "Wait for the Marshall on that one. We'll find out who sent them."

The Comanche warrior nodded at the Mayor and turned to Ivana,

"You okay?" he asked her.

"Thanks to you, we are now." With that comment, Ivana threw arms around Spotted Wolf and crushed him in a bear hug.

Marshall Dillon and his deputies showed up moments later and took the surviving attacker into custody. Mark surmised the thug would clam up about who he worked for and would magically bond out on someone else's dime. After Mark was elected Mayor, a former Australian Barrister transported to Elsewhen and then to Freetown; Madeline White became the first Judge. Thus began a formal legal system, warts and all. Marshall Dillon cursed that the days of merely bashing or shooting someone to stop crime were over. Mark reminded him such was the cost of civilization.

Mark saw the way Ivana looked at the Comanche and knew the two would soon be an item. An hour after the incident, Mark, as an adopted uncle, managed to talk to the Comanche alone.

"Spotted Wolf, you know Ivana will not be content to follow you all over and cook your meals, tan the hides of your game kills, and do all the hard labor around the campfire. She is not a Comanche nor a captive.

A small smile formed on the American Indian's mouth.

"You know of the Comanche ways, Pistolman."

"Yep. Where I come from, there are many books on the Comanche and other tribes."

Spotted Wolf shrugged. "I have been here some six winters. I know the old ways are gone. The Great Spirit brought me to Elsewhen as you, Blue, and Red calls it, for a reason. I think that reason is to live a new way."

Mark stuck his hand out to shake. "As the young women's adopted uncle, I will always keep an eye on them."

"Of course," answered Spotted Wolf. "Family takes care of family."

Later in the evening, after Ivan and Marianna had told Susan what had happened, Mark was able to pull his Elsewhen wife aside. "Ivana will soon be someone's wife."

"I know, Mark. Her eyes twinkle when she talks about the Indianer. But she knows the way of this world already."

"Well, Susan, they have an aunt and uncle as family. We can help ensure they both have dowries."

Susan smiled at Mark. "We will make this work, my love. We will make an excellent place to live in this world you call Barsoom."

Mark laughed. "Yes, my Dejah Thoris. I believe you are right. Now. Time to eat."

"Then to bed, my love. As usual."

"But of course, my love, but of course."

# 5
# INTERLUDE

Sheriff's Detective Ron Smith hated this part of his job. Sitting across from him at his desk was Mrs. Cheri Stone, wife of missing Mark Stone, retired federal agent. It had been a week since Mark Stone was declared officially 'missing.' Since then, there had been no trace of the man. The Jeep SUV was gone; there was no activity on Mark Stone's credit cards, and attempts to 'ping' the former agent's cell phone had come up negative. A BOLO for the vehicle was in effect with the Washington State Patrol, yet no one had reported seeing it since Mark's disappearance.

Cheri Stone was an attractive middle-aged blonde of above-average height. Mark Stone's wife saw no reason why her husband would just up and leave her. Nothing in his preliminary investigation pointed towards a man fleeing an unhappy marriage, a hidden mistress, or some unknown substance abuse. Mark had called Cheri a few miles from their home and then vanished.

"Detective, you have found or heard nothing?" Cheri asked with the beginning of a quiver in her voice.

"Sorry, Ma'am. I have nothing new. We still have an all-points bulletin out for him, as well as contacted his previous agency and the FBI, just in case someone who he arrested or crossed paths with when he was active grabbed him."

"I cannot imagine Mark just driving off. If he were angry about something, he would have said it."

Ron Smith paused for a moment before he once again broached an uncomfortable subject. "Mrs. Stone, is there any chance he went off to visit someone. Like another woman?"

"No, not like this. We may not have children at home, but we have four dogs he loved and cared for, despite being upset with me. I cannot imagine him not calling a day or two later, even if he were so upset that he was with—another woman." The wife of the missing agent dabbed her eyes with a tissue to keep tears from running down her cheeks.

"I know these are tough questions I ask," said the Detective. "However, I have to eliminate all possibilities."

"Are there still no places where Mark could have run off the road, the Jeep hidden in the brush?" Cheri asked.

"We even ran a helicopter with a FLIR over a ten-mile square area. Homeland Security does not like it when a recently retired senior agent just disappeared, so they provided the Blackhawk with the infra-red capability."

Cheri sat and stared at her hands as she fidgeted with her wedding ring set. Ron Smith could not imagine the anguish she was going through. Decades of marriage and have your life partner disappear minutes after speaking with them? The Detective hoped he and  his fiancé would never have to deal with this situation-ever.

"We'll keep this case open, Ma'am. I know your husband told you about how law enforcement does things over the years, so please believe me that we do not like unsolved investigations like this."

"I know, Detective Smith. Please keep me informed. If he doesn't come back soon, I'll have to take some legal steps."

"I understand, Ma'am. Please call me anytime."

Ron Smith walked her out to the front exit and watched her enter her car and drive off. He went back to his desk and sat down. In the file was a driver's license photograph and some personal photos Cheri Stone had provided. The Detective examined the man in the pictures as he mumbled. "It's as if you fell into a Black Hole, Jeep and all." The Detective felt a shiver up his spine. He set the photos down and called his fiancé. He would take her out to dinner after work. Ron Smith needed some real-world assurances as to how life on Earth was supposed to work. People disappearing in broad daylight just a few minutes from home          were spooky.

Mark Stone jerked awake in a cold sweat. A female voice asked, "What is wrong, dear?" As gentle hands caressed his shoulders, a shudder went through his body.

"Bad dream, Cheri—I mean, Susan."

The raven-haired buxom beauty in bed with him kissed his cheek as she hugged him. "You are dreaming of Old Home, yes?"

He patted Susan Von Braun's hand as he exhibited a sheepish smile. "Yes. Sorry. It was like Cheri, my wife there, was trying to talk to me."

Susan kissed him again and smiled as she spoke. "I used to have such dreams the first couple of years I was here. I dreamt of friends, family, and lovers."

Mark put his arm around his Elsewhen Wife. "You were not married. That creates a different bond. And different guilt."

"It has been over a year since we met, my now-husband. I know it is hard to believe, but our Earth is but a memory, And we are soon to bring new life to Freedom Town, Mister Mayor."

Mark placed his hand on the stomach of his new wife, many years his junior. "Who would have thought I still had that ability at my age?" The former Senior Special Agent stated.

"But you do. And as much as it pains us to admit it, the chances of us ever seeing our Earth again is almost nil. So we make the best of this reality, this world."

He kissed Susan slow and passionately. Then he patted her tummy. "Excuse me while I enjoy the indoor plumbing you so efficiently obtained."

"Doctors and Mayors should have the best as we do important work in this world of mixed times, places, and people."

Mark chuckled and then walked to the bathroom.

Susan laid back and gently caressed the lower abdomen where new life developed. "I hope you do not mind If I borrow and use your husband, Cheri Stone," she whispered. "He saved my life, and I have come to love him. If we should ever meet, I hope you will understand."

Susan heard the toilet flush and watched as Mark Stone padded his way back to the bed. As he crawled in next to Susan, he spoke. "I wonder if time passes on Erath as it does here, on Barsoom, Dejah Thoris."

Susan giggled as she hugged her very own John Carter. "It may, and it may not, Mark. But there is one constant among the various universes."

"What is that, Susan?"

"Love, my dear. Always love."

# 6
# THE FLYING MOFANGOS

S crew," said Major Susan Finch. She tried to clean up her language and not use a curse word with a similar meaning but started with an 'F' and numbered in one less letter. However, there were times like these as a C-17 Globemaster command pilot that demanded harsh language.

"Any luck, Ginger?" the black-haired woman asked her redheaded copilot Captain Ginger Roberts.

"No joy. I cannot raise anyone on any freq. It's like every single communication tower and radio station, even good time civilian, dropped off the face of the Earth."

"Any chance of something like a solar flare? Could it have fried all the broadcast stations and control towers on this side of the globe?"

"You mean a Carrington Effect? That flash we flew threw was weird, but—you would think it would fry some of our systems also. Plus, I cannot even get static. Our military has some shielded radio and computer systems that should be putting out at least a carrier wave."

Susan spoke over her shoulder to the third person in the cockpit. "Well, Lieutenant Liu? Any ideas?"

The young woman was flying as a 'spare' aircrew member to help relieve the other pilots and obtain some experience. This mission was her first flight overseas and into the combat zone of Afghanistan. Already it was not expected.

"No, Ma'am. It's like we flew into some pristine space with no human traffic."

"Try your cell phone, Billi," said Susan. "Maybe we did have some kind of an onboard systems failure."

"Yes, Ma'am."

As the young dark-haired Chinese American tried her cell, Susan looked out the port cockpit window of the massive transport aircraft. The atmosphere was crystal clear, with some hints of cumulus clouds on what looked like a spring day. Then the command pilot noticed something... *odd.*

"Ginger, when is sunset today?"

"Why, not for another five hours in this part of the world."

"Captain, Lieutenant, look out the windows. What do you see?"

The two women looked out each side of the cockpit. Ginger began to curse. "Motherf— the Sun is setting. We haven't flown that far and fast. We just took off from Kabul an hour ago.”

"Ah, Ma'ams?” Billi Liu said with a shaky voice. "Weren't we flying due South out of Kabul? The Sun should be setting.on our starboard, in the West.”

"Yes. Why—oh shit.” Susan's six-pack muscular stomach tied itself into a knot as she realized the aircraft seemed pointed due North.

"Check the compass, Captain. The manual one.”

Ginger took a lensatic military compass from the pocket of her flight suit. She unfolded the cover and sighting piece and then held it up to the starboard cockpit window as far from any aircraft metal possible.

"Thank God. The Sun is setting in the right direction, according to the Mister Compass. Somehow we got turned ass-backward. Out internal aircraft system must have gotten screwed by that—flash we flew through.” Ginger frowned as she continues. "But that doesn't explain how we did a one-eighty, and none of us noticed. “

"I think the Colonel would be up here screaming if we had pulled a tight turn back towards Kabul,” said Susan. "Ginger, see if you can reset the aircraft navigation system. Billi, take over my seat. I have to go and talk to the rest of the passengers and crew, and I do not want to broadcast it over our com and upset the air evac patients.”

Ginger smirked. "Good luck with Colonel Complex.”

Susan unbuckled and rose from the left seat command pilot position and walked to the access door as Billi slid into her vacated position. "I have the aircraft, Captain."

"Yes, you do. Now, don't do anything rash until I figure this crap out."

Susan went out of the cockpit door and down the access stairs. The cockpit in a C-17 sat high up in the massive aircraft, and one had to walk down into the huge cargo bay. Onboard the Aeromedical Evacuation configured C-17 were two-three person Critical Care Aeromedical Transport Teams (CCATT) and a five-person standard Aeromedical Evacuation Team (AET). Susan knew this medical staff Assigned to the 446th Aeromedical Evacuation Squadron, flown missions with them before. They were not a problem. The problems involved Lieutenant Colonel Bruce Fish and a last-minute special ops team who called for an immediate airlift.

Col. Fish's nickname was Col. Complex, as he had a severe Short Man's Complex. A trained surgeon in the Air Force Reserve pulled some strings to fly on this mission to Afghanistan to check a block for service in a Combat Zone. He was not a regular member of the 446th AES; instead, he performed surgeries at stateside military hospitals when he was not working at his usual civilian gig. As a surgeon, his reputation was good. As a human being—the jury was still out.

"Seen the Colonel, Chief?" Susan asked her Flying

Crew Chief Portia Williams. The African American Technical Sergeant kept the C-17 up and running maintenance-wise. She and Susan worked well together, assigned to the C-17 for two years.

"In the back, Ma'am. Glaring at our late arrivals."

"Staff Sergeant Smith and Senior Airman Jablonski, our Loadmasters. They around?"

"They are hiding in the shadows, keeping out of the Colonel's sight," Portia replied to her Command Pilot. "All due respect to the Colonel's rank, but he is one misogynistic asshole."

"All due respect to his rank, I have to agree, Crew Chief."

Susan carefully picked her away around all the ICU medical equipment brought on board to support the two CCATTs. Susan and the team picked up eight wounded servicemen and women at a secondary airfield on the outskirts of Kabul. Two were ambulatory with minor shrapnel wounds, and the other six were not. The CCATTs were onboard as two of the wounded were severe burn victims, with another facing life as a double amputee. The other three non-ambulatory had suffered various gunshot and shrapnel wounds. Towards the rear of the cargo area sat a Marine Corps Gunnery Sergeant with a Corporal, the two ambulatory patients.

A ninth official patient was part of the 'late arrivals,' a Special Operations troop suffering from acute appendicitis. An unofficial tenth patient was an Afghani with cuts and contusions, who sat in handcuffs.

Susan stopped and took a deep calming breath.

"Here goes," she whispered, then walked forward. Colonel Fish was glaring at the beat-up HUMVEE where the three remaining SPECOPS personal sat. In the vehicle with them was the handcuffed Afghani. The man with appendicitis was with the AET nurses as they monitored his condition.

"Colonel." Susan lightly touched the man's shoulder. A cargo jet was noisy in the rear.

Bruce Fish turned around and faced her. Susan thought he had lifts in his shoes as he did not seem tall enough to match her 5'7" height.

"Major. How is the flight progressing after our delay? Thanks to these—people." The Colonel leaned in a bit to deal with the ambient noise.

In addition to being short, Fish also had a receding hairline he tried to hide with a buzzcut haircut.

"We have hit a snag, Colonel. I know you were planning on performing that appendectomy when we landed at a base, but there is now a glitch in that plan."

"Glitch?" the Colonel said with a frown.

"That flash we flew through we thought was heat lightning? Well, it screwed up our navigational equipment."

"I can help you with landmarks, Major," interjected a new voice. Susan and Fish turned to look at the speaker.

"Mister Jackson," replied Susan. "We can try. I just do not want to—worry anybody, especially the patients. I could land this beast on a dirt road if I had to; a C-17 is designed for unimproved airfields.

"Why would you risk that, Major?" asked the Colonel.

"Why don't we walk to the cockpit, and I'll explain it, gentlemen."

The tall, wiry, and dark bearded special ops warrior flashed a wide grin. Jake 'Stonewall' Jackson had been around many blocks not to recognize what the Major was saying.

"Don't want to make the troops nervous. I get you."

Fish harrumphed and then spoke. "Why do you need to be part of this discussion?"

"Because the Major has some sealed instruction that if someone with my call sign, Free Range One, calls for assistance, I have priority."

The Colonel glared at Susan.

"Why don't I know this as ranking individual on this aircraft?"

"Need to know, Sir," replied Susan. "You were a passenger until there was a need for your surgical expertise with Jackson's man. I am the commander of this ship. Push comes to shove. I can tell Jackson to take a flying leap."

"And piss off D.C.," Jackson added.

"Won't be the first time a command pilot pissed off some desk jockey. Now, shall we go to my office?"

Jake Jackson laughed as Fish fumed. A few minutes later and Billi Lui exited the left seat so Susan could have back her spot. Jake looked out the cockpit side windows. "Those do not look like any Afghan Mountains, not to mention the trees look too thick and resemble large cedars in the States."

"Then, where are we?" demanded Fish. "Pakistan? Uzbekistan? "

"Can't be," said Susan. "We have not been in the air long enough."

"Major, I still can't raise anybody on the radio," interjected Ginger. "Lt. Lui tried her cellphone. Nothing."

"That is impossible!" blurted Fish as his face reddened.

"Well, Colonel, it is now reality," said Susan. "I am going to start a large one hundred klick circle as a search pattern. I have about 2,000 miles of fuel left. If we find a spot I can set down in, I will."

"You won't land until I tell you to land," demanded Fish with a bright red face.

"Colonel, with all due respect, I'm the skipper of this boat. I'll land when I deem it fit."

Fish began to sputter as Jake tried not to laugh. "Okay, Captain. Keep your eyes peeled. Hopefully—"

No one had noticed that Fish had his service automatic concealed under his BDU shirt. The first inkling was when he shoved the barrel in Susan's face. All personal had at least a sidearm assigned while in a combat zone. However, usually, only the aircrew wore them when the aircraft was operational.

"Listen, Bitch—"

"Colonel, shooting a hole in this C-17 at this altitude is not a good idea."

"Shutup! I'm in command now. You will continue on a heading through Pakistan and find a friendly airfield to land. Then—"

Jake had his hands wrapped out the pistol and twisted from the Colonel's grasp before the man realized it. In the process, Jake broke Fish's trigger finger. The Colonel yelped and then shut up as the SPECOPS warrior slammed the officer's head into the aircraft bulkhead. Fish collapsed to the deck.

"Jesus Christ, Jackson. If that gun had gone off—"

"You think this is my first rodeo, Major? It would not go off."

Susan took a deep breath to stop shaking. "Just please don't do that again. My orders said if you called, I come running. Now, let me try and salvage this mess."

Jake dragged the unconscious officer from the cockpit. A team member he called Smitty helped him carry the Colonel back to the strapped downed HUMVEE. A quarter of an hour later, Jake returned to the cockpit.

"Any news?" he asked the two pilots.

"We think we saw some smoke from south of us

as we dropped down to a lower altitude. We headed that way."

"Then what?"

"We find a place to land this beast. No use flying until we run out of fuel."

"What if the fire is from a hostile camp?"

"Well, Mister Jackson, that is where you and those two ambulatory Marines come in. You help protect the plane and patients until we get into the air."

Jake laughed. "Hope you have some extra firearms and ammunition. My man with the SAW is down to two rounds. Smitty has a single bullet for his Glock. I have a personal snubby thirty-eight, and we have the fifty cal mounted on the confiscated Afghani Forces HUMVEE. All our rifles are empty, as are our other pistols."

"That's it?"

"Other than some Hadji weapons we took as intel and souvenirs. I'll show them to you later. Oh, and I still have the Colonel's pistol."

"Have you checked with the Gunny Sergeant yet, Jackson?"

"No, and please call me Jake. I think we are going to be dealing with this situation for quite some time. I'll do that right now."

The SPECOPS operative walked over to two Marines seated along the aircraft bulkhead. A massive black Gunnery Seargeant rose to meet Jake.

"Can I help you?" The Gunny had a deep voice.

"I hope so. Jake Jackson, special operative. If you have any small arms, we may need them."

"Why?"

"We may have to land in an unsecured area, Gunny…."

"Jefferson. William Jefferson. Sitting next to me is Corporal Jesus Ramirez. Now, you are talking about landing in a hot zone?"

"Yes, Gunney. My men and I are very lite on ammunition. So the aircraft commander, Major Finch, and I were wondering—"

"That asshole Colonel is not involved, is he? He tried to tell us to leave our weapons behind. Something about this being a medivac flight, so no guns."

"The Gunny and I are not about to explain why we left our rifles for the Hadjis to use," added the small and wirey Corporal. "

"No. I took the Colonel's pistol from him after he got squirrely with it," replied Jake. "He now has a busted finger and a headache."

Gunny Jefferson looked at the Corporal. "Want to grab the B-4 bags?"

Corporal Ramirez turned and went to a section of fold-down seats a few yards away. He came back with two bulky standard-issue canvas barracks bags. Jesus struggled a bit with the bags, which told Jake they were heavy. The Gunny picked one up as if it weighed near to nothing and opened it up.

"Take a look, Jackson."

In the bag were three M-16A4s and an MP-5 submachine gun. A smaller cloth bag contained several rifle magazines and two clamped together MP-5 magazines. All seemed to be at least partially loaded. As Jake looked at the bottom of the bag, he saw several boxes of shells of various caliber.

"Think you can spare a few rounds?"

"I think I can arrange that. The other bag is a stripped-down M-240 with a two hundred round belt, a couple of pistols, and a twelve gauge."

"We each have a couple of loaded mags behind our body armor," said Ramirez, "away from prying eyes."

"Smart move. If I can get about a hundred rounds of .223, I'll be happy," said Jackson. He called out across the noisy cargo area.

"Hey, Smitty, I have something for you."

A short, stocky, bearded towheaded man walked up to the group of three.

"Hey, Boss. I have something for you, too." Smitty held up a thirty-caliber ammo can. "This was hidden behind the spare tire. It looks like a little over a hundred rounds of a bunch of stuff. There are a few fifty calibers mixed in also."

"Sort out there, Specialist. We'll add it to about a hundred rounds the Gunny is lending us."

"Will do."

"Hey, Gunny, have you met Major Finch,

the pilot?"

"Not yet."

"Well, come on. No time better than the present."

Susan was about to mount the stairs to the cockpit when she saw Jack and the broad Gunny Sergeant approach.

"Major Finch, Gunnery Sergeant Jefferson. Carrying around some shrapnel but still operational."

"Glad to have you aboard, Gunny. Jack, here fill you in?"

"Yes, Ma'am. Just tell me where we are needed when we land, and I and Cpl. Ramirez will be there."

"Thank You. Now, I get to go to the cockpit and see about setting this beast down until we figured out what to do next."

"Okay, Major," Jack replied. "Just let us know when we have to put our tray tables up and fasten our seatbelts."

Susan could not help but smile at the old joke. She made her way back into the cockpit. Ginger was in the left seat now as Billi held down the copilot position.

"So, what do we have?" asked the Major.

"Looks like the smoke is coming from some type of town. There is a small river that runs buy it, and a dried-up river bed about two and a half klicks what passes as North in this place."

"How long and flat is the river bed, Ginger?"

"About 2000 meters, and it looks flat from up

here. Of course, we won't really know until we do a low-level fly-by."

"Okay. Decision time. What do you two pilots think?"

The Captain and the First Lieutenant looked at each other. Ginger nodded at Billi.

"Major, I think we try a landing. This is all too weird just to keep circling."

Susan looked at Ginger with a 'and' expression on her face.

"Same here, Boss. I keep thinking about the Bermuda Triangle."

"You know most of those missing ships and things were found over the years."

"But not all, Major. Not all."

Susan used the private intercom connection to the Crew Chief and the Loadmasters. He explained to Tsgt. Portia Williams, Loadmasters Staff Sergeant Erica Smith, and Senior Airman Maria Jablonski, the bizarre situation.

"So, have you sidearms on, locked, and loaded. Sergeant Smith, take Jablonski and double-check everything is tied down tight, especially the medical equipment and patients. This landing may be bumpy."

"Ma'am, I have to ask," said Staff Sergeant Smith. "Who broke the Colonel's finger?"

"Our SPECOPS guy, Jake Jackson. The Colonel got

squirrelly with his pistol. So Jake took it away from him."

"You don't say?" said Chief Williams. "It couldn't happen to a nicer asshole."

"Well, just don't let him get ahold of your sidearm. I think he holds a grudge."

"Nobody complaining about the all-female crew?" added Portia.

"No. Ma'am. They wouldn't dare."

Susan explained the over general intercom situation. At the statement's ending, the senior ranking doctor after Fish, Major Carol North, cut in.

"Major, how long will we be… delayed? I have three critical patients and an appendectomy I have to take care of."

"You can perform the appendectomy?" asked Susan.

"Yes, I have done it before. We have everything we need, and I have plenty of nurses with the AES team on board."

"Okay. I need to speak with you, Major, once we are on the ground."

"Roger that. Okay, everyone. Let's get ready for landing."

Susan swung the C-17 wide and noticed a good-sized lake, which was the river's headwaters that passed near the supposed town. She flew over the settlement at some two thousand feet, then swung the large cargo aircraft around to line up on the river beard.

"The riverbed looks solid and not too rocky, Major," said Ginger Roberts.

"Good. The Sun is setting, so I want to sit down before it gets any darker. Hang on and call out, Ladies, if you see something that will ruin our day."

Susan Finch did a textbook unimproved field landing. Using as little brakes as possible and reverse engine thrust, Susan brought the C-17 to a halt a hundred meters to the end of the dried river bed. The solid ground told Susan the remains of the river were ancient. The river itself was about a mile away as the crow flies.

"Chief, security out," Susan called on the radio.

Jake heard the broadcast and slid out the side access door. Smitty and the other team member, Marco Franzetti, were on his tail with loaded assault weapons. Each had a thirty-round magazine. The discovered ammo can provided a magazine worth of forty-five ammo for Jake's tricked-out 1911 and a few nine-millimeter rounds for Smitty's Glock. Marco Franzetti had the Colonel's Sig Sauer as a backup.

The Gunny and the Corporal exited with M-16s and full loads. The five armed men formed a ragged 360-degree coverage around the C-17 as the Crew Chief opened the rear access doors and lowered the loading ramp. The two Loadmasters coasted the HUMVEE with the mounted fifty caliber down the slope and braked to a stop. Erica was trained in the Ma Duece, so she handled it as additional firepower. The Flying Crew Chief stayed at the top of the loading ramp with her sidearm readied.

Susan shut down the aircraft engines and let the turbine blades run down. Then she was up and moving with Ginger. Billi Liu stayed, armed, in the cockpit to repel all boarders. The two pilots hurried through the aircraft, checking on the medical personnel as they weaved around the patients. Then they were at the bottom of the access ramp.

"Looks a bit like the Southwest, but with more trees," said Ginger.

"The river helps provide more water for vegetation. But there may be a rainy season," replied Susan.

"You don't think we're in Kanas anymore, do you, Major?"

"No, Captain. I do not."

"We are definitely over the rainbow, ladies," said Jake Jackson as he walked up with his rifle at the ready. "Lookup in the sky,"

The two pilots looked up and cursed. In the darkening sky were two Moons. One was close to the size of Luna; the other was smaller and seemed to be chasing the larger.

"Welcome to Barsoom, Ladies. Who gets to be Dejah Thoris?"

As night fell about the C-17, Carol North operated on Donald Hoffa, the last SPECOPS team member. Major North kept the medical teams busy with the patients to not allow them to dwell on the problematic situation.

"I expect to see some Munchins and a wicked witch," said Jake.

"Maybe it will be a giant rabbit with a pocket watch," replied Ginger.

Susan sat on the edge of the ramp and stared into the night sky. "This is effing impossible. I keep looking for familiar star formations, and they just are not there,"

Major North walked down the cargo ramp, removing her surgical gloves. "Surgery is a success. The patient is resting comfortably. "

"Thanks, Doc," said Jake.

Doctor North looked up into the night sky. "This is not a dream, is it?" she asked.

"No, Major, it is not," answered Ginger.

Carol North looked at Susan, then spoke. "I have serious problems. I have two severe burn patients who need long-term treatment and rehabilitation, or they will die. Infection from severe burns is nasty and fatal. The double-amputee will survive physically, but I wonder if mental health is in the cards."

"How are the medical staff holding up?"

"Numb and distracted by their duties right now. Tomorrow—"

"I wished I could tell you, Doctor; we could just fly out of here. But there is no magic doorway back."

"Well, Susan, the double-amputee and one of the burn victims are female. Disfiguring injuries are rough on women in our society. People expect to be nice to look at."

"If I may interject," said Jake. "We can hang together and try to find out what or who caused us to be here, or we can go stark raving bug nuts. Everyone is going to have to make their own decisions. I don't see the chain of command lasting past the first week here on Barsoom."

The four humans stood silent. Then Susan spoke. "Let's all try to get a good night's sleep before we talk about making decisions. Jake, you have overnight security set up?"

"If I can use your three enlisted, yes."

"You can use Lt. Liu also; she is the low woman on the totem pole."

"Well, time to get back to the patients," said Carol.

"May I bend your ear about a medical problem, Major?" asked Jake

"Sure, why not. Come and walk with me."

As the two slow-walked up the ramp, Jake whispered, "I have a kilo of uncut heroin plus some poppy seeds. In case we need more—pain killers."

"Where did you get that from, Jackson?"

"Ask me no questions, and I will tell you no lies. I also have a small amount of powdered opium and a couple of joints of weed. Not to mention a bottle of hooch."

"How did you all get this?"

"Major, this was Afghanistan. Even with so-called good and faithful Muslims, money talks and bullshit walks."

Jake shook Susan awake from her cot on the cargo area floor.

"We have company." He handed her a cup of coffee. "MRE blend. The best stuff around,"

"God, it wasn't a bad dream. I hoped I would wake up home with my husband and two boys."

"Well, Major, we'll have to deal with that later. There are two men on horseback coming this way."

"Call me Susan. No six-legged monstrosities?"

"No Dejah Thoris either. They are both males."

Susan slipped into her flight suit as Jake tried not to look at her bra and panties. She was good-looking, married, or not. She slipped on her Tactical vest with her pistol and followed Jake down the ramp. At the bottom, Gunny Jefferson was watching the two slow-approaching riders through his tactical rifle scope.

"They have a white flag and all. We have bets if they speak English or not."

"Might want to hold on to your money, Gunny,"

replied Susan. "I bet you there are no banks or ATMs around." She looked at Jake.

"Want to walk out and meet them."

"Good idea. No need for those guys to see the inside of the C-17."

Jake turned towards the HUMVEE. "Smitty, you have the Fifty?"

"Sighted right on them, Boss."

"Well, Major, we may only have twenty rounds to the Ma Duece, but Smitty will make them count."

"I hope we don't have to use any of them."

The two 21st Century humans began a slow walk towards the two riders.

"We dodge viruses from China, try to help pull our soldiers back from killing zones all over the world, and we get—this shit," said Susan.

"How many of your people are married?" Jake asked.

"Ginger has a wife at home with a bun in the oven. Billi Lui is single but close to her family. The three enlisted all have husbands, with Crew Chief Williams having four kids at home."

"Four? Man, how does she do it?"

"She's tough and smart. She'll be a good backup in a fight, Jake. How about you?"

"Three exes and four kids. I don't do marriage well."

"I guess. How about your men?"

"They are all married with kids."

"All married? Why do they keep doing—this."

"Good money. My guys get fifty thousand a year tax-free plus ten dollars a day per diem once we hit the road. I get a few hundred on a debit card or local money for expenses that take care of them in the field. All our equipment and weapons are supplied. They have excellent health care for their families, plus bonuses and found."

"Found?" queried Susan.

"Any money and valuables we take off of the bad guys we can keep unless the Gov't says it wants the funds recovered. And yes, I keep my guys honest about whacking people for their stuff."

Susan looked at Jake as they walked. "So, it's the money?"

"And we are all adrenalin junkies. I say we will all be burnt out in ten years if we aren't dead. I keep my guys alive. I have a pool of operatives. These three are the best."

"What about your captive, Jahan? I hadn't asked before as we had bigger fish to fry."

"Jahan Ayubi will get cut loose. He is only an excellent intelligence asset in our world, not Barsoom. The answer to your unasked question is no; I doubt we will make it back to Earth. Sorry."

"Man, you are hard."

"Which is why I do not do marriage well. But all

those medical types will have to harden up. They have some difficult decisions to make about themselves and their patients."

Susan stayed silent as what Jake said sank in. Difficult was not the right word for the decision-making process. Impossible was the correct word.

They were within hailing distance, and Susan called out, "Major Susan Finch of the United States Air Force. Who, may I ask, are you?"

The rider with more gray in his beard called back. "Mark Stone, the Mayor, Customs and Immigration for Freetown. I thought I recognized a C-17."

"You from the 21st Century?" Jake called out.

"I am. Marshal Matt Dillon here is from 19th Century Texas. He was a real-life Texas Ranger and our law keeper."

"Marshal Dillon? Really?" mumbled Jake.

"So," continued Susan, "your town is Freetown. So where in Holy Hell is Freetown? Where the Hell are we!?"

The man identified as Matt Stone paused for a moment then answered. "Most of us call it Elsewhen. A few say it is Limbo or Purgatory. All I know is people from different times and places show up. I popped into this existence about six months ago. Marshal Dillion has been here for almost three years."

"I take it nobody knows how people come and go," said Jake. "Or can people go back?"

"If they have, we have not heard from them," said the Marshal.

Susan seemed to shake a bit, then stood a bit straighter as she calmed herself.

"Well, maybe we'll be the first. Our great flying machine still has some fuel in it. We can watch for an anomaly and lift to meet it."

"Mine happened on the road," said Matt.

"Then we will rush towards it whatever vehicle we can muster."

"So, what is in Freetown?" interrupted Jake. "You have beer?"

Matt laughed. "We have some beer, wine, some hard alcohol from a still we made. It's possible to use alcohol as fuel for that HUMVEE you have yonder."

"Electrical power?"

"A bit. My former Jeep SUV doubles as a small power station. We have two former Russian young ladies who are good with mechanics and engineering. We are trying to construct a water wheel generator on Free River to provide power for the town. We are almost there."

"But no video games or the Internet yet," said Jake.

"No, sir. You'll have to find something else to rot your brain."

As usual, Matt Dillon gave Mark a quizzical look as the people talked about items he had never seen nor experienced."

"So, how do we emigrate to Freetown?" asked Jake.

"There may be a delay in that," said the Marshal. "You will have been noticed by a Chinaman who fancies himself as Emperor."

"Emperor?" said Susan as she again found her voice.

"He is actually the rebel who overthrew the son of the original Chinaman who crossed into this world almost a hundred years ago. The first Emperor came with soldiers and followers.

"And the Emperor set up shop and filled a vacuum."

"You have it, Major," said Mark Stone. "The Emperor and his son collected as much of the technology and metal people bring as possible. Metal here means money. On this planet, most of the heavy metals are buried deep or under the oceans. Then the current Emperor, a refugee from the 20the Century, overthrew them. "

"There are oceans?"

"Yep, Major. Too bad you did not fly over them. We could use a recent eyewitness account of the coasts. Freetown and Beijing are both well back from the Great Ocean coast and what people call the Other Sea."

"So, you say this current Emperor is a problem?" asked Susan.

"That is an understatement. The Emperor allows

us to exist as we are far from Beijing and act as both a buffer and trade post to the peoples and land out West of here."

"Other aircraft have crossed over into—Elsewhen then. And this Chinese strongman grabs them all if he can. By force, I imagine."

"Yes, Ma'am," said the Marshal. "And in Freetown, he has some merchants who still favor him. They will send a carrier pigeon or a rider to make sure the Emperor knows you have landed. He will send a bunch of soldiers to seize everything. Including you."

"You have held out so far, yes?" asked Susan.

"By the skin of our teeth, "answered Mark. "I was elected Mayor to counter the Emperor's influence. But we have a limited militia. Just enough to defend Freetown. So, unfortunately, we can offer minimal assistance when his troops show up."

"Jesus. We dodged those viruses from China and winded up fighting another problem of a Chinese government."

"So, as Mayor, I must tell you that Freetown would like you to delay trying to move into town until we figure out if the Emperor's boys will track you here."

Susan looked at Jake. He shrugged then spoke. "If we took off and flew west, what would we find?"

"Germans and Amazons, from what the few immigrants and traders tell us. Neither are very friendly."

After a few more minutes of conversation, the

two new arrivals took their leave and walked back to the C-17. Susan remained quiet, lost in thought. Just before they reached the others, Susan spoke.

"I have to tell everyone that hope is almost nonexistent. This is not going to be easy."

"Just keep it short and sweet. People will have to work things out on their own. Don't expect everyone to remain in a military-run environment. Especially single people."

"I know. I can't let anyone run off with our equipment. The medical capability aboard the C-17 is way above anything in this world."

"That, my good Major, is a bargaining chip. And an industry the group can use to survive. So, sell that to them."

As Jake kept watch, Susan explained the situation to the staff and awake patients a half-hour later. As she finished, Colonel Fish broke in. "You must be insane to believe you can just people walk off. Everyone signed up, volunteered for this."

"That was on Earth. Have you seen the two moons, Colonel?"

"It must be an optical illusion, a mirage."

"Then, where are we? Who were those two men Jake and I talked with?"

The Colonel began yelling. "I'll have you all up on charges of desertion!"

"Colonel, give it a rest," said Gunny Jefferson. "We are strangers in a strange land. We must survive. I have a family at home also. But I also know we are not going back to them anytime soon."

"May I say something, Susan?" asked Major North.

"Of course, Carol."

The Doctor stepped forward. "We just lost the two burn victims. They needed a hospital. We have other patients to care for and ensure they survive. That includes an amputee."

She scanned the group.

"If we stay together, become a family, we can help each other and the people in this world. We have medical expertise and capabilities decades advanced from some Chinese Empire. We can use this C-17 as a hospital and go about scrounging for additional equipment and medicine. We may even discover flora and fauna we can use in our medicine."

Carol North paused, then began again. "I have a husband on Earth. This is not Earth. He would want me to survive until, maybe, we find a way back. However, as Susan said, you all have to decide for yourselves." Doctor North stepped back.

"Thank you, Doctor. Anyone else?"

Tsgt. Williams stepped up, her cheeks wet with tears. "Y'all, I have a husband and four children at home. I don't know if I can see them, hug them again. I'll stay with my pilot. I know if there is a chance of going home, it's with the Major. But I understand if some of you without family waiting may want to strike out on your own."

There were murmurs among the group. The Colonel went off again. "I am ranking officer here—"

"Oh shut up," a Medtech called out. "What are you going to do? Courts-martial us? There are no courts-martial here."

Fish kept sputtering and stammering, then turned on his heel and stormed back into the C-17.

"Take ten minutes," said Susan, "then let us know what you all want."

The military personnel broke up into small groups. Carol North walked over to Jake. "Thank You. They are not in pain anymore."

"You did the right thing, Doctor. Remember that."

Carol squeezed Jake's hand. "You're a lot like my husband. The strong and smart type."

Jake laughed. "Wait until you see me drunk, Doc."

The Doctor walked back to the aircraft. Susan stepped up to Jake. "Your idea seemed to work."

"So far. No matter what, I'll stay with you."

"Why?"

"I saw you in your skivvies. Now I can fantasize."

Two single Medical Technicians said they wanted to head towards Freetown. After some discussion, they were allowed to take their sidearms. The rest of the personnel stated they would stick it out at the C-17- except for Colonel Fish. He stormed up to Jake, broken finger and all.

"I want my pistol."

"Okay. Marco!"

"Yeah, Boss."

"His pistol, please."

The shooter brought the pistol to Jake. The SPECOPS supervisor cleared the weapon, ejected the live round out of the chamber. He then slid the magazine into the pistol butt.

"I keep this round. Don't try to chamber a shell until you're a mile away. If you do, I will shoot you."

Fish flushed bright red.

"I'll see you in Leavenworth Penitentiary," the Colonel hissed.

"Hey, Toto. We're not in Kansas anymore."

The angry and short man stormed off towards the nearby town.

"You think that's a wise idea?" asked the pilot.

"I predict he'll be shot within forty-eight hours."

Susan shook her head. "That is the waste of a surgeon."

"That is a waste of a human being."

The military members combined their resources to make a communal meal. As they did, a Respiratory Technician reported seeing a warren of giant jackrabbits. Jake and the Gunny went out to set some heavy-duty snares. Within an hour, the two men had snared three oversized jackrabbits.

"Well, if we can scam something to use as a large pot, we can have rabbit stew," Jake said.

Susan and Carol went to see Sergeant Guadalupe Silva, the double amputee.

"I know this sucks, Sergeant, but we'll come up with some legs for you," said Carol North.

"Hey, Major, Don't worry about me. I'm in a real-life science fiction novel."

"You're tough, aren't you?" said Susan.

"Yes, Ma'am. I'm still alive. No time to give up yet."

The men and women set up some makeshift dining tables and set a meal up. Once again, Jake stood watch. Someone started saying the Lord's Prayer as Grace, and all joined in.

"There are no atheists in foxholes," Jake said softly.

Later on, Susan brought him a mess kit of food.

"Thanks, Susan."

"You're welcome. Someone needs to relieve you."

"No problem, I have it planned out."

"How long have you been doing this, Jake?"

"Running and gunning? Fifteen years. I've been all over the world. I even worked with the Flying Mofangos."

"The Flying Mofangos? I never heard of them."

"Part of the Air Units with Customs and Border

Protection. They worked around Puerto Rico on drug interdiction. They were as crazy as I was."

"What did you do with them?"

"My team did an extraction. The government used us as we were 'unofficial,' but the CBP pilots extracted us from a jungle airstrip. Their aircraft had a few bullet holes for war stories."

Jahan Ayubi walked up with a soft drink in his hand.

"Am I free to go?"

"Yep, Jahan, you are. Sorry, we screwed you over and dragged you to a new world, but, well, tough shitski."

"You have done me a favor, Jackson. I no longer have several groups fighting over me. Nor am I on my way to be a human bomb."

"Well, we can give you a few coins but no weapon. Sorry."

"I will take the coin and then leave in the morning. The doctors here are very nice. Major, if you could tell them that for me."

"I will. And you can tell the doctors yourself in the morning."

"Okay. Now, I will go rest."

After Jahan walked away, Suan asked, "What did he do that made him a target?"

"He was a courier. Jahan ran information and sometimes money between the various groups. Thus, he knew who many of the main players were. His ex-girlfriend turned him in."

"Ah, yes. Jake. A woman scorned."

"You can say that again.'

The Emperor's soldiers came the following day. There was one hundred calvary with metal chest plates, a half dozen with lances, and most others with some type of rifle. The NCOs and Officers had flap holstered pistols. As the security detail sounded the alarm, the cavalry formed a line facing the C-17. The back ramp was up and locked, with the HUMVEE setting out just past the ramp drop area. Manning the Fifty was Donald Hoffa, propped up with some straps and drugs to keep his stitches from breaking loose. He had refused NOT to be part of any armed response. Being in the HUMVEE meant he did not have to run around.

The evening before, the Airmen, Marines, and SPECOPS had gone out scrounging and brought back some not too large logs and set up a couple of barricades for concealed firing positions. Behind one were Jake, Susan, and Billi Liu. The Lieutenant held a bull horn as the consensus was the Chinese would try to communicate demands first, then take by force if ignored.

A smartly uniformed Chinese horseman trotted out to within fifty yards of the C-17. The man unrolled an ornate scroll and proceeded to yell its contents at the group of military. Billi Liu translated as he read.

"It is a form of Mandarin. They must be from a

time close to 1000 A.C.E.—some of the forms sound a bit archaic."

"What's the gist of it?" asked Susan.

"In the name of His Imperial Majesty, we are to surrender ourselves and all our property, including the C-17, to this cavalry unit. Failure to do so will result in pain and death."

"What law do they claim we violated?"

"We are trespassing on Imperial Property. And all metal belongs to the Emperor."

"So," said Jake, "do you want to respond 'nuts,' or is there something else you want to say?"

Susan paused for a moment, then said. "Billi, tell him we are doctors who will be treating them for gunshot wounds if they attack us."

After the Lieutenant used the bullhorn to transmit the message, the Chinese junior officer spun his horse around and galloped back to the formation some two hundred meters back. There was a quick consultation with the unit commander; then, the officer fell back into the cavalry line. The six lancers were positioned in the middle, bracketing the commander. The senior officer yelled out a command; the lancers pointed their weapons at the C-17 as the other mounted soldiers removed rifles from scabbards. Another order and the horsemen began to trot towards the aircraft.

"Wait for them to fire first?" asked Susan.

"Hell, no. They clearly have deadly intent," said

Jake. Then he yelled out, "Pick your targets, semi-auto, fire when I do."

As the horse soldiers passed a prepositioned sighting stake at one hundred meters, Jake fired. The .223 round hit the commanding officer and unhorsed him. Hoffa cracked off a single fifty caliber round and blasted a horse into pieces. All trained marksmen, the other rifle shooters, fired with deadly effect as the Chinese discharged their black powder weapons. Lead bullets ricocheted off the HUMVEE and the C-17 as some of the calvary tried to charge the defenders. Others panicked and fled. Franzetti threw their only grenade, a Chicom production, which exploded among the surviving lancers. The center of the attack fell apart, and horse soldiers scattered.

"They are clearly not used to organized and armed resistance," observed Jake.

He signaled his two ambulatory SPECOPS men, and the three slowly searched the kill zone for survivors. Two wounded were picked up by Medtecs and carried into the C-17 for treatment and questioning by Billi.

"I count four dead horses and thrty bodies," Smitty called out.

Jake walked out further to where he had shot the commander.

"Headshot," he mumbled. "All that practice pays off."

He stripped the breastplate of the body, found the

dropped pistol.

"Colt Navy Clone," he said. "Interesting."

The two Loadmaster recovered the dropped weapons, assisted by the Gunny and the Corporal. Franzetti began to butcher the dead horses for fresh meat.

Susan met Jake as he walked back to the defensive positions.

"What do we do with the bodies, Jake? They will bloat and stink."

"Funeral pyre. If we can access a bit of your aviation fuel and get it lit, we can burn the bodies. We can use the HUMVEE to move them a hundred meters and make a burn pit."

"I never thought I would be so nonchalant about all this—death," Susan finished as she looked at all the bodies.

"We do what we must. We lucked out. The Emperor's boys underestimated us, are used to being bullies. So, Thirtyone dead, all theirs. We have two wounded Chinese we will have to kick back somehow, but we suffered no casualties."

Just then, Ginger Roberts walked up with three horses. "Look what I found."

"I did not realize you were a horsewoman, Captain," said Jake.

"Used to ride a lot before I became a pilot. Now not so much."

"We can use the horses to help move the bodies," said Susan.

"Burial?" asked Ginger.

"Cremation, a funeral pyre. I think many Chinese believe in that anyways. No matter, as we cannot have rotting corpses."

"Yes, Susan. You're right. I'll rig some tow ropes for these fellas." Ginger led the horses away from the carnage.

"You have a tight crew, Major," Jake stated.

"We have flown together a lot. They are all good people. But a week, a month from now, when the reality sets in…."

"Most will do fine if we set good examples. And give them some say in their future."

"No more orders, Jake?"

"Think like a mercenary unit. Elected leaders who serve until they get people killed. You follow your leader until you unelect. That is how I operate."

"Hmmm. That sounds good."

They heard the sounds of a raggedy motorbike, and Jake had his rifle at high ready.

Up rode Mayor Stone with a rifle slung across his back. He dismounted as Jake asked, "What, no, horse?"

"Horseback and I don't do well on my butt."

"Well, Mayor, we repelled boarders," said Susan.

"The soldiers will be back. Next time they will come in more numbers or sneak up and take by stealth."

"Oh, great. Maybe we should fly out, try another place."

"Major, it's all the same real estate, just different dangers. Trust me. Here, you have friends."

"You're our friend?" asked Jake.

"Yep. A few bottles of beer and homebrew hooch for you. Come in and trade some of that metal you collected off the bodies."

"That's how things work here?"

"Yep. To the strong go the spoils. I wish it were different, but it's not."

Jahan walked up with a pistol stuck in his belt and a bolt action Needle Rifle strapped across his back. "I have weapons and ammunition from the dead. I hope you don't mind.'

"Just don't point them at us," replied Jake. The civilian soldier looked at Mark Stone.

"You want to give Jahan a ride to town, Mayor?"

"He's not going to get himself shot like your Doctor, is he?"

"What happened?" asked Susan.

"He went into one of our two local whore houses and proceeded to tell them they needed to hire him as all kinds of diseases probably infected them. The Madam disagreed, there was an argument, and she tried to have him thrown out. The Doctor went for his pistol with that broken finger of his, then decided to switch gun hands. The bouncer shot him between the eyes. Now the bouncer has his pistol."

"No trial?"

"Why? The local magistrate happened to be visiting the Madam and saw the whole shebang. We treat whores in Freetown as licensed sex workers. My Elsewhen wife is the local doctor, so of course, she examines the ladies of the evening."

"You have a wife on Earth, then?" asked Susan.

"Yep. No kids there, but I don't think I'll make it back."

"You do what you have to to get by," opined Jake.

"You said it. By the way, Susan hired those two medical technicians from your crew. They have good jobs and bright futures. Ten years from now, they will be doctors themselves and can go to new free settlements."

"Plan to expand, huh?"

"If we don't, someday the Emperor or some other dictator will crush out this little corner of liberty. Right now, the Dragon Forest and Northern Mountains make the Emperor, the Romans, and Camelot on the seacoast think twice about a long campaign. Seeing your aircraft made him take a chance, and there was a large patrol nearby. Carrier pigeons travel fast."

"Will you let us stay an independent entity?" asked Susan.

"You are hereby recognized as the independent territory of Globemaster. As the Secretary of State for the city-state of Freetown, I will write up a formal treaty of recognition and understanding."

Jake and Susan laughed as Jahan smiled. Americans were so strange.

"And with that, I will depart. Jahan, hop on the back. I bet you are used to rough motorbikes ride."

"Yes, I am. "

The Mercenary and the Major watched the motorbike rattle away.

"I have a question, Jake."

"Go ahead."

"You think we can all qualify as Flying Mofangos?"

"But of course!"

It would take some time, but the crew of the C-17 would make a go of it in Elsewhen. But... those are stories for a later time.

# 7
# THE HIGHWAYMAN

Once of the Emerald Island on Earth, Lorcan Quinn sat above the trade road leading from the Great Mountain Range towards New Beijing and the Emperor. This road, like several similar, wound through the mountains near the valley passage of the North River. The tall, slender, and muscular Irishman sat on his rocky perch some one hundred English Yards from what his contact said was the route of the exclusive trade caravan. This wait was the second day of his venture, and Lorcan was weary of the chill and boredom.

"I will give it one more day," he said in the King's English as he finished his lukewarm tea. Since coming to this Limbo or Purgatory, which the elder inhabitants called Elsewhen, Lorcan found English was a reasonably common language. However, Gaelic Irish speakers seemed limited to only Lorcan. His first friend here, Mathew Rhodes, explained that Mandarin Chinese was the primary power in the area, with other Asian, English, German and Italian-Roman speakers at various points of the compass.

Lorcan smiled at the thought of Mathew. Just as much a rogue as the Irishman Highwayman, Lorcan Quinn would have been dead or enslaved if Lorcan had not met him that first day. The ruling Chinese grabbed all 'newcomers' and would enslave them with a desired skill, knowledge, or wanted physical attributes. Resist, and they killed you.

"Sounds a lot like some English Lords I knew," replied Lorcan.

"Yes, my new friend from the Irish Potato Famine," said Mathew. "The Emperor of New Beijing treats all non-Chinese as serfs or low caste subjects. We are round-eyed barbarians."

Mathew was a small man but was quick with a blade and a gun. Mathew had introduced Lorcan to the revolver and repeating firearms, as well as to a history that was Lorcan's future on Earth.

"1848 is the last year you remember?" Mathew asked.

"Yes. Then God or Satan yanked me here."

Mathew, the American, laughed. "Tis neither as they say. An unknown person or thing yanked me from Atlantic City in 1930. Some people from later times explained something about other universes and timelines, meaning people from everywhere and every time come here against their will. Now we all try to survive in Elsewhen.”

It took Lorcan a while to understand the words and concepts Mathew mentioned. However, Mathew had been a bit of a Highwayman himself with a crime organization or syndicate. Thus, he understood the idea of robbing those who could afford it. Mathew arrived a couple of years before Lorcan and quickly learned the ropes. In Lorcan Quinn, he had seen a kindred spirit.

Lorcan looked through the spyglass again. He was in his third year in Elsewhen, plying the only trade he knew well. As a starving Irishman, Lorcan soon learned how to hijack wealthy English officials and merchants on the various highways in English Occupied Ireland. Mathew helped him hone his skills with more modern weapons than 1848 AD muskets and cheap single-shot pistols. After Mathew had settled down owning a whore house the year prior, Lorcon struck out on his own.

“Hide here anytime you wish,” Mathew told him from the town people called New Chungking. “We are far enough from the Emperor here to dodge his interest but close enough to New Bejing to get good business.”

Lorcan stretched and checked the large matchlock musket’s rest, braced between a couple of boulders. Lorcan acquired it barely four days prior as he was en route to this ambush spot. A large and mad Spainaird just newly arrived, based on his fearful demeanor, had tried to relieve Lorcan of his Chinese-Mongolian ponies with the threat of the matchlock. The Irishman shot the attacker in the face with his flintlock boot gun, making the first trip to Elsewhen with Lorcan. He finished the man off with his shillelagh. Lorcan vaguely remembered tales of Conquistadors from his school days and assumed the Spaniard was one. He stripped the dead man of all his metal (metal was wealth in Elsewhen) and boots plus the matchlock powder and ball.

Mathew assisted Lorcan in the original search for firearms and other weapons befitting a Highwayman. Thus, the Irish transplant already possessed two fifty-caliber Hawkins rifles (Chinese copies), a fifty-caliber Chinese rimfire horse pistol, an original Colt thirty-one caliber pocket revolver, and of course, his original flintlock boot pistol. A year previous, Lorcan had possessed a lever-action rifle which Mathew identified as a copy of a Volcanic. Lorcan traded it in with some gold for the Chinese horse pistol when the weak "rocket ball" ammunition bullet bounced off a Chinese soldier's breastplate at point-blank range.

Now, the Irishman sat with the matchlock pointed at the path the caravan must take if his informant was correct. His mount and pack pony, Loran thought the creatures of the Mongolian and Chinese plains were too short to be considered real horses when compared to Europe steads, were hidden in an enclave of rocks some one hundred yards back up a game trail. The matchlock fired a three quarter inch ball that would take down a horse in seconds. Lorcan had used a file to place one rifling groove at the end of the smooth barrel. Hopefully, the slight spin on the groove put on the round lead ball would improve the accuracy of the smooth-bore musket. Or, his attempts at gunsmithery could be an abject failure. Lorcan shrugged. If he had to flee, so be it.

This attempt was his seventh highway robbery. The fourth one had netted him unforeseen riches as he stumbled upon a military paymaster and the escort. Rather than a 'hands up' on the road, Lorcan shadowed the small group to their campsite for the night. The Highwayman snuck into the campground after midnight, unhobbled the mounts, and sent them loudly scattering. As the escort rushed to recover their horses, Lorcan dashed into the camp, used his shillelagh on the paymaster, and escaped with two small lockboxes stuffed with gold and silver. It was ten minutes before the escort soldiers realized what had happened. By then, Lorcan galloped away.

The downside of such a successful robbery was the Emperor sent many patrols looking for the bold Highwayman. One did not rob from the Emperor and expect to live. For some three months, Lorcan had soldiers hounding him in the Great Mountains. The Irishman stashed most of the riches in a tiny secret cave he found, once a small viper pit. Any returning snakes would dissuade anyone from poking around. He took the rest of the monies and bought his pack pony, presents for Mathew's whores, and supplies for the road. The patrols kept him from robbing any caravans. Lorcan resorted to stealing from two small merchants just for sufficient horse feed and dried meats. Thus, when an informant at a roadhouse he frequented late at night mentioned an exclusive caravan coming from Fishers City en route to Beijing, Lorcan knew he had to chance it.

Now, one dead Spaniard and one acquired matchlock later, Lorcan waited and watched. He took a swig of sour wine from the last robbery and sat down in the shade of a boulder.

"Tomorrow morning, and I leave. Mathew might have a job I can do until the heat is off, as he would say."

After he said that, Lorcan saw a dust cloud rise from several hundred yards down the roadway. The amount of dust told the Highwayman the transport vehicle or animals were moving at speed or oversized. He brought his spyglass up to his eye. Once he had a good focus, Lorcan swore. Four mounted soldiers led a fancy stagecoach pulled by six Chinese horses some three hundred yards away. As the incline towards Lorcan increased, the steads slowed to a trot; now Lorcan saw there was a single file of pack horses trying to catch up.

"Damn. It must be a royal family procession of some sort," he said.

He had moments to make a decision. Should he try to take on the group or let them pass?

"Ah, Hell. In for a penny, in for a pound."

He mounted the massive stock of the matchlock

against his shoulder and sighted down the crude set of sights. At some one-hundred yards range from the coach, he pulled the simple trigger, and the serpentine lit match rope ignited the powder charge, a *boom*, and the three-quarter-inch ball flew towards the target.

Lorcan aimed in hopes of hitting a member of the four-person mounted escort. Instead, the massive round struck the left lead horse of the coach. The equine collapsed at the impact of the lead ball. The coach itself was nearly upset in the road as the five remaining horses came to a crashing halt. Lorcan had chosen this spot for an ambush as there was a twenty-foot drop off on the far side of the road, which limited the escape routes. A typical caravan would be stopped by sniping and convinced to drop some valuables for passage. This group was no natural assemblage of merchants and travelers, and now Lorcan was in a bit of a pickle.

Horses screamed in pain and fear as they were brought up short by their dead coach mate. The coach might flip as the horses slammed together. However, the coach traveled at a trot rather than a gallop. The two civilians minding the four-pack animals that followed the coach kept them from crashing into the halted conveyance. The coach's driver was an expert as he kept his beasts from trying to break free in every direction as his assistant clambered down to unhook the dead horse. The officer in charge of the troops yelled orders, and two of the riders maneuvered their mounts around the panicked coach horses in an attempt to pull the dead horse out of the way of the royal coach.

The ambush spot was a narrow passage between the rocky upward slope and the drop-off on the other side. Lorcan's initial shot, despite the plume of black powder smoke, went unnoticed. He moved the matchlock out of the way and brought up one of his two Hawken rifle clones for a shot. The officer scanned the mountain slope for the attacker he knew was there as he yelled at the men to get the coach free and moving.

"Now, to make the best of a bad situation," the Highwayman mumbled as he sighted, then fired the fifty caliber rifle at the led pack animal. Hawkin rifles' reputation on Earth for accuracy was excellent. These Chinese copies on Elsewhen were the same. The lead pack animal collapsed in a heap and was dead within seconds. Now Lorcan knew he would have the merchandise on that animal if nothing else.

The lead civilian yelled out, unholstered a revolver, and shot at the black powder plume from Lorcan's rifle. The Irishman knew the more he fired from his perch, the sooner he would be targeted. This situation went with the territory of being a robber. Sometimes the victims shot back. Lorcan preferred not to shoot people, but sometimes it was unavoidable.

With practiced ease, Lorcan grabbed up his second loaded rifle, aimed, and shot the lead pack animal wrangler as bullets zipped close. The man toppled off his mount, and the horse bolted. The lead to the dead packhorse jerked loose as the deadman's horse tried to gallop around the stalled coach. The officer in charge yelled at a young trooper in Chinese that Lorcan understood: "Get him!"

With his sniper perch exposed, Lorcan knew he had to make a choice. Flee now, or keep resisting in an attempt to gain more treasure? One young soldier decided for him as the cavalryman urged his horse up a small game trail that leads to Lorcan's concealment. Lorcan crouched down and pulled his tried and true boot pistol out. The Highwayman had taken many a shot with this lite dueling pistol from his days in Ireland. The young mounted soldier's head came into view as he passed a boulder, and Lorcan shot the man in the face. The soldier topped off his horse, dropping a lever-action rifle. The mount panicked and tried to back down the trail. Lorcan unholstered his small .31 caliber Colt revolver and scrambled after it, staying in the cover of the rocks and boulders.

The dead packman's horse now became entangled in the attempts to move the dead coach horse out of the way. The assistant coach driver managed to cut the harness and straps loose from the dead horse as the two remaining horse soldiers used ropes to pull the body away as the free horse whinnied in fear and bumped into the other animals. The officer dismounted his stead and tried to help lead the remaining five attached horses away from the dead one.

The remaining pack animal wrangler tried to control the three live pack horses and guide them to follow the coach. Lorcan recovered the shot soldiers' rifle and found a newer and more robust version of the Volcanic copy stressed to shoot forty-four caliber shells. He quickly returned to his original perch. Cocking the newly acquired rifle, Lorcan aimed and at the rump of the right front coach horse. The bullet left a bloody crease. The horse let out a scream and surged ahead, the other four steads following suit. The assistant driver was yanked off his feet and drug by the panicked horses down the road. The sudden actions knocked the young officer off his feet, and he sprawled in the dirt. The terrified animals yanked the coach forward, almost upending it. The coach wheels crushed the fallen officers left arm, his screams adding to the cacophony of sounds.

The royal coach driver hung on for dear life as the conveyance teetered near the edge of a drop-off, then righted itself. The galloping horses propelled it down the road as the occupants began to shout above the din of injured animals and people. One of the soldiers helped the assistant driver onto the back of his mount and took off in pursuit, with the remaining cavalryman chasing after him. The party forgot the two dead men and the injured officer as everyone fled with the royal coach. The remaining pack animal wrangler let loose three horses and galloped after his fellow retreating Chinese.

Lorcan scrambled down the small game trail to the

main road. He managed to stop the three remaining pack animals from fleeing and quickly tied them off on a jagged boulder. The Highwayman approached the injured officer with the lever-action rifle covering him as the young Chinese man lay crying and moaning in the road's dirt.

"Don't move, or I will shoot you," Lorcan said in passable Chinese. The officer tried to move to look at the Irishman but screamed in pain as the crushed bones in his left arm shifted. Lorcan saw a flapped pistol holster and removed a Chinese clone .44 Colt rimfire revolver. Even a wounded man was dangerous.

"We will hunt you down like a dog, barbarian," the young officer finally hissed through pain-clenched teeth. "Your guts will be torn out and fed to dogs while you are still alive."

"Not today, boy," Lorcan replied.

He went to the dead wrangler and recovered his pistol, a .38 Colt rimfire, plus a coin purse. Lorcan kept an eye on the wounded officer as he grabbed some saddlebags off the dead packhorse and transferred them to the other three. As he prepared to leave the scene before someone recovered their nerve and came galloping back, he asked the officer, "Who was in the Coach?"

"The Emperor's royal niece and her consort, barbarian. You will pay dearly—"

"Oh shut up, pigshit," growled the Irishman. "You will be lucky not to lose that arm and spend the rest of your days as a street beggar."

Lorcan led the three pack horses up the game trail as he made his way to his two animals. He stopped and took another .38 revolver off the dead soldier and then coaxed the three beasts as fast as he could after loading firearms onto the pack animals. He left the matchlock behind as unneeded weight.

Within a quarter of an hour, he was back at the hiding place of his two mounts. After checking loads of the three acquired pack animals (and removing some coinage and jewels for transfer to his horse's saddlebags in case he had to make a run for it), Lorcan hit the trail. The Highwayman stayed in the saddle for almost twenty-four hours, stopping only to rest the animals. He finally bedded down at a small farm whose owners accepted his periodic presence in exchange for some needed money. Lorcan did not stay long as, despite his experience at hiding his trail, he knew the Emperor would not rest until his head was on a stake. Messing with the man's niece was not a good idea. With a few hours of rest, he hit the trail again. After three days of hard travel, Lorcan was at Mathews Emporium in Nan Guan /South Pass township. Some fifty English miles south of the outskirts of New Beijing, Mathew ran the town. However, he was under the watchful eye of the Emperor.

Lorcan came in the dark of night. Mathew had his people stash the pack animals in a secure stable and put Lorcan in a particular hidden room in the brothel. The

Highwayman slept an entire day. He was awoken by two young maidens who knew him well with a feast of local delicacies. Lorcan ate, had a bath with the two comely women, then shared some aperitif with rice and fish rolls. Mathew came up at the finish and shooed the young women away. The two sat down with some good Irish Whiskey.

"The words got out you made a big score," said Mathew Rhodes.

"That information traveled fast."

"There is something called the telegraph. The talking wires are in various small forts and posts the Emperor has built. Freetown has been getting on his nerves, so he has started expanding his ability to respond with force."

"Huh, I heard rumors of something new, Mathew. I thought it was just so many tall tales."

"Well, The Emperor is waking up to the fact that New Rome, Camelot, and Freetown are no longer afraid of him and his people. Lorcan, you might want to use this treasure to find a new line of work."

"And what would that be, Boyo? I started doing this against the English assholes when we were starving, and I know no other life."

"I can keep you hid here for a couple of more days. After that, well…"

"I understand, my friend. Your ladies here are your family. And you have a wife and child now also."

Mathew shook Lorcan's hand.

"You are a good friend. I would say my best here in Elsewhen. After things cool down, especially if the Emperor is deposed someday—"

Lorcan laughed. "That's what we said about the Royals in my day. Though I understand Ireland was a free country in your day and after."

"There, blood was spilled, Lorcan. Where ever we humans go, we spill each other's blood, it seems."

"Well, if I may visit with some of you young ladies some more, then I will be off. I promise."

Lorcan left the following day. Mathew helped him sell the pack animals to people who would modify the brands. The Highwayman gave away silk scarves and clothes to the women in the Emporium and some jewelry to Mathews s wife, Eve. Plus, a couple of toys for Mathew Junior. Mathew said he would liquidate whatever else he could and send it to him. They packed all the easily disposed items on his remaining packhorse, plus the extra weapons he now had. Mathew found some extra ammunition and powder for the firearms and bid him adieu.

A day on the trail and Lorcan Quinn decided his destination. He had heard a lot of this Freetown over the last couple of years. It was way out West and seemed to be a grand mixture of people and times. Lorcan also heard there were a lot of Americans there. When the Famine hit in 1847, many of the Irish headed to the Americas. Lorcan had wanted to suck out one more bit of revenge from the English before he left.

Then he wound up in Elsewhen.

The Highwayman spent two more weeks dodging Chinese Patrols as he wound down to the Lesser River and headed West. He traveled at night and followed the river as much as he could. Loren made it through the Lesser Mountain range with little difficulty. Somehow he made it through the Cedar Mountains without running into any Dragons. The Lesser River became a creek by this time, and Lorcan followed a couple of trade roads used by smaller merchants and caravans. He traveled along with a couple as security against robbery (what a turnaround). The merchants told the Highwayman of trade routes and peoples he had heard about in bars. Lorcan shrugged them off as myths. They also warned him of new arrivals with destructive war machines and giant iron birds. Lorcan smiled politely and said to himself he would have to see all this to believe it.

At the beginning of the third week, the Highwayman came down off some foothills of the Cedar Mountains and received his first view of the Freetown area. Off to the northeast of the so-called city limits was an odd metal machine. Lorcan avoided that object and slowly rode into the town proper. There were quite a few plumes of smoke from fireplaces and cooking stoves, which told him the town was more civilized than many areas. He saw a small lookout tower and rode towards it.

A young lad yelled down at him. "Are you peaceful?"

Lorcan laughed. "Are you? That determines my actions."

"Check in with Marshal Dillon, three blocks down. If you don't check-in, he will come looking for you."

"Thanks for the warning."

He found the office and a large man sitting on the wooden sidewalk in front of the office. The Marshall watched the Highwayman dismount without moving from his chair.

Lorcan recognized him as a large man who could explode into violence if the need arose. "Hello. Are you Marshal Dillon?"

"Yes. And your name is?"

"Lorcan Quinn. Late of the Emerald Isle."

"How long in Elsewhen?"

"Just a bit past three years."

"Staying or passing through Freetown?"

"That all depends on how friendly everyone is, Marshal."

Marshal Dillon slowly stood up. "Follow me down to the Mayor and Senior Immigration and Customs Officer, Mark Stone."

Lorcan walked his two horses as he followed the Marshal. He watched people come and go between the numerous shops and storefronts. Many were of European cultures and non-Chinese racial populations. After living in an area where relatively free people were at the most twenty percent Non-Chinese, Lorcan felt almost like he was back on Earth. Everyone seemed to have a decent standard of living with no beggars on the streets.

They arrived at a newly constructed two-story building. Sitting out front in a padded chair was a middle-aged man in Western Americana clothes and cowboy-style boots. Marshal Dillon called out to the slightly graying man.

"I see you are working hard, Mark Stone."

"Someone has to test the new local liquor over ice. I see you have a new friend."

"Welcome, Lorcan Quinn. He is thinking of immigrating."

Mark stood up and shook Lorcan's hand after the Irishman secured his horses. Mark Stone had a firm handshake and fixed the Highwayman with a steady gaze. "So, you are tired of living under the Emperor's heel."

"Yes, Sir. Let us say I have not endeared myself with the Emperor or his subjects.'

"How did that come about?"

Lorcan smiled as he answered, "My chosen pursuit was as a highwayman, a road agent who preys on the caravans of the Chinese government."

Mark paused before answering, "You plan on continuing that career path here?"

"No, Sir. I am hoping to start a new life. To be

honest, I have some of the Emperor's people looking to have my head on a stake."

Mark smiled as he spoke. "Most of us here have pissed off the Emperor to no end. And, we have resisted the attempts by his soldiers to impose his will on us. That resistance led to many dead soldiers. Yet, Freetown and its residents are still here."

"My friend Mathew Rhodes says the Emperor is building forts and strongholds to support new attempts at control over people like you."

"Yep, We have heard the same, But we have some weaponry tricks up our sleeves. If you saw the large aircraft in the northeast, you will get the idea. So, you are proficient with firearms?"

"Yes, to include my shillelagh."

"I thought that was an Irish accent. So, you wish to be a militiaman?"

Lorcan shrugged. "If you mean, defend the town, yes. But I am not into marching and uniforms. Give me a horse, and I can harry the enemy with the best of people."

"Well, as a militiaman, you get a chit for a bowl of soup, bread, and cheese once a day at some of our more excellent dining establishments. I assume you have brought some treasure with you from your previous career."

"Yes, Sir. Have you a bank? But I also do not want to sit around drinking my profits away every day."

"We have a fine bank, Lorcan. I guarantee its

honesty as I am on its Board of Governors." Mark glanced at the Marshal. "You still need a deputy, Matt?"

"I could use another, Mark."

"Well, I was told in my thirty years in law enforcement that it sometimes takes a thief to catch a thief. Lorcan, do you think you could help keep order in town with that shillelagh you're carrying?"

Lorcan laughed. "I? As a Gardia? The Sassenach heads will explode when they hear that."

"I have to ask," continued Mark Stone, "How many Englishmen did you shoot or kill?"

"I shot and killed two Redcoats. I also stabbed and beat two Boyos who tried to take my profits."

"No honor among thieves. And how many people in Elsewhen?"

"As of the last affray, I have shot and killed four, smacked around a few others. The shootings happened when someone tried to shoot me."

"I'll have to show you a poem written after your time on Earth," said Mark. "It fits some of your life."

Mark and Matt looked at each other. Then the Marshal spoke. "Do what you're told, don't abuse the citizens, and I can use a strapping young man as yourself."

"So, shall we shake on this?" asked Mark.

"Of course," Lorcan replied.


A week later, Lorcan was standing at the front door of his small but cozy one-room shack. Freetown was on a building spurt, and one of the more successful projects was tiny abodes for the new immigrants. They were built on side streets as well as at the west end of the expanding township. Lorcan discovered Freetown had an average of one hundred new arrivals each week. Thus, he was a welcomed addition to the police force. The citizens of the area liked his pleasant demeanor and Irish humor. His good looks made him popular with the young ladies, both in the bordellos and out.

Lorcan stretched and finished his tea. The Chinese had excellent 'tae' as the Irish called it, or 'cha' as the Chinese named it. He would walk over to the communal indoor plumbing washroom and toilet to clean up a bit before beginning his afternoon rounds. After all the time on the road as a Highwayman, cold camps and all, the last week was like Heaven.

Lorcan had the former Chinese copy .44 caliber Colt rimfire conversion on his hip and his smaller .31 caliber Colt cap and ball in a shoulder holster. Of course, he carried his shillelagh. The Highwayman went to the communal washroom then began his shift. He stopped by the First National Bank, checked with the staff, and flirted with a couple of female cashiers. While there, Lorcan also checked his new bank account. Here he was a Deputy Marshal and also was one of the larger depositors in the bank.

He continued walking through Freetown and headed towards Ma Bells to ensure no early afternoon drunks were causing problems. Lorcan saw three riders bunched together, coming down the street. As they neared him, the Irishman froze. The leading horseman looked familiar in the face, but the wooden left arm ending in a hook sealed the identification. The lead rider was the Chinese officer with the royal coach crushed arm. Lorcan would bet the other two men were the surviving soldiers from his raid on the royal caravan. He could imagine the conversation they had with the Emperor was to bring back Lorcan's head or do not come back.

Lorcan slid his .44 from his holster and held it behind his right leg. He stepped out into the street towards the three riders, and the officer looked at him. As Lorcan's face registered in the mind of the Chinese officer, the former Highwayman spoke.

"Looking for me?"

The three Chinese men's eyes widen, and hands went towards holstered guns as Lorcan raised his pistol and shot.

Marshal Dillon and Mayor Stone examined the three dead soldiers as they lay in the street. The town Doctor, the Mayor's wife Susan, had officially declared the men deceased.

"Nice shooting, Deputy," said Matt Dillon.

"Do I still have a job?" asked Lorcan.

"Why not?" asked Matt Stone. "They came looking for you as secret agents, not as uniformed representatives of the Emperor looking for a robber. Plus, we do not recognize extradition to a government which rapes and murders people who disagree with His Lordship."

"Well, they did start to draw their pistols."

"Which gives you even more justification. Relax. These dead men wrote their obituaries when they signed on with the Emperor."

"Take the rest of the night off, Lorcan," ordered Matt Dillon. "We'll let things settle down before you walk your rounds again."

"Thank you both. You are good friends."

Lorcan walked towards Ma Bells House of Entertainment. He'd get a good meal, some passable Irish Whiskey, and some female friendship to take his mind off of three dead bodies in the street. Was he a bad man? Lorcan asked himself. He did not ask for life as a Highwayman in Ireland under the oppressive yoke of the English. Then, he was in Elsewhen, with a tyrannical Emperor. He mentally shrugged. He would let God sort it out on Judgement Day. Here he seemed to have friends and soon family, he hoped. Plus, a chance for a new life on the regular side of the law.

But right now, he needed a nice shot of Irish Whisky.

# THE HIGHWAYMAN
by Alfred Noyes

## PART ONE

The wind was a torrent of darkness among the gusty trees.
The moon was a ghostly galleon tossed upon cloudy seas.
The road was a ribbon of moonlight over the purple moor,
And the highwayman came riding—
  Riding—riding—
The highwayman came riding, up to the old inn-door.

He'd a French cocked-hat on his forehead, a bunch of lace at his chin,
A coat of the claret velvet, and breeches of brown doe-skin.
They fitted with never a wrinkle. His boots were up to the thigh.
And he rode with a jewelled twinkle,
  His pistol butts a-twinkle,
His rapier hilt a-twinkle, under the jewelled sky.

Over the cobbles he clattered and clashed in the dark inn-yard.
He tapped with his whip on the shutters, but all was locked and barred.
He whistled a tune to the window, and who should be waiting there
But the landlord's black-eyed daughter,
  Bess, the landlord's daughter,
Plaiting a dark red love-knot into her long black hair.

And dark in the dark old inn-yard a stable-wicket creaked
Where Tim the ostler listened. His face was white and peaked.
His eyes were hollows of madness, his hair like mouldy hay,
But he loved the landlord's daughter,
  The landlord's red-lipped daughter.
Dumb as a dog he listened, and he heard the robber say—

"One kiss, my bonny sweetheart, I'm after a prize to-night,
But I shall be back with the yellow gold before the morning light;
Yet, if they press me sharply, and harry me through the day,
Then look for me by moonlight,
  Watch for me by moonlight,
I'll come to thee by moonlight, though hell should bar the way."

He rose upright in the stirrups. He scarce could reach her hand,
But she loosened her hair in the casement. His face burnt like a brand
As the black cascade of perfume came tumbling over his breast;
And he kissed its waves in the moonlight,
  (O, sweet black waves in the moonlight!)
Then he tugged at his rein in the moonlight,
and galloped away to the west.

## PART TWO

He did not come in the dawning. He did not come at noon;
And out of the tawny sunset, before the rise of the moon,
When the road was a gypsy's ribbon, looping the purple moor,
A red-coat troop came marching—
  Marching—marching—
King George's men came marching, up to the old inn-door.

They said no word to the landlord. They drank his ale instead.
But they gagged his daughter, and bound her, to the foot of her
narrow bed.
Two of them knelt at her casement, with muskets at their side!
There was death at every window;
  And hell at one dark window;
For Bess could see, through her casement, the road that he would ride.

They had tied her up to attention, with many a sniggering jest.
They had bound a musket beside her, with the muzzle beneath her
breast!
"Now, keep good watch!" and they kissed her.
She heard the doomed man say—
Look for me by moonlight;
  Watch for me by moonlight;
I'll come to thee by moonlight, though hell should bar the way!

She twisted her hands behind her; but all the knots held good!
She writhed her hands till her fingers were wet with sweat or blood!
They stretched and strained in the darkness,
and the hours crawled by like years
Till, now, on the stroke of midnight,
  Cold, on the stroke of midnight,
The tip of one finger touched it! The trigger at least was hers!

The tip of one finger touched it. She strove no more for the rest.
Up, she stood up to attention, with the muzzle beneath her breast.
She would not risk their hearing; she would not strive again;
For the road lay bare in the moonlight;
  Blank and bare in the moonlight;
And the blood of her veins, in the moonlight,
throbbed to her love's refrain.

Tlot-tlot; tlot-tlot! Had they heard it? The horsehoofs ringing clear;
Tlot-tlot; tlot-tlot, in the distance? Were they deaf that they did not
hear?
Down the ribbon of moonlight, over the brow of the hill,
The highwayman came riding—
  Riding—riding—
The red coats looked to their priming! She stood up, straight and still.

Tlot-tlot, in the frosty silence! Tlot-tlot, in the echoing night!
Nearer he came and nearer. Her face was like a light.
Her eyes grew wide for a moment; she drew one last deep breath,
Then her finger moved in the moonlight,
  Her musket shattered the moonlight,
Shattered her breast in the moonlight
and warned him—with her death.

He turned. He spurred to the west; he did not know who stood
Bowed, with her head o'er the musket, drenched with her own blood!
Not till the dawn he heard it, and his face grew grey to hear
How Bess, the landlord's daughter,
  The landlord's black-eyed daughter,
Had watched for her love in the moonlight,
and died in the darkness there.

Back, he spurred like a madman, shrieking a curse to the sky,
With the white road smoking behind him
and his rapier brandished high.
Blood red were his spurs in the golden noon;
wine-red was his velvet coat;
When they shot him down on the highway,
  Down like a dog on the highway,
And he lay in his blood on the highway,
with a bunch of lace at his throat.

· · ·

And still of a winter's night, they say, when the wind is in the trees,
When the moon is a ghostly galleon tossed upon cloudy seas,
When the road is a ribbon of moonlight over the purple moor,
A highwayman comes riding—
  Riding—riding—
A highwayman comes riding, up to the old inn-door.

Over the cobbles he clatters and clangs in the dark inn-yard.
He taps with his whip on the shutters, but all is locked and barred.
He whistles a tune to the window, and who should be waiting there
But the landlord's black-eyed daughter,
  Bess, the landlord's daughter,
        Plaiting a dark red love-knot into her long black hair.

# 8
# FLYING TIGER

Mark Stone walked arm in arm with his Elsewhen wife Susan Von Braun down Main Street of Freetown. He had talked her into a stroll to work off the steak and eggs breakfast on their day off. Raven-haired beauty Susan smiled at her mate and squeezed his arm.

"Now what, my husband? What other activities do you wish on our day off?"

Susan was the primary doctor of Freetown, and Mark was the Mayor, so they rarely had much time off as the town grew like a bad weed. The rare case of a form of democracy and individual rights in the alternate universe of Elsewhen was attracting more and more humans of all nationalities and ethnicities. The original ethnic Chinese majority was no more, now replaced with a combination of other Asians, Americans, Germans, and a smattering of Africans, Russians, and a Comanche.

"Well," answered Mark, "we can do some window shopping. A Chinese merchant with a long train of packhorses arrived yesterday. Plus, our adopted nieces Ivana and Mariana are providing manufacturing capabilities thanks to modifying my Jeep for use as a basis for a factory."

"Well, we are getting a percentage from that industry," added Susan.

"Also, our friends at the C-17 Globemaster are using their skills and equipment to produce gasoline from that pool of crude oil they found," said Mark

"How many people live in Freetown, husband?"

"Well, when we first arrived, there were just about six thousand souls. With people walking and riding here, plus others dropping in like the C-17 aircraft—"

A loud engine noise mixed with crackling drowned out the rest of the conversation. A badly smoking single-engine airplane zoomed overhead as people up and down the street ducked and cried out. Mark saw a rear fuselage that his past aviation interests spoke 'P-40" to him, and then "China" when he saw the well-known winged tiger emblem over a Chinese National Sun. The aircraft continued down Main Street and a hundred yards past the town limits sign. It then bellied into a wastewater pond, a soccer field length to the south.

Younger Susan mounted a borrowed horse as Mark ran to grab his motorbike. Marshal Dillion and his two Deputies galloped down Main Street after Susan as

Mark tried to catch up. The water in the pond helped to suppress the fire as Susan urged her mount close enough to clamber onto the wing. As the two Deputies arrived and joined her, Mark yelled out. "Susan! Get out of there. It's still smoking."

"The younger they all, the more they think they are immortal," called out Matt Dillon.

Mark watched from the edge of the pond as Susan and the two Deputies lifted and dragged a pilot from the stricken craft. Mark helped the Deputies lay the aviator on dry land as Susan began an examination for injuries.

"He has a wound in his leg, but the flames did not reach him," Susan said as she checked his breathing and pulse.

The pilot suddenly choked and jerked up to a sitting position.

"Lazarus, rising from the dead," Mark said. The pilot tried to focus his eyes on the Mayor as Susan kept trying to get him to look at her.

"Americans?" the man asked.

"For the most part. Susan is German."

The pilot looked at Susan, who smiled. "Your leg wound is not too deep. I'll have it stitched and bandaged at the office in no time."

"Nazi?" the pilot managed to add.

"After my time, I understand. So no."

"You have a name, Lieutenant?"

"Edward Leibolt, American Volunteer Group, serial

number—"

"Whoa, hoss. You are not a POW."

"How'd you all get into Burma? Or is this China?" asked the fighter pilot.

"This isn't China, nor Burma. We have some explaining to do."

A half-hour later, Susan was patching Edward Leibolt up on her operating table. The Flying Tiger pilot kept looking from Susan, to Mark, to Marshal Dillon. Finally, he spoke.

"So let me get this straight. Like a story from a science fiction or fantasy magazine, I am not in China, nor Burma anymore. Nor am I on Earth. Right?"

"That's right," answered the Mayor. "Another planet in another dimension. Wait until you see the two moons at night."

"My husband keeps talking about Barsoom," Susan added with a smile.

"But I gotta get back to the Tigers, my unit. Colonel Chennault is going to wonder what the hell happened to me."

Mark paused and looked at Susan. She nodded affirmatively.

"Son, I was a big World War Two plane buff growing up. I read a lot about the Flying Tigers and the P-40. So, what I am going to tell you will come as a bit of a shock. The opium sedative Susan gave you may help."

Edward Leibolt rested comfortably as Susan, Mark, and Matt talked in the outer office.

"Well, he took the fact he will be considered Missing In Action forever pretty well," Mark said.

"If I can be here and not go crazy, a flying machine pilot should also," the Marshal opined.

"He is young and tough. He will make it," said Susan.

"Now, I'll get with Christopher Walken and our nieces. We'll see what we can salvage from that shot up P-40."

"So, it is not his aeroplane?" asked Matt.

"Rules of salvage. Leibolt crashed it, and we saved him. So we get first dibs. Besides, it is actually U.S. Government property."

"It may be Chinese property since Chiang Kai-shek paid them for their services, husband.'

"Well, I don't see him around. So, Freetown gets it for payment of services rendered. The Lieutenant got a good patch up out of the deal and is not dead as he normally would be."

"The local Emperor may disagree," said the Marshal.

A week later, after help from the former USAF crew of the permanently grounded C-17 Globemaster ( thanks to Major Finch and Jake Jackson Spec Ops), bits and pieces of the P-40 sat in a large barn.

"Mayor,"a voice called out.

"Here," Mark said as he wiped the grease off his nose. He had always wanted to get hands-on with an old Warbird.

"Vistors approaching. Emperor's soldiers."

Mark stood a half-mile from the east entrance to Freetown. Several hundred yards away were one hundred mounted soldiers of the Chinese Warlord who claimed to be the Emperor of this part of Elsewhen.

"Well, Matt. I guess they dodged another meeting with Susan Finch and Jake Jackson at the Medevac bird."

"They have to save face by ignoring their defeat in seizing that flying machine. It was so much simpler when all we had were trains and steam engines."

"Yes, Marshal. And a lot more people in your time died in childhood, so it was a trade-off."

A single rider with uniform plumage denoting a junior officer rode to within earshot of the two men. With a flourish, the young man produced a scrolled declaration and began to read from it loudly.

"Marshal, you understand Chinese better than I can."

"It is the typical everything belongs to the Emperor. He demands the crashed flying machine be handed over or suffer the consequences. Typical dictator and warlord talk."

"Then why does he not just sent an army? Why this nickel and dime stuff?"

"Costs money and I think he is afraid to let too many soldiers leave the Capitol Area. I think he is afraid of being overthrown."

The two dozen Militia members dug in some prepositioned fox holes. Mark figured he could count on them getting off at least one good volley. Red and Blue, the two frontiersmen, were out in the hinterland, so they were missing two of their best shots. The Militia was a new attempt at central planning, but most people in Freetown were not big on following someone else's orders.

Mark turned and looked. "Ah, here they come."

Edward Leibolt and Christopher Walken pushed a small cart up the road to Mark and the Marshal. A tarp covered an object on the coach.

"Just in the knick of time, gentlemen."

"Well, Mayor," said the Flying Tiger, "we had to load the belt with some loose shells."

"Well, we just received the ole request from our favorite Emperor. So we may need your toy there."

The Chinese Officer yelled what had to be the equivalent of "Time's Up." He spun his horse around and spurred the mount back to the formation. Mark looked through a spyglass he had scammed and watched the Junior Officer report back to the Commander. Moments later, the Chinese Commander began yelling commands, and the mounted soldiers removed their long guns from their sheaths. In a double line formation, the calvary started to walk towards Freetown positions. Mark turned to Edward and Christopher.

"Bring the thirty caliber up. At my command, shoot their horses."

They threw the tarp back, and the former Browning wing gun from the P-40 Tomahawk swung upon an adjustable mount. As the calvary formation broke into a trot at three hundred yards, the machine gun barked. Horses went down, screaming with pain. The dying mounts trapped riders as other horses panicked and tripped over the fallen. A smattering of shots zipped by the Freetown positions, and Mark signaled the Militia to fire a volley. These took some riders off their saddles, and the horses ran wild. The calvary formation broke by the time it hit one hundred yards. The survivors fled.

Mark went out with the Militia and recovered dropped weapons, plus checked for survivors. As he walked back to the original position, Edward approached him.

"Killing my former allies is- unsettling is the word."

"Well, my Flying Tiger friend, this whole existence is unsettling. I should be home watching television, something you never saw."

"Do you remember me listed as MIA?"

"Yes. The USAF never found your plane. I think you are listed somewhere connected to the Tomb of the

Unknown Soldier. Now you have a chance to finish out your life here."

Leibolt shook his head.

"I guess I'll have to make the best of it. Maybe working with the crew of the C-17, we can make a workable plane. I miss flying."

"Or, one can land in our laps. Come on, and I'll buy you a beer after we clean up this battlefield."

"The Emperor won't stop trying to take what he wants, will he?"

"Yep. I think next time, the Emperor will bite the bullet and send an entire army. He needs to save face after two significant failures."

"You would think in a new world people would try and get along, be better."

"Well, Ed, you can take the nasty monkey out of the ugly jungle, but you can't take the nasty out of the monkey. Come on—a beer awaits us."

# 9
# THERE BE MONSTERS

Mark Stone was getting a haircut and beard trim at Alfie's Barbershop, run by an expatriate of England (specifically of Cockney descent) when young Johan Andersen came bursting into the shop.

"It ate our cow! The monster dragon ate our cow!"

Mark, Mayor of Freetown, sat up in the barber's chair. "You mean it killed and is eating your cow. The standup dragons are not big enough—"

"No! It is huge. It is on all four legs. Like a giant alligator in the schoolbooks."

Mark frowned as he took a towel from Alfie Bass and wiped his face and hands. "Let's get the Marshal and go see, Johan."

Mark Stone and Matt Dillon followed the young lad to the Anderson family farm. In tow were two Town Militia, Red MacBeth, and Blue Baxter. The two former

U.S. frontiersmen were the primary fresh meat suppliers for the town and had seen about every type of creature there was in the world of Elsewhen. Thus they were perfect people to bring along when investigating a so-called "monster."

The four men rode up on horseback to the combination farm and ranch located about two miles west of Freetown. Matt Dillion had the young Johan on the back of his horse as they approached the scene.

"There it is!" yelled the youth. "Look, the monster!"

The horses, getting a whiff of the beast, began to shy and jerk. All four riders dismounted with their weapons and tried to keep the equines from fleeing.

"Well, I'll be danged," said Red. "That thar thing matches those tracks we saw last year."

"You know what this is?" asked Mark.

"No, Sir. We just saw the tracks."

The owner of the tracks was a gigantic cross between a Komodo Dragon and an oversized Iguana. Mark saw this beast lying stretched out, apparently sleeping off the meal of the cow.

"I don't know if my fifty caliber breach loader rifle can kill that thing," said Mark.

"Our rifles will take down a Buff," said Blue. "But that beast is a lot bigger than any buffalo I have seen."

"What do we do, Mayor?" asked Marshal Dillon.

"Blue, can you high tail it to the Globemaster

people? Ask them if we can borrow their Humvee with the Ma Duece on top."

"What do we do, Mark?" asked Matt Dillon.

"We move over to Johan's house—and wait."

An hour later, the responding men and Johan's family heard the approach of the Humvee.

"Well, I guess Blue jawed enough, so they brought their machine," opined Red.

Mark walked out and met Jake Jackson and Marco Franzetti, the two special forces troops from the C-17 group. Blue crawled down from the top hatch position near the mounted Ma Duece fifty caliber machine gun.

"Man, this contraption can move! That was fun."

"Thanks for coming, Jake," said the Mayor, Customs, and Immigration Official for Freetown as he shook hands.

Jake Jackson used a high-end sniper spotting scope to survey the beast. "That damned thing must be at least thirty feet long and massive," the Special Ops supervisor said as he set aside the spotting scope.

"Think we can convince you guys to use a couple of your limited in number fifty caliber rounds to take that think out? We have a limited amount of cows and meat beeves around."

Jake looked at Marco Franzetti. The other man shrugged. "Why not, Boss? We can make lizard boots from the skin."

Marco manned the Ma Duece as the others watched. Ingamar, Johan's father, stood by with his son.

"Mister Mayor, may we have some of the flesh and skin also? A cow is not cheap."

"We'll divide it up. Hell, we can have a 'Gator Day feed if it tastes like an alligator."

Two minutes later, just as the carnivorous lizard noticed the humans and roused itself to action, two loud reports sounded as the Ma Duece did its thing. Franzetti's aim was true as both armor-piercing rounds hit just behind the creature's ear hole. The beast lurched up, twisted and snapped, then died. The group of humanity watched it a good five minutes before they approached.

"Saw a rattler once bite a man after it were cut in half," Blue said as the men approached the elongated body.

"Which is why we are taking this slow, gentlemen," said the Mayor.

After ensuring the monster lizard was dead, Ingemar produced some axes and butchering blades for the task of cutting up the beast. Jake and Marco drove back to the grounded C-17 and returned with a chain saw.

"Where did you get that from?" asked Mark.

"The Crew Chief," said Jake. "She carried it in case they needed to chop some trees down to take off again from the boonies."

"Woman after my own heart."

"Well, if you expect a second wife," interjected

Franzetti, "you'll have to arm wrestle a big black Marine Gunny Sergeant."

"That way now, yeah?"

"It's been a month since we were drug from Earth to Barsoom," said Jake. "It is starting to sink in the chances of finding a hole in time and space to get home is extremely remote."

"Yeah," interjected Marco. "Major Finch is starting to put the moves on the Boss here."

"God, man, you are such a gossip, Franzetti."

"Hey, Boss, what other fun do I have? There is no strip club."

"I take it that you gentlemen have not partaken of our fine bordello establishments in Freetown."

"Not yet," answered Jake. "People are trying to see if they can get coupled up on the C-17. There are many single females, but I do not think they want to share a man with a whore. 21st Century morals, and all that stuff."

"Huh. Well, Jake, live here over six months like me, and the various Earth ideas begin to fade."

Red and Blue were expert butchers and came to love the chain saw. Mark Stone said they were working on refining some gasoline from some petroleum pools located south of town.

"We'll pay you back for the gas," stated the Mayor.

"Hey, mi casa is su casa, Mayor," replied Jake. "We Earthlings are definitely in this together."

Just then, Franzetti shouted a warning from his Ma Deuce perch. "We have company!"

The men looked to where he pointed. On a slight rise, a half-mile away was a horserider. The horse itself looked much larger than the Chinese mounts, and as Jake looked through the spotting scope, he whistled."

"That rider looks like a woman in a rather ornate set of metal, leather, and lace armor. With a big honking sword."

"Any guns?" asked Mark.

"Looks like a large scabbard with some type of big game gun."

"Amazon," said Ingamar Anderson.

"Come again?" asked the Mayor.

"Amazons. Female warriors. Chinese merchants in years past mentioned them."

"That's right, Ingemar. You've been here near to ten years."

"We heared of them also," stated Red. "They live way out west, is the story."

"Maybe they hunt these big bastard lizards," said Mark.

"If they do, that rifle of hers must be a giant killer," replied Jake.

The mounted warrior watched for another minute, then turned and galloped down the far side of the rise and out of sight.

"Think she'll be back?" asked Jake.

"I don't know. However, as Mayor, I would not be surprised."

Two days later, Freetown had the first 'Gator Feed.' Mark Stone was always trying to create unifying activities for the varied population of Freetown. With the Chinese Emperor temporarily put off after his failed attempt to obtain the C-17, Mark needed to remind the Chinese, European, Asian, American, and Heinz 57 members of Earth humanity that they were all in it together.

Matt Dillon sauntered up to him as everyone enjoyed the various cuisine and versions of prepared lizard meat. "We have a guest," said the lawman.

"Who? Not some Emperor toady, I hope."

"She is moving in slow, from the West."

Mark turned to his local spouse, Susan Von Braun.

"I need to check out this visitor, my dear."

"Then I will also come, my Mayor," stated the dark-haired beauty. "For I speak several languages—"

"Yeah, yeah. I know. Come on, then, you stubborn German you."

Susan laughed and linked arms with him.

The three walked down Mainstreet and soon saw the subject of Marshal Dillon's consternation. Walking a great stead of old Earth Medieval times was the Amazon. She had removed her conical helmet to reveal flashing blonde hair, done in intricate braids. A long-bladed sword in scabbard was across the young woman's back. The Amazon was a good six feet in height, with curves and bumps in all the right places that even her armor could not conceal.

"Man, she would be the fantasy hero of many a comic book back on Earth," said Mark Stone.

"Well, my husband, whatever you are saying, she is quite—stunning."

The woman met the three in the middle of the street. She showed an empty right hand in greeting and said something like, "Guten tag."

Susan replied in Hoch Deutsch, then some Sud Deutsch. After about five minutes of stunted communication, Susan turned to Mark and whispered. "She speaks an archaic form of German, or maybe Frankish Gaul if there is such a form. She came here to see who killed her Dragon. That word came through."

"Well, we'll have to find Franzetti—"

"Englander? American?" The Amazon suddenly interrupted as Mark spoke aloud.

"Yes, American," replied Mark Stone. "You speak American?"

"Little," the statuesque woman replied. "You people—they come—year past."

The warrior woman held up a hand to pause the conversation and then dug around a small pocket in her armor. After a minute of searching, she pulled out a blue piece of cloth. Sewn-on it was 'USAF.'

"Well, I'll be goddamned." Mark smiled and took the pocket emblem in his hand and laughed. The Amazon grinned and smacked his chest with the back of her hand.

"You just made a friend, I think," said Matt Dillon.

"American?" the woman asked the Marshal.

"Yep. But Texan primarily."

The Amazon cocked her head a bit and said, "Texas."

"Yes, Ma'am."

With a broad grin, she repeated the backhand blow.

"Mark," the Mayor said in his best imitation of a "Me Tarzan" moment.

"Chabra," the Amazon replied and struck her chest with the palm of her hand.

"Susan," Mark said as he pointed towards his spouse. "You—eat? Drink with us?"

It was quickly like an old home week. Chabra walked down Mainstreet as if she were part of a parade. Mark could tell her eyes were taking everything in, but she had a friendly smile on her face. When a young Asian girl ran up to the warhorse of days old, Chabra laughed and hoisted the young child up onto the saddle. Mark Stone could tell Chabra had that killing edge of a professional soldier, yet was well socialized. Thus, no psychopathic warrior cult as far as Mark could see. He would keep an eye on the new arrival.

Jake and Marco Franzetti walked up to the small

group with mugs of beer in both hands. Jake pushed one towards Chabra.

"Hello there, my Amazonian friend. Drink with us?"

Chabra laughed, grabbed the proffered drink, and chugged it down. She then struck Jake with the back of her hand.

"American!"

"You got it," said Franzetti. He handed his extra beer to Chabra, and she laughed.

The warrior swept her hand to include Matt, Mark, Jake, and Marcos. "Who—kill Dragon?"

"I did," Marcos replied as he held up a silver chain on his neck. Attached to it were a colossal fang and a fifty-caliber shell casing. Chabra's eyes widened a bit when she saw the shell, then whistled in appreciation. In a flash, she pulled a long straight rifle round and gave it to Franzetti.

"That looks like a Sharps 50-110 at least," said Mark Stone.

"You know your shells," interjected Matt Dillon.

"Nice," said Franzetti.

Chabra laughed and smacked the man in the chest.

"Klingon mating ritual," said Jake as Susan gave him a quizzical look.

Chabra was soon a center of attention. Major Susan Finch introduced herself, and when "United States Air Force" was mentioned, Chabra again laughed and gave the officer the "Friend' cuff to the chest. As the day progressed, the story unfolded.

Just over a year prior, 'USAF' showed up at the Amazon's queendom. Chabra stated the Amazons had lived in the West Mountains for centuries. Iron Mountain was theirs. They used raw materials to make iron and steel weapons. Sometime in the vague past, they began making massive firearms to hunt the Dragons. The oversized monitor lizards lived in the southern end of the West Mountains and also moved out to the High Plains and a small desert to the south. Young Amazons like Chabra (she was twenty-one a month ago) hunted the Dragons as rites of passage and kept them from decimating livestock and local fauna.

Chabra had come this far to the East not only to track this specific Dragon but also to work off some youthful exuberance. When 'USAF' appeared, they brought some new weapons and a new male gene pool. Plus, five military women, one who was a nurse. Chabra was a bit too involved with the newcomers. The Elders sent her out to work off her rampaging hormones and track and kill the Dragon. This specific beast had killed a young Amazon tending a herd of cattle. Revenge was the word of the day.

It had taken Chabra three months to track the Dragon here, a first for one to be this far East. Then, the citizens of Freetown had done her job. Chabra pondered the matter for a day, as strangers were always dangerous.

Then she saw the party from afar and decided now was the time to make contact.

As the Two Moons chased each other across the heavens, the celebration finally broke up. Chabra and Franzetti disappeared to parts unknown.

"Hope she doesn't hurt him," said Jake. "I'll need him if the Emperor's goons show up."

That night in bed, Mark explained to Susan the situation. "That tag is old school, before the USAF went all subdued, camouflage."

"So that means, Mark, that once again, there is no rhyme nor reason as to who comes to Elsewhen."

"Nope. Time here is not linear. We get people from all times and eras. However, I may need to take a trip to Chabra's home."

"Why?"

"Americans. 20th Century types. With plenty of iron. They can help us make Freetown into a Free State. Screw the Emperor and his thugs."

Franzetti limped back to the C-17 the next day. As Jake and the others laughed, the man said, "Never sleep with a She-Bear."

"Where'd she go?" asked Jake.

"Home. We swapped shells, and I gave her the fang to prove the beast was dead, and she did her duty."

"So why didn't you go with hey, loverboy?"

"Are you kidding me? I'd be in a male harem or

stud farm. That is how they do things. Women pick the men."

"Think of all that sex you'd have with all those zaftig ladies."

Marcos groaned, gestured obscenely, and hobbled away.

# 10
# TANKERS

Where in Holy Hell are we?"

Sergeant First Class Mike Virgil yelled from the commander's hatch of the M-48 Patton tank as he tried to find a familiar landmark or terrain. An E-7 Sergeant as a tank commander of a single AFV was a bit rank heavy, but this was not a standard tank mission. He and his three-person crew were in Israel this spring day in 1968 as part of a classified exchange program. The U.S. Army wanted to pick the Israeli tankers' brains after the lightning war of 1967. However, with Viet Nam in full swing, someone up the Chain Of Command in the U.S. Army Armor Command wanted to keep the mission on the down-low. Thus, one handpicked crew with a brand new M-48C diesel-engined main battle tank arrived in the Land of David.

"This is not on our map grids, Senior Sergeant," stated his Gunner, Staff Sergeant William Jefferson. Again, an E-6 tank gunner was rank overkill. However, the Staff Sergeant had combat experience from Viet Nam, which Mike did not. Bill was a Black American, a Negro with a Purple Heart in a time of some racial discord. Those facts, plus an upcoming election, were probably factors considered by some ranking officers.

"Shut her down, Jack," Mike called over the tank intercom system to his driver, Corporal Jack Rhodes. Jack was an experienced tank driver who had been en route to Viet Nam when some 'Rabbi' grabbed him and sent him to this non-combat assignment. Mike would have to question Jack more as to who he knew up the chain.

The low man on the totem pole, the loader Avram Adan, did have an actual 'Rabbi' in the Israeli armed forces. According to a note, Mike Virgil found in the operations file that the Private First Class was related to some high-ranking Israeli officers. Mike soon found out Avram seemed to have a relative of some kind in every town where the Americans traveled. Not for the first time did Mike wonder why the young man with the flashing smile chose to work his way up the chain of command in the U.S. Army. 'Israeli Spook' came to mind when the tank commander thought on the subject. No matter, as Avram's ability with the local languages plus his Hollywood good looks opened doors, his connections did not.

"Dismount guys, but keep your eyes open," commanded Mike. All four men were soon standing in front of the M-48, each scanning a different compass quadrant.

"This not the part of Israel we were in a little while ago, Sergeant Virgil," said Avram. "This not the Negev Desert out from Beersheba. This area is more a grassy plain, dry but not a desert."

"So the fire and maneuver range—it isn't here."

"No, Sergeant. Neither is that jeep we were following."

Mike was so fixated on figuring out where they were; he forgot about the Israeli jeep guiding them to the range area.

"Damn. Toto, we are no longer in Kansas. Troops, a complete accounting of all of our resources. Water, food, fuel, weapons, and ammunition. Now. I'll try to raise someone on the radio for a few minutes. Got it?"

"Roger that, Sergeant Virgil," all three men responded. They may be a thrown-together crew due to the unique mission, but they were still professional Tankers. Mike climbed up into the commander's cupola and tried to raise someone on the radio. All Mike obtained was various forms of static. He eventually stopped to save the M-48's batteries.

A half-hour later, he climbed down from the turret as his three crewmen compared notes from their ammunition and supply check.

"So, guys, what do we have to work with, seeing as I can't raise anyone."

"We have twenty U.S. supplied training rounds for the main gun plus five Willie Pete smoke rounds," said William. "The Israelis gave us three old AP rounds, plus two new HE rounds they wanted us to test,"

"So we have thirty 90MM main gun rounds. Even the training rounds can put a hurt on infantry." Mike looked at Cpl. Rhodes. "What do you have for me?"

"Thaks to Avram here, we have a scrounged Uzi and a fifty-round box of nine-millimeter. The Ma Deuce has fifty-round boxes of fifty caliber rounds and the thirty-round belt of tracer ammunition for the coax machine gun. Other than that, we each have the six-round magazine in our pistols that Mother Army allowed us."

Mike shook his head in disbelief. "They and the Israelis were so afraid we'd somehow shoot up the place or lose ammunition or something. Here." Mike tossed a box of ammunition to Jack.

"A fifty bullet box of .45. I know I'm usually by the book, but this sucks. Load thirty-round magazine for the M-3A1 Grease Gun, then divide the rest among you three."

"Fuel wise, Jack? What do we have?"

"Enough to get us around two hundred miles if the going is a bit rough."

Mike looked at PFC Avram Adan. "You checked the food and water?"

"Yes, Sergeant. We have a case of C-rats, our canteens, two water skins, a six-pack of Israeli Coca Cola, and—well, a case of beer."

Mike snorted, then spoke. "Leave it to the scrounger to come up with some contraband on a tank. Well, at least we have supplied to get us by until we find a piece of civilization or some body of water."

"We're not in Israel anymore, are we?" asked Avram.

"I don't think so. I am still trying to wrap my brain around—"

"Engine. I hear an engine," said the Staff Sergeant.

"Shit—battle stations, people."

*That's all I need,* thought the Sergeant First Class as he clambered up the M-48. Caught flat-footed by a bunch of Ayrabs.

Mike quickly had his binoculars out and scanned the horizon as the other three took up the driver's, loader, and gunner positions.

"Load with a training round," commanded Mike.

"Loading with training," William called back."

"Get ready to crank her up, Jack."

"Yes, Sergeant."

"Plan is to fire a training shell as a warning, then load with the Willie Pete in case we have to bug out. We lack the right ammunition to make a battle of it."

In one minute, everyone was in their assigned crew position. Mike used his high-powered binoculars to look at the dust cloud of the approaching vehicle.

"That does not look like one of ours," said the

Sergeant First Class.

"Maybe an Israeli border patrol vehicle," said Avram. "They have developed some odd-looking desert transport vehicles."

"Through my main gun sights, it looks like it has U. S. markings," stated William.

"Adjust the Ninety for a shot, Gunner. See if the people in that vehicle notice."

William Jefferson used his main gun controls to depress the tank cannon and line it up on the moving target. As he tracked the stranger, the occupants must have noticed the targeting as the vehicle abruptly braked to a stop just over a football field away. A figure in some unfamiliar fatigues stepped out of the transport's passenger side and waved a white cloth.

"I think they want to talk," said the Gunner.

"Okay," replied the tank commander. "You three cover me while I walk out and talk to them. That looks like U.S. military markings on the jeep-type vehicle."

"You think that is wise, Sergeant?" asked driver Jack.

"We have to find out where we are and what happened. Plus, that is what I get paid for in this here Army. Load up the Grease Gun while I'm gone."

"You be careful, boss," said Avram.

"Always, Private."

Mike climbed from the commander's cupola and dismounted the M-48. He had his Colt .45 locked and cocked with a round in the chamber as he walked towards Mike, the unfamiliar vehicle. Two figures in sand-colored uniforms came towards Mike. He saw the smaller person had a Red Cross emblem on the left sleeve as the strangers walked nearer. Mike next clearly saw the smaller person was female.

"Senior Sergeant Mike Virgil, United States Army. I am the commander of that tank."

"Lieutenant Luli Gong, U.S. Army Nurse, assigned to the local Medivac Unit. Next to me is Mister Robert Masters, local special operations. "

"Ma'am." Mike saluted the Lieutenant as he identified the officer's silver bar on the unique desert camouflage.

"How'd you get to Afghanistan?" asked the muscular and bearded man, the officer called a special operator.

"Afghanistan? This is Israel."

The three military personnel all stood and stared at each other for a few moments. Mike broke the stunned silence. "I said before—this is not Kansas."

"And I am not Dorothy," said Luli Gong. "I have this weird feeling I stepped into a new episode of the Twilight Zone."

"Your vehicle is not familiar to me, Lieutenant."

"It's called a HUMVEE, short for High Mobility Multi-Purpose Wheeled Vehicle," interjected Masters. "This one is an expanded capacity vehicle for medical teams. Standard issue from the late 1980s on.”

"1980? This is 1968," said Mike.

"Why do I get the feeling I just stepped into a bad science fiction movie?" asked Luli Gong.

The three quickly compared notes. The most important task at hand was Robert Masters had a very wounded comrade that the Lieutenant was trying to get to a MEDIVAC. Special Operator Jesus Garcia needed someone to take some lead and steel out of his body soon if he were to survive. Marine Corps Corporal Susan Running Deer, the Humvee driver, kept an eye on the wounded man as the three tried to figure out the next move.

"I'm no Doctor, but I need to try at least to repair some of Garcia's damage," said the Army nurse.

"Bring him down to the tank. We have some medical supplies and can set up some shade for him."

"Thank you, Sergeant. We can also put our heads together as to how we all got here. Wherever 'here' is."

Five minutes later and the two groups made introductions as they tried to make wounded Jesus comfortable.

"I have a few morphine syrettes locked up, Lt. Gong."

"Thanks. Sergeant Virgil. But what I need now is someone with some knowledge of surgical procedures."

Just then, Jack Rhodes stepped up. "Ma'am, my dad was a veterinarian. He had me help him as he wanted me to be a Vet also. I helped in many a surgery on some poor dog hit by a car. I mean, they weren't human, but I learned how to stop bleeding, cut into bodies, and clamp veins, arteries."

Mike looked at Jack. "What in Hell are you doing driving a tank?"

The thin, toe-headed young man shrugged. "I thought it would be fun."

"Well, young man, you and I are at this moment, doctors," said the nurse. "Help me get Jesus set up in the back of the Humvee. Wash up with this alcohol. We need to get this goat rope done, or we may lose him."

"Here." Robert Masters handed Luli a small tied-off condom. "The remains of a heroin eight-ball."

"What are you doing with that, Masters?" asked Mike.

"In Afghanistan, it doubles as money. Now, it may help with some pain control."

"We had tons of shit in Viet Nam," interjected William.

"You saw action?" asked Robert.

"Yeah. Two weeks as the only Black tank commander and then ambushed with two rocket grenades during convoy duty. Wounded me, severed a fuel line, and the tank went up in flames. I was sent home."

"How'd you wind up—here?"

"They wanted to discharge me on a medical. I said

upper command just wanted to get rid of the only nigga tank commander around. They let me stay in, with the racial problems going on, then sent me here."

"He's the only one with combat experience in the tank, Mr. Masters. I was a staff wienie who, for some reason, they would not let me go for a combat position."

"You type and write well, right?"

"Yep,"

Robert laughed and then replied, "It never changes. Office skills mean more than combat skills to some generals."

"I've been trying since I joined just after the Korean War. So they send me here instead, and I fell into a rabbit hole."

"Okay, I need some extra light over here, guys," the Lieutenant called out.

"Got it, Ma'am."

The operation went surprisingly well. Running Deer and Avram stood a watch on top of the M-48 as the rest did what they could to help. Jesus was soon resting comfortably with a bit of help from the heroin so they could save the morphine syrettes and ampoules.

"Thanks, Doctors," said Robert Masters. Luli and Jack both laughed at the honorary medical licensing. Mike walked up to the small black-haired Susan Running Deer. She had not spoken a word since driving the Humvee to the tank.

"Hey, Corporal, may I ask how much ammunition you have for your M-16?"

"It's an M-4, Sergeant. I have six-thirty round magazines. I have an M-17 pistol under my body armor."

"Well, I may have to ask for your help. My commanders and the Israelis limited our ammunition and weapons on this goat rope."

The Native American fixed him with an intensive gaze. Mike felt like she was looking into his soul. Finally, she spoke.

"So we are not in the dreamworld some of the Elders talked about?"

"I don't think so. I poked myself with my knife, and it hurt, so I am not dreaming."

"I'm part Kiowa and Comanche, Gunnery Sergeant. We don't give up easily. I won't stop trying to get back home."

Mike realized being an E-7, he was equivalent to a Gunnery Sergeant, so he did not correct Susan. He also realized this small and quiet Marine was probably tougher than just about everyone there, except for Masters. That special operative had that edge only specific people had. Mike stuck his hand out to shake.

"Thanks, Corporal. I need all the John Waynes I can get."

"Begging your pardon, but he died years ago. And he was just an actor. I'd ask for Crazy Horse or Quannah Parker."

Mike discussed the situation with Robert Masters as he seemed to have a wealth of combat experience. Until they figured out where they were, everything was dangerous.

"So, Sergeant, you have primarily training ammunition in the tank."

"For the main gun, yes. I mean, the unrefined iron core of the training rounds would screw up a civilian car, shatter into shrapnel if it hits a hard enough object. So, the twenty rounds are worth something."

"And you have about two hundred rounds of fifty caliber and below with which to shoot at people, places, and things."

"You got it. What do you have?"

Robert laughed. "We bugged out fast, so I have a thirty caliber sniping rifle with three rounds, an M-17 with one round of nine-millimeter ammunition, and a captured Chicom 57 MM recoilless rifle I was bringing back for Intelligence. Jesus had a SAW, Squad Automatic Weapon with him when we jumped in the Humvee. I think he had a few rounds with it."

"So, if we find out we are in a hostile place, we are limited as to what we can do. "

"Unfortunately, Sergeant, that may be the problem."

Mike paused for a few moments. His training involved ceratin military parameters, even in unconventional warfare, but not even knowing where you were, who was a friend, who was enemy? Mike was not trained in those types of situations.

"Any suggestions, Mister Masters?"

"Call me Robert or Rob. You and the Lieutenant are the military people. I'm just a special operations guy."

"However, you have a helluva lot more military combat experience than I and the others."

"Sergeant, Mike, I started in the Marines, did a stint with DELTA FORCE. Then connected with some private contractors who various government agencies employ. I go where they send me but have no desire to order people around."

"So, the Lieutenant and I get to make the decisions for our troops."

"Yep. I'll offer advice and make sure Jesus stays in one piece. You two get to decide where and how we go." The Spec Ops man paused, then continued, "When the shooting starts, if it does, your training takes over. Just remember your training and then apply it as it fits."

"Thanks for the advice, Rob. Call me Mike. If we don't find a way home soon, I think rank won't mean much."

Mike and Luli decided it was best to bivouac at where the tank sat for the night. They set up a campsite, and Luli sedated Jesus for a comfortable night's rest. Avram dug out some C-rations, at which Robert

Masters grinned.

"I heard about C-Rations, but MREs, Meals Ready to Eat replaced them. We have a couple in the Humvee."

William Jefferson had a sly grin on his face as he tossed a can at Robert. "Here. I barely opened it. Chopped ham and Eggs."

"Don't abuse the inexperienced ones, Sergeant," warned Mike. "Find him something else."

"Let me try it, Mike. I have some hot sauce with me."

"Your funeral."

The Spec Ops guy was soon chowing down. The four tankers were astounded when Masters said he liked Chopped Ham and Eggs in a can.

"Hey, I've eaten a lot worse."

"Special Operations Group people eat snakes and scorpions, I hear," said Avram.

"If you are talking Viet Nam, I will have to say they trained to eat a lot of stuff, but I was never there."

"The large elephant in the room, Rob," said Mike. "About what years are we talking? Since we are in the Twilight Zone."

"I came from 2021."

"What happened with Viet Nam?" asked William.

"Paris Peace Accords, we left. President Nixon was impeached, so after the U.S. went, Congress stood by while the Communists invaded. If we make it back to our times, stay out of Viet Nam, It was just one big goatfuck."

Williams spits into the campfire. "Assholes."

Luli walked up to the group and sat on a log—someone had moved up to the camp.

"Jesus is sleeping comfortably."

"Thanks, Doc," said Robert.

Luli laughed. "My husband is in medical school—" then stopped. "Gentlemen, I have to ask. Are we going to find a way home? I just looked up in the night sky and saw two moons."

The rest of the group looked up at the darkening sky and watched a larger moon chased across the sky by a smaller one.

"Ah, *fuck*," said Mike. He had a wife and three children at home.

"Glad I'm divorced," said William.

"Twice divorced, with three kids," added Robert. "My exes are going to have a hell of a time collecting child support if I am listed MIA by the contractor."

"Every science fiction story I ever read had a way back," said Jack. "We just have to find it."

"I hope you are right, my fellow Doctor. Until then, I guess I'll make a bed near the patient." Luli rose then asked, "Is Jesus married?"

"Yes. With six kids. He wanted to spend more time with them as that stupid Virus from China winds down."

"When he wakes up, I guess I'll have to tell him about the two moons."

"I'll tell, Ma'am. We've been together a while."

Mike set up a watch schedule. Robert demanded he is included. "I'm not military, but I'm a shooter."

"You know how to use the Uzi Avram scrounged?"

"Yep. I'll train the rest."

"Load your pistol with some of the leftover bullets from the loaded magazine. We are definitely in this together."

"Roger that."

Mike twisted and turned, barely dozed off when it was his turn for the sentry. He thanked his stars that the C-Rations had coffee packets in them. He took the last shift in the morning to make sure everyone woke on time. An early morning decision about the direction of travel loomed. The group had to move and figure where they were.

Mike heard the whinnying of a horse and stood upon the tank. The sun of the planet was peeking over the horizon and framed a series of approaching figures. Mike observed a single file caravan of small horses and carts, with a couple of ox-like creatures pulling one transport. He tossed a rock down on William and woke him. The gunner clambered up on the tank, and Mike pointed to the animals and human shapes approaching.

"Load the main gun with a training round. I'll wake the others."

"Gotcha, boss."

The group was up and taking defensive positions

within a minute. Luli looked through Mike's binoculars at the caravan. "By damn, they look Asian. Maybe Chinese like me."

"Do you speak Chinese?" asked Mike.

"Yes, Cantonese and Mandarin. My parents made me learn."

"Care to go with me to meet them? They may tell us where we are."

"Of course."

Mike and Luli jumped down from the M-48.

"I'll cover you with my scope," said Robert. "Three bullets should help if you need to beat feet back here."

"William has the main gun ready also."

"Might want to put the drivers in their vehicles, In case we have to take off quick."

"Good idea, Rob."

The caravan came to a halt some hundred meters from the tank once they realized it was not just a significant rock formation. Mike and Luli slowly walked out to meet the arguing Chinese men and women.

"That older man is the father and boss," said Luli. "He is talking about someone following them and the misfortune of \meeting barbarians on the road."

The Lieutenant called out a greeting in Mandarin, and the stunned man sat silently on his mount for several moments. Then he called back, looking at Mike. "Of course, this man is a traditional Chinese who want to talk to the man in charge."

"What do you want to do?"

"You can be the boss. This matter is about survival, not gender politics."

Mike had Luli asking about where they were. Was there a town nearby or a water source? Luli frowned.

"He says he can see we are barbarians from outside—the word he uses for here translates as Elsewhen. I get the impression people like us dropping in happens all the time."

"So, does he have information on water and civilization?"

"He points what seems to be West unless the sun here does not arise in the East. There is a town or settlement in that direction, but he is vague."

"Who is following them?"

"He says Soldiers of the Emperor. It sounds like soldiers head in the same direction as this family, and he is trying to stay away from them."

"Okay. Does the man have water for sale?"

A curt reply told Mike the man did not want to trade. Next, the father/boss was yelling at his eight-person family unit to hurry up. Mike counted three carts, ten horses, two oxen, and a goat. The family members glanced nervously at the tank as they made their way West. When the merchant traders were a couple of hundred yards past, Mike and Luli returned to the campsite.

"They say there is a town or something to the West," explained Mike to the others. "They won't give us any details. But soldiers of some Emperor are following them and are not nice, it seems."

"I suggest we let them get an hour ahead, so we know they are going on the correct path and not trying to throw us off," stated Robert.

"Sounds good. Shall we break camp? Is Jesus awake?"

"Yes. I already told Jesus the situation. He'll deal with it."

"Okay. Shall we move along? Emperors make me nervous."

An hour later, just as the group was about to drive off, a horn sounded. Mike stood up in the turret and looked towards the sound of the trumpet. He cursed as he saw horse riders with pendants approaching along the path used by the caravan.

"Shit. They were closer than we thought."

Mike nudged his gunner with his foot and then spoke on the intercom system. "Calvary. And they do not look friendly."

"The main gun loaded with a training shell, boss."

"Okay. Acquire the target, William. A training shell among their ranks should dissuade—"

Something significant and fast spranged off the turret moments after a loud report. Mike automatically ducked, then he looked through the tank commander's periscope. He cursed as he saw a wheeled field cannon.

"Assholes have gunpowder! Gunner, Shell, gun."

"Identified, boss."

"Fire."

"On the way."

The shell struck the gun's carriage, smashing it as the gun crew was amidst the reloading sequence. The shot tore the man swabbing the gun barrel into pieces before it struck the weapon and broke it apart.

"Target, ceasefire. Great shot, William. Reload with like round."

"Roger that."

Mike called over the radio to the Humvee. "Take off. The Emperor is not friendly."

"Copy that," replied Susan Running Deer. "Moving."

The Humvee took off like a raped ape as a squadron of cavalry appeared on the vehicles' right flank. Mike stuck his head out of the commander's cupola and watched Robert Masters use Jesus's SAW to fire two short bursts at the mounted soldiers. Two horses and riders went down, with the third sprawling over one of the downed mounts.

"Gunner mounted enemy."

"Identified."

"Fire."

"On the way."

Mike watched the training round zip through the attacking squad of horsemen. The solid piece of metal pierced three horses, taking the rider's legs off as they ripped the equines.

"Driver. Move."

Jack Rhodes accelerated the beast of metal known as an M-48 to twenty miles an hour.

"Coaxial machinegun?" William asked over the intercom.

"No, load, Smoke, WP."

"Up." Loader Avram called out.

"Identified," Williams stated. An M-48's gun was not really stabilized to fire on the move, but Mike had an area target.

"Fire."

"On the way, boss."

The white phosphorus shell struck one horse and rider straight on and exploded. Pieces of burning hell landed on other mounts and the riders. The tank crew could hear the screaming of men and beasts as the M-48 rumbled by the now shattered cavalry formation. Mike stuck his head up and looked behind the tank. A column of some two dozen cavalry was galloping to catch up with the M-48. Mike pulled his pistol from its holster and stuck it out of his hatch. He popped off three quick unaimed rounds with the .45 and was rewarded with a horse and rider on the ground. A bullet ricocheted off the turret.

"Trouble, Sergeant?" Avram called out.

"Gunner, target behind." Mike let William transverse the turret.

"Training round, troops."

"Identified," replied William.

"Up." Avram let them know the round was in the gun chamber.

A cavalryman faster and gutsier than the rest caught up with the M-48 and managed to leap from his horse and grab onto the now rearward-facing main gun barrel. As he swung himself up onto the tank, William called out, "On the way."

The muzzle blast atomized the cavalryman as the solid shell flew towards the rest of the mounted formation. The muzzle blast knocked down two mounts and riders as the shell continued on its path of destruction, decapitating two additional soldiers. The still-solid shot whizzed onward, removing a pendant from the end of a flagpole on a royal coach. As the round lost its momentum, it dipped down to strike the Rear End Charlie of the baggage and supply train. The cart driver died, and a smoldering fire began thanks to the small tracer on the shell base.

The remaining cavalry reined in their mounts as they stared at this metal beast that shrugged off bullets and fired cannon shells. Mike called on the radio to the Humvee.

"Status?"

"A couple of miles ahead, Gunny," replied Susan.

"Slow up a bit so we can catch up. I think those Chinese are reconsidering their pursuit of us."

Susan slowed the Humvee down to ten miles an hour as the M-48 caught up. They continued on at that speed until they crested a small hill.

"We have a pond up ahead and our not-so-friendly Chinese merchants," radioed Robert Masters.

"Good. We'll stop and take on as much water as we can. Plus, we can tell the father about the pissed-off Chinese troops."

The father and boss of the merchant family was not happy to see them again. Not only did they bring him bad news about the Emperor's soldiers, but they interrupted a salvage operation.

"That is a Huey Slick helicopter sitting in the large pond," said Sergeant Jefferson.

"I saw my share in Viet Nam."

"Another war machine drug somehow to this weird place?" said Mike.

"That senior merchant called it Elsewhen," replied Luli.

"Hmmm, Isn't that still U.S. Government Property?" asked Robert.

"You know, my special operation friend, I believe you have a point," said Mike.

"Lieutenant, can we borrow your language ability again?"

The merchant, with the name of Xin Dong, was none too happy with the news. His three sons suddenly produced revolvers as the merchant screamed at Luli and Mike. A three-round burst from Running Deer's M-4 changed the conversation's tone, one of the sons falling to the ground with a bullet in his foot.

"Hey. Assholes!" the Marine called out. "I have had just about enough of this shitty place. Now, do you want me to show you what a pissed-off female Kiowa-Comanche warrior can do? "

The merchant and his sons did not need Luli's translation to get the gist of the message in Marine-speak. Mike and Robert made them drop the pistols in the dirt and step back.

"Colt Navy clones. Whadda knows," said the special operator.

"So we are in a place where people from all times and places can visit," said Jack Rhodes. "This is a science fiction story."

"Come on; We'll hook a tow chain to that Huey and drag it out with the tank," replied Mike.

An hour later, the remains of the crashed helicopter were sitting on the edge of the pond. In addition to a couple of massive catfish who had made the Huey their home, they also contended with the remains of South Vietnamese military bodies. They also recovered the body of an American pilot.

"There should have been two American pilots," said William. "They were transporting some Viet Namese Militia. Look at the old surplus World War Two weapons."

Based on the bodies (fed on catfish) and the weapons' conditions, the Huey had been there for two to four weeks. Again, whatever was yanking people and things to Elsewhen, they had no rhyme or reason. Xin Dong stood by glowering until Mike gave him two wet and slimy M-1 Garands to play with and get functioning.

"Box of thirty calibers for our coaxial gun," said William. "I just have to clean and oil it."

"The Huey's door gunner M-60 is still here," said Mike."Why they took so long to put M-60s in our tanks, I'll never know."

"What to do with the remains?" asked Luli.

"Cremation is the best answer. Lots of Viet Namese were Buddhist, and our one lone American I don't think will mind. I'd sure like to know what happened to his dog tags."

"I think the co-pilot survived and took them with him," Robert said.

"To where?" asked Mike.

"Maybe towards the town Xin Dong wants to visit."

"Visitors!" Avram doing a lookout on the top of the tank, called out.

"Chinese soldiers?"

"Yep. A whole crapload."

Everyone scrambled to their vehicles. Mike had Jack crank up the M-48 and turn it around as Avram and William loaded the main gun.

"Over a decade of no action and now, in less than a day, all this."

"No rest for the wicked, Sergeant First Class," said the loader with a smile.

The Chinese column had formed up in a long line a thousand yards back. The results of a quick count my Mike's results were just under a thousand soldiers. Plus, two field pieces like the one the tankers had knocked out.

"Okay, gentlemen. We fire a dozen training rounds. First, we take out the field gums. Then, take out the cavalry. We use Willie Pete, then the two HE the Israelis wanted us to test. "

"If I had time to clean up that thirty caliber ammunition, we could mow them down."

"Well, William, we don't. Hopefully, we can put the fear of God into them, and they leave."

A single rider broke off from over a hundred cavalrymen carrying a white flag and galloped to within fifteen yards of the M-48. He reined his horse to a stop, stuck the flagstaff into the dirt, and unrolled a scroll. In a booming voice, he read a short and terse proclamation. The man then rerolled the scroll, pulled the flagstaff from the dirt, and galloped back to the Chinese Emperor's forces.

"What did he say, Lieutenant?" asked the tank commander.

"If we surrender now, all will be forgiven. The One and Only Emperor of Elsewhen owns all he surveys and demands we surrender the metal mechanical war wagon. If not, we will be treated as common thieves and hanged."

"Hell, he shot first."

"Emperors do what they want. He expects us to bow down, to kowtow."

"Gunner."

"Yes, Commander."

"Targets, the two cannon, "

"Identified."

"Fire when ready, on both targets."

"Roger that."

Moments later, William called out, "On the way!"

"Up," Avram called out as he slammed a new shell into the chamber of the 90MM. Seconds passed and another "On the way!" from the gunner.

Mike saw the first shell rip off the left cannon's wheel through his commander's periscope and spin the weapon around. The following shell struck the second cannon dead on its barrel. A loud explosion occurred as the cannon chamber and its contents exploded due to the obstruction. Pieces of the exploding field artillery piece peppered the nearby Emperor's soldiers, and several went down, wounded and dying.

"I don't think they like our answer," said Mike.

"Sorry, that first shot was a bit off. "

"Good enough for government work. Load a Willie Pete round."

"Up," Avram called out.

Mike stuck his head out of the tank hatch and looked around. A hidden squadron of cavalry appeared on their left flank, galloping hell-bent for leather.

"Gunner, transverse left, target."

"Identified."

"Fire."

"On the way."

The Willie Pete smoke round exploded among the packed riders. White Phosphorus chunks set men and mounts burning as the galloping fell over the fallen. Suddenly, Mike heard the familiar thumping of a thirty-caliber machine gun.

"I got the Sixty going," called out Robert. "This Pig was designed to work dirty and wet."

"Hot Damn! Give it to them, Masters!"

The steady beat of the M-60 was music to his newfound combat ears. All those years of waiting and training finally paid off. The flanking cavalry formation shattered, the survivors and riderless horses made a hasty retreat.

"Hey, Sergeant," called out the driver, Jack. "They are not giving up."

Mike looked to the front quadrant and saw several hundred riflemen march inline towards the tank.

"What, they think this is Gettysburg or something? Man, I wished we had canister rounds." He called on the radio to Robert.

"You still have M-60 ammunition?"

"Yep. A couple of hundred rounds at least. I have an M-2 Carbine, I think, will work."

"Bring them upfront. Corporal Running Deer, watch the flanks and rear."

"You got it, Gunny. By the way, the Merchants are beating feet out of here."

"Let them. One less worry."

"Gunner, Training, troops."

"You don't want the HE?"

"No. We'll use the solid shot training round to kick up some rocks at the infantry. It might make them reconsider."

"Say when. Mike."

"Find a boulder you can shatter in front of the infantry. It should produce some shrapnel."

"Got it. Avram, do the honors."

"Up."

"Identified."

"Fire, gunner."

"On the way."

The solid shot round struck a boulder the size of a beachball. The rock shattered, and with pieces of the non-hardened steel flew towards the line of soldiers some twenty-five yards in front of the impact. Mike watched six soldiers fall, either wounded or dying. The Chinese Officers ignored the casualties and kept screaming at the troops to advance.

"Damn, Willie Pete, William."

"Identified."

"Up."

"Robert, you have the M-60 ready?" Mike called out.

"Climbing up on your beast as we speak. I'll fire from around the turret."

"Got you. Hang on, Rob. Fire when ready, William."

"On the way."

The WP Smoke round hit a Chinese officer straight on just as the line of soldiers stopped. The officer's bodyparts and accouterments spattered and slapped at the infantry along with the white phosphorous. As pieces of the burning mineral did the dirty work, Robert began to fire bursts from the M-60. The center of the attacking formation broke and scattered. The remaining officers ordered the infantry to form a line and fire their rifles, which occurred only sporadically. Robert ducked behind the turret as lead bullets hit the tank.

"Gunner, training round, troops."

"Want me to try the ricochet concept again?"

"Yep. One last time."

"Up."

"Identified."

"Fire."

"On the way."

The shot sliced through several humans before it hit a pile of loose rock. Pieces of metal and stone slammed into nearby troops. More infantry scattered, this time the Officers with them.

"I think these guys are used to people surrendering and not fighting back," said Mike.

Robert fired a parting burst of machinegun fire to hasten the retreat. Mike climbed out of the tank, jumped to the ground, and made his way to the Humvee. He saw an unfamiliar face. Jesus Garcia grinned through his thick mustache as he spoke.

"Can't a wounded guy get some rest around here? You must be Sergeant Virgil."

"Call me Mike. Robert does. You comfortable back here?"

"The Lieutenant has it set up as pleasant as possible. You worry about getting the rest out of here in one piece, with all this shooting going on."

Mike smiled. "I'm working on it."

After a very quick powwow, everyone grabbed what salvage they could off the Huey and fill some spare containers with pond water. They would boil the water later. William watched from the M-48 as the Emperor's soldiers tried to re-organize for another attack. Mike planned to bug out before they could.

"We ready to move out?" the Sergeant First Class called out. He got thumbs out all around just as a trumpet blew. Ten seconds later, the Humvee and the M-48 accelerated away from the oasis. No one wanted to stick around to see what the horn note meant. The two vehicles soon left the Emperor's troops in the dust.

A half-hour later and Susan in the Humvee contacted him on a standard frequency. The equipment was decades apart, but the necessary frequencies stayed the same.

"Gunny, I have someone from a grounded C-17—that's a newer type of air transport—asking who we are, where we're from."

"Where are they?"

"Some smart ass said go West, young man, go West."

Mike Virgil laughed. The American military, they must be. Yanks were incurable smartasses.

"Tell them we're en route. If they give us some landmarks, we can figure the distance."

"Roger that, Gunny."

Mike sat in the command copula of the M-48 and mused on the realities of this place called Elsewhen. The ones with families would have it worse, himself included. A drop through a hole in time and space into a new universe was great in a novel, not in real life. Few people ever talked about those left behind.

*Hopefully,* he thought, *they could adapt.* Then

again, Susan Running Deer said it succinctly. She would never give up trying to get back.

"Hmmm," Mike mumbled to himself. "Not a flawed concept. Never give up, nor surrender. I might see June and the kids again someday."

Until then, at night, he'd look at the twin moons and ponder as he helped others stay alive. Masters was right. Good training helped.

# 11
# THE EMPORER'S WISHES

iam O'Grady jerked awake at the sound of the suspended gong strike. The man had installed the device below his veranda to prevent pounding on the massive entry door or loud screaming to get his attention. As Liam's eyes focused, he saw an Asian female face in repose on his right. As he slowly shifted to his left, he came up against a pair of very feminine feet with painted toenails. On the other side of the feet was a light-skinned attractive female Caucasian face. Memories of a night of debauchery soon rose to his frontal lobe.

Someone struck the gong a second time, and Liam crawled over the female bodies in his bed.

"I'm coming!" he called out in Mandarin Chinese. "Keep your pants on."

Liam stepped out onto his second-story veranda of the combination arms factory and living quarters. He looked down and saw a mounted messenger of

The Emperor.

"You rang?" Liam called out.

"The Emperor Wishes your presence, Master Armorer. Now."

*Ah shit,* Liam thought. Something went wrong.

"Do I have time to wash the smell of sex off me, my good sir?"

"Of course. The Emperor does not wish to smell your crass bodily odors."

"Please tell My Emperor that I will be there within the hour."

"Do that, Master Armorer. The Emperor has received bad news." The mounted messenger turned his ornate outfitted horse and trotted off towards the Palace with that final statement. People on the streets of New Beijing quickly dodged from the path of the messenger. No one dared to interfere with the Emperor's business.

Liam thought he knew what the 'bad news' was and had a fleeting thought of beating feet out the largest city gate on Elsewhen. Even fleeing with Liam's most trusted bodyguards would not ensure his survival. It was best to face the music. One of the most important members of the Emperor's Court looked at the three exquisite female shapes on his bed, now just stirring from sleep.

"Well, ladies, it's been fun."

The Irish American expatriate was out of his quarters within a quarter-hour and using the local form of a rickshaw. The small muscular man pulling the two-wheeled conveyance made record time to the Palace compound. Liam wore a silk suit, leather Roper boots and carried his walking stick shillelagh. The streets of New Beijing could be rough for the incautious. Liam slipped a small clone of a Colt Pocket Pistol into his right boot top before leaving his home and workplace. If someone in the Emperor's Court decided to 'off' him as a favor to His Exaltedness, Liam would not go without a fight.

Liam gave the rickshaw operator a colossal tip and walked through the official entrance to the Palace grounds. All the guards knew Liam and saluted him as he passed. Hell, they all carried weapons Liam had procured for them. As he walked towards the Emperor's royal court office, Liam thought about how he had come to be here and in Elsewhen proper. For everyone not born on this version of Barsoom had their own unique story.

Liam O'Grady's father was a gunsmith and owned his shop. Liam picked up the trade but wanted to explore the world before settling down to help his father. Thus Liam had joined the Army and wound up as an Armorer thanks to his civilian expertise. He spent a stint in the rear areas of Viet Nam, suffered a few rocket and mortar attacks. During the Tet Offensive, the Irish American went on a supply convoy to take weapons and ammunition to troops in the field. He soon learned what it was like to be shot at and to shoot back.

After Viet Nam, Liam stayed in the Active Duty Army for six years and remained in the U.S. Army Reserve. Liam had made some contacts with the Military-Industrial Complex when he went to industry conferences presenting new weapon systems to the people who would use them. Liam considered taking a job with some big-name like Colt, Remington, Winchester instead of working with his father when 'it' happened.

Liam was out on a 'black powder hunt,' a sport of increasing popularity as various hunters tried their hands at shooting replica as well as a few original flintlock and percussion cap firearms. Liam had a personally constructed Kentucky Rifle and a brace of old Horse pIstols he wanted to try out in the field. One minute he was with a couple of friends; the next minute, he seemed to fall into another world.

It took Liam some minutes to get a grasp on his new situation. Then he heard some loud voices yapping in some Asian language. Being armed and trying to figure out where the hell he was, Liam approached the arguing persons. He saw four Asian or Chinese mounted soldiers slapping around a family of peasant farmers. Liam's memory of what happened next was clear.

The stocky-built armorer slung his rifle, found a hunk of a thick tree branch. He then snuck up on the soldiers. One soldier stayed mounted, holding the reins of the other mounts of his fellows. Liam slammed the tree branch into the side of the head of the mounted man, knocking him off his saddle and to the ground. One soldier was in the process of slapping the peasant farmer around when he heard the commotion behind him. As the man turned, Liam punched the soldier's jaw with a broad fist. The man went down, and another soldier yelled a warning as he reached for a holstered pistol. The young woman he was abusing grabbed the hand, reaching for the gun, and bit it. The horse soldier beat at the young lady's face to make her let go, and Liam slit the man's throat with his hunting knife. Grabbing the dying man's pistol, he shot the fourth soldier in his face as this man tried to grab a rifle.

Liam spoke no Chinese but made it clear what he wanted accomplished. The group quickly tied the two unconscious men. They stripped the dead men of all their valuable items. The farmer's family and Liam took all metal and weapons and packed them on two captured horses. Then Liam followed them to their village.

The armorer spent a month with the farmer's family while he examined the captured weapons. Two of the pistols were clones with Chinese markings of Colt Navy cap and ball circa 1851. One rifle was an almost exact duplicate of the anemic Volcanic lever-action developed by the early Smith and Wesson. Another recovered one was a near duplicate of Liam's Kentucky Rifle converted to a percussion system. Using the Chinese weapons and the ones that 'came' with him to this place called Elsewhen in English, Liam endeared himself with the villagers by killing two nasty wild boars which were messing with their crops as well as a 'standing dragon' a miniature Godzilla which preyed on humans and livestock. The six-foot-tall dinosaur died with a fifty-caliber bullet in its softer throat.

At the end of the month, Liam decided it was time to move on. Any day he expected to see soldiers of the Emperor the peasants feared appearing while they looked for the killer of the other soldiers. Liam decided it was best to grab the bull by the horns. The Irishman packed up his few possessions, talked the villagers out of a burro, and set out East, the direction of New Beijing. Liam confiscated a Colt Clone pistol and added it to his weapons. He thought his two Horse Pistols, replicas of Remington rolling block fifty caliber single shots, would be unique enough to serve as an entrance key to the higher-ups in the New Beijing Government. The villagers told him that the Emperor demanded all firearms belonged to him.

During his stay in the village, Liam learned some Mandarin and discovered some of them knew English and German. The Lesser Mountains Liam dropped into was like Grand Central Station in NYC for new arrivals and merchants traveling West. He dodged a couple of small forts placed to keep the peasants and passing strangers under control. The Emperor was sensitive about any challenges to his authority.

A week and a half of traveling on foot brought

Liam insight of New Beijing. Twelve-hour days walking ate up the miles. He made sure he did not overtask the burro, kept the load light. Liam met a couple of merchant caravan on this North Trade Route, which went West through the Northern High Plains. Liam was slowly learning the geography of his new home. Based on the force of gravity, he felt, this planet was Earth-size. However, even the merchants talked in generalities about distance and location. Out West could be a week or a month's walk.

Liam used coins taken from the soldiers he beat and shot, plus some scrap metal he picked up to pay for food and information on the trail. It also bought him passage on a ferry across the New Yangtse River, Due South of New Beijing. Liam knew he was nearing the city when he saw the haze of smoke hanging over some low hills.

"That smoke. I hope it means smelting like the villagers said," the Irish American mumbled.

He strayed in an Inn a mile from the main gate into the Palace grounds. Liam was renting a locking room and explained in the international language of violence to the inn staff that someone would have extra holes in their body if his things disappeared. A thumb across the throat seemed to have the same meaning everywhere. Liam then went to the public baths and soaked his weary body. The locals understood as his room was in one piece when he returned. He bought a clean tunic for the hoped-for audience with some bigwig, ate some rice balls, drank some plum wine, and went to sleep. In the morning, Liam picked up his burro from the attached stables, loaded the concealed weapons on it, and walked towards the Imperial Palace.

The two guards at the main gate were young and bored. They started yelling at him once they saw he was non-Chinese. Liam ended the verbal abuse when he showed them the handgrip of a Horse Pistol.

"I have special weapons and knowledge. Please tell the Emperor."

Someone up the chain of command must have put the fear of God and the Emperor in them as they hustled him off to the side. One of them then ran into the courtyard as Liam scratched the donkey's ears. Within five minutes, someone referred to as a majordomo appeared. His name was Chen Bai. Liam would discover the man was a claimed 'cousin' of the Emperor.

"You are English?" Chen asked in accentless English.

"I am Irish-American. Liam O'Grady, armorer extraordinaire at your service."

The majordomo spoke in rapid Chinese to the two guards, which sent one running.

"You deal in weapons?"

"Where I came from, I fixed, built, helped design things that go 'boom.' So, yes sir, I deal in weapons."

Chen gave him another once over examination,

then held a hand out, palm up. Liam handed him one of his Remington pistols. Chen tried not to look interested but failed.

"You could build—this?"

"Give me some decent metal, yes. But I understand anything but copper is in short supply."

"I see you have been talking to some merchants on the road," said Chen Bai. "Tell me, Liam Irish-American, who is your allegiance to here in New Beijing?"

"My allegiance is to keeping me alive and in one piece," replied Liam.

A smile finally appeared on Chen's face as he spoke. "I think we have a place for you."

An hour later, Liam was seated in a large greeting area on soft cushions. A comely young Asian lady ( more like a girl in age) kept him supplied with iced wine and traditional sweetmeats. She spoke no English, Spanish, German, or Gaelic as Liam tried all of them. She limited her communication to smiles and, "Would you like more ice?"

Suddenly a young soldier in a very ornate dress uniform strode into the room and announced, "His exalted Emperor Yang Bing the mighty, ruler of all he surveys, enters. Bow and show obedience to His Excellency!"

The young serving girl prostrated herself on the thick carpeting. Liam stood and bowed deeply. It was dangerous, but he needed to demonstrate some individual self-respect and power. If he acted like a toady subject of the Emperor, people would treat him as such. Then again, the Emperor may not like independent people and kill him on the spot. Being a stranger in a strange land was not easy—or safe.

Chen approached Liam and hissed, "Kneel," but the Emperor strode by him and shoved the Remington pistol in his face.

"You can make these?" the ruler spoke in unaccented English. Emperor Yung was taller than what Liam remembered as an average Chinese male. He also seemed muscled, more like an athlete than a pampered rule. His jet black hair was cut short, was not in the queue or long, and braided as Liam had seen among the other Asians. Liam recognized a fellow military member.

"Yes, sir, if I am given sufficient metal and a trained blacksmith or two to assist me."

"Ammunition also?"

"Again, your excellency, if I have sufficient metal—"

The young Emperor yelled some Chinese at Chen, which sounded to Liam like a command to bring someone named Zhang Li. Liam stood silent as the Emperor kept examining the massive single-shot pistol. Some five minutes passed, and a man in a silk top and trousers arrived. He bowed low to his ruler and began to speak in Chinese with averted eyes.

"Speak English so our Caucasian guest can

understand," said the Emperor. "He needs to hear your answers." The Exalted Ruler tossed the heavy pistol to Zhang Li. The man caught it, figured out how to operate the rolling block action, and looked down the barrel.

"It is massive but not complicated, My Emperor," replied Zhang Li. "Our revolvers contain more bullets, though not as thick—"

"They are also more complicated, easily broken by the peasants we draft as soldiers. You have never presented this design. Why not?"

"My Emperor, I and my assistants use as models those weapons which are brought by others to Elsewhen."

"Yet you, the Master Armorer, cannot develop any originality, despite all the various weapons provided. Hmmm. That is a mystery. Give me back the pistol."

The armorer stepped forward with eyes averted and handed his ruler the pistol. The Emperor opened the rolling bock action and inserted the round of ammunition provided by Liam.

"Liam O'Grady, you have other shells for your pistols?"

"Yes, Emperor Yang Bing. A limited supply but—"

The Exalted Ruler aimed and fired the fifty caliber bullet into the chest of Zhang Li. The man toppled backward and died. Liam started making mental calculations about his chances of escape when Yang Bing tossed the now empty pistol to him.

"You are now the Master Armorer of New Beijing. Chen will show you your quarters and work area. It will be up to you if the assistants should be kept on or—terminated. They have become lazy and slow under this piece of pig excrement, now bleeding on the carpet. CHEN! Get him out of here, and replace the carpet." Yang Bing turned and walked off as if nothing of import had occurred.

"Get to work, my new armorer, and do not fail me," the Emperor called over his shoulder as he departed.

It was just a few months short of six years since the Emperor shot the previous Master Armorer. And now, Liam was wondering if his blood would be decorating the new carpet. Well, he thought, he would not go down without a fight; it was against his Irish nature.

Liam stood in a smaller anteroom just outside of the Royal Office. He had been here innumerable times before, working on the various projects designed to arm the Emperor's Army. Liam had fought official bureaucratic inertia leftover from the ancient Chinese Confucian system of centuries, now transplanted to Elsewhen. Thus, he improved the lever-action rifles based on the old Volcanic design but was still stuck with bureaucratic resistance to melting the old ones down into usable recycled metal. So he had Henry/Winchester rifles with better ammunition, but not for everyone. The revolvers his workshop factory produced were much superior. He developed a five-shot actual Horse Pistol revolver firing rounds similar to the Remington rolling block he brought.

Since he was limited in meltdown and recycling, Liam went the same route the U.S. Army made post-Civil War. He used a similar breach loading conversion to the Trap Door Springfield and began a slow transformation of the large caliber rifles and muskets on hand. Liam built a few new Remington rolling block rifles and pistols, and then the Emperor presented him with a pristine Mauser bolt action rifle circa World War One. With that, Liam started work on obtaining sufficient materials to start production.

Then, the Emperor demanded cannon. It seems an upstart place called Freetown on the far outskirts of the so-called Western Province was causing him problems. New inhabitants/immigrants with modern weapons were implementing a representative republic/ democratic rule. That could not be allowed. Thus, Liam created a crash program, produced three bronze cannons with four-inch bores, helped train a cadre of 'Cannon Cockers, and added some new model repeating rifles and better revolvers. After sixty days, a one thousand man force army moved towards a showdown with this Freetown.

That had been over a month ago. Scuttlebutt was that things had not gone well.

The Emperor walked into the room with no fanfare. As Liam started to bow low, Yang Bing commanded, "Sit." So Liam sat.

The Emporer rang a small bell on his massive desk and sat down opposite Liam. A comely lass brought in a large tray with several decanters and glasses filled with ice cubes.

"Scotch or Irish Whiskey?" the Emperor asked. "Or something else?"

"Irish, please, Sir."

The young lady poured the drinks, then disappeared. The two men sipped their drinks, Liam waiting for the Emperor to speak first. After a minute of silence other than the noise of icecubes shifting, Yang Bung said.

"You have probably heard about the—expedition to Freetown."

"I have heard rumors, My Emperor. But to be truthful, people are afraid to talk."

"Afraid of the Emperor's wrath?"

"Yes, My Emperor."

Yang Bing laughed. "Fear is a useful tool in achieving power and control. Sometimes, it interferes with a ruler getting the truth." Yang Bing took a long drink of his whiskey, then spoke.

"Out of a thousand armed personnel, two hundred killed. Another two hundred wounded. The majority of the dead were cavalry, with the loss of over a hundred horses."

"What killed them, My Emperor?"

"What you call a tank. This massive metal beast

the cannon shot bounce off of like pebbles. And the crew fired shells with lit phosphorous. It burned to the bone, many dying hours later."

The Emperor emptied his glass, refilled his, then refreshed Liam's. That action told the Irishman he just might come out of this meeting alive. "Six artillerymen killed, one cannon blown apart, and the other two badly damaged. And of course, they had machine guns."

The Emperor stood up suddenly. "Let me show you something."

Yang Bing unlocked a bottom drawer on his oversized desk and removed something wrapped in silk. As he unwrapped it, Liam whistled.

"A Mauser M-96 pistol. One of the first successful semi-automatic pistols."

"We Chinese called it the Box Cannon. It came in a combination of a wooden holster and stock. I've meant to have a duplicate stock holster made, as I lost the other on my trip to Elsewhen." He sipped his drink, then continued. "I was a young Lieutenant in the Imperial Army during the Wuchang Uprising, trying to decide what side I was on. In 1911, Sun Yat-Sen was about to take over China. I had learned English at a missionary school, so I understood more than most what was happening. Then, poof! I was near New Beijing."

"You came alone?" Liam asked.

"Funny, you should ask. Chen Bai was a young revolutionary soldier who was yanked here at the same time. He became my fast friend."

"And, My Emperor, if I may ask, how long ago was that?"

"Close to twenty-five years ago. Some mounted Chinese troops of the warlord ruling New Beijing showed up with muzzleloaders and bows. I shot all six of them. Chen and I took their weapons. We soon found some villagers who hated the warlord, as well as a wandering Ronin Samurai, who was willing to work with a Chinese man."

"How long did it take you to overthrow the warlord?"

"A week. Bai was quite the bombmaker, and the warlord was an opium addict. Someone has been growing opium long before I showed up. Plus, I found a means to pay off the Assassins Guild."

The Emperor smiled. "I tell you my complete history as you are the only person other than Chen Bai I consider a friend. I also wanted you to know that I would not ask a friend to do something I had not done."

"Which, My Emperor, is?"

"Reform my Army. Rebuild it. Then invade Freetown. I cannot let that thorn in my side fester."

Liam finished his drink in one gulp. "I am best at making weapons, not using them, Emperor Yang."

"You sell yourself short. You have military training. You are smarter than most people here."

Liam poured himself a drink, then refreshed Yang

Bing's glass. "What about the current commanders?"

"The three senior officers from the expedition are being beheaded at this moment. Chen is handling it."

"So, if I fail, it's the executioner's ax?"

"You won't fail. Neither will you drag yourself back with your tail between your legs as the others did."

Liam saw there was no way out. Unless he wanted to sneak off in the dead of night and try to ride like hell, and he was a lousy horseman.

"Well, My Emperor, I guess I was just drafted."

Liam left the Emperor and caught another rickshaw home. He had a couple of assistants who could take over some projects as he tried to whip the expedition's remains into a decent military force. Damn, he enjoyed his concubines, the life he had carved out here, and did not want to go to war again. Viet Nam was enough for him. Liam knew he could apply for a job with the Assassin's Guild. They were constantly bugging him and others for better weapons. However, he also knew their initiation was to go out and assassinate people.

Liam paid the rickshaw drive and stood looking at his small but comfortable empire. Liam had money, and precious metals stashed away. But where would he go? The Irish-American stood and thought for a moment, then shrugged his shoulders and unlocked the main door. He'd sleep on it. Who knows, maybe when he got to Freetown, he could switch sides.

As he had told Chen those years ago, his allegiance was to keep himself alive and in one piece. That concept had never left him.

Liam walked upstairs to his suite. Man, he had to admit, he'd miss his concubines.

# 12
# THE EMPORER
# HAS NO CLOTHES

**M**ark Stone sat and stared at the fuzzy video on the well-worn laptop computer. Others at the conference table at Ma Bells Emporium had perused the images previously. Now it was the Mayor, Immigration, and Customs Commissioner for the city-state of Freetown to see the oncoming threat.

"I see at least fifteen hundred armed Chinese soldiers moving our way."

"A regular merchant says its at least three thousand, with a half a dozen cannon and a catapult or two." The comment was from Marshal Mat Dillon, Freetown's senior law enforcement official.

"Sorry about the fuzzy picture," added Major Sue Finch, commander of Globemaster's community, named after the C-17 aircraft she flew into Elsewhen some six months prior. "We cobbled together the drone and camera from stuff on my plane. "

"Beggars can't be choosers, Major," replied Mark. "The pictures are sufficient to show our not so friendly Emperor is probably looking for the Tankers after what they did to that first invasion force."

Words from passing merchants and new immigrants relayed that the massive force of Chinese troops that stumbled on to Sergeant First Class Mike Virgil and his tankers was a punishment force en route to Freetown. The community now overseen by Mark Stone and company was a thorn in the Emperor's side he was no longer willing to ignore. Plus, he received a bloody nose when some calvary tried to take possession of the Globemaster C-17. The Emperor's soldiers seemed used to being bullies. When resisted by trained warriors, they broke quickly.

He looked at Chris Walken, another Executive Board member and owner/operator of the local gun and armament shop.

"How are the militia guns coming, Chris?"

"We have one hundred Sharp's clones in 45-70." The tall and slender man answered. "However, we have only had a half dozen recruits trained in them ."

"Why so few?"

"Ammunition bottleneck. We have just one thousand new brass shells made, along with primers."

Mark looked at the newest member of the Board. James Chou. He was American Chinese, late of Seattle, Washington. He fell through the Rabbit Holesome three months ago and took over the large jewelry and precious metal shop at Freetown entrance. The previous owner lost an argument with a local Chinese Tong. The Executive Board, with the help of some of the local trained soldiers, 'installed' James into the strategic business. Freetown needed Jewelers and metalworkers to manufacture ammunition and weapons.

"So making decent brass shells is somehow out of your employees' capabilities. James?"

"I admit some are dragging their feet," replied James. "There are those who are still upset over how the previous owner was unseated. Plus, I was forced on the business. Then some do not want to seem to be taking sides in a fight with the Chinese Emperor."

"Time for them to chose sides, James," said Mark. "I know I am not a President with emergency powers, but—"

"Actually, Husband, you are," Mark's Elsewhen wife and the local senior Doctor Susan Von Braun said. "Things are past being a mayor. The growth of Freetown to over ten thousand souls means a change in the power structure. Especially since you formed a military."

*Why must my local wife be so damned smart?* Mark asked himself.

"So, then, I start declaring martial law? How about

we deal with the weapons issue at hand first, then I start pulling a Lincoln and habeas corpus."

"Well, soon-to-be-President," said Chris, "I do have over a hundred black powder grenades and landmines. I also reloaded two of Sergeant Virgils expended tank shells with black powder. He now has a canister load and an old fashioned cannonball he can shoot."

"We should convince him to be part of the Board," said Matt Dillon.

"It's that military thing," replied Mark. "He swore allegiance to the U.S.A., and that M-48 is U.S Army property. He defended himself and his crew when they took apart that previous invasion force."

"I accepted the new reality," said Sue Finch. "After all, Freetown does have the principles of the Bill of Rights. And it is about survival."

"Your time and his are separated by over fifty years. His ideas are much more in tune with those in World War Two."

"Well, Mark, the personnel of the area called Globemaster, is willing to throw in with Freetown. Jake Jackson has a small catapult he built to throw black powder bombs. He can help Chris build some more for use near town."

"I could use Gunny Sergeant Jefferson to complete some quickie military training with our militia."

"He'll do it," the Major responded.

"Anyone heard from Misters Franzetti, Quinn, and Masters?" asked Matt Dillon.

"Nope," answered Mark. "They are still in the land of the Amazons."

Susan Von Braun laughed. "Probably being used as a stud service."

"Well, Wife, if they are, I wish they could still bring us in contact with the Amazon leadership and that group of U.S. Military that fell into their laps. We sure could use some additional trained troops."

Mark looked at the laptop again. "How far out is this group?"

"About two days," said Chris Walken.

"Ah, shit."

Mark Stone used a pair of scrounged binoculars to survey the battlefield to the East of Freetown. During the last forty-eight hours, most residents of Freetown slept little. Starting a half-mile from the small tower lookout post that marked Freetown's Main Street entrance, a No Man's land had been created. Numerous punji stick pits and a few large tiger traps now sat concealed in the path of the invading force. A half a dozen small bomb-throwing catapults spread out behind an abbreviated minefield backing up the pits and traps. The Globemaster person had been a godsend in using their machinery for manufacturing needed equipment. Gunny Sergeant took over the training and command of the

Militia, now some semi-trained rifle and bowmen. Mark figured they were suitable for about ten minutes of fighting before they would begin to break. He cursed himself for not taking a more aggressive stance towards the defense of the new city-state. Mark allowed himself to be distracted by the birth of twins by Susan. He did not have any children in his original world and time, so it was unique.

The Russian sisters Ivana and Marianna used the machine shop built around Mark's former Jeep SUV to produce copies of the WWII Russian PPS-43 as if they did such work in Russia every day.

"We studied how they made things in The Great Patriotic War," said Ivana. "What is so strange about that?"

The sticky point was no ammunition supply. Had Mark started preparing even a month before—

The Mayor cum President was able to convince Sergeant Virgil and the personnel who came with him to fight the oncoming invaders. The M-48 Tank was a strategic weapon that overmatched the 19th Century technology of the Emperor's army. There was a chance the Chinese may surprise him with something brought by a recent "immigrant." Mark would have to deal with that when the time came.

The Globemaster personnel would defend their aircraft with their military weapons as neither they nor Freetown could risk losing that resource. Mark decided if he lived through this, they would need to build some Hadrian's Wall around Freetown and the C-17.

"Chris, I should have had an expedition to the Great Smash Dump, or Heap, whatever you call it. We could bring back tons of useful metal and stuff if the stories are true."

"The stories are true, Mayor," replied Chris. "I have talked to people who saw it, brought a few pieces or items to sell to me. The problem is out of every ten who has taken the journey, only about five have returned,"

"Well, I think I have the right people here to put a lie to that statistic. But it's too late for today. Here, take a look."

Chris surveyed the approaching force and whistled. "Damn. There are over three thousand Emperor's people in that column. Most seem to have weapons."

"Yep. Time for me to get down off this tower and help command the troops."

"I have a question, Mark."

"What's that?"

"If they try to parlay, will you?"

Mark paused for a moment. "If they actually sent someone to treat with us, yes. But the Chinese reading an ultimatum to us like they usually do? They can kiss my ass."

Mark descended from the tower and walked over to the M-48 Tank. Mark called out to Sergeant Virgil was sitting on the edge of the commander's cupola.

"You ready for this?"

"Well, Mayor, I have a hundred rounds of scrounged fifty caliber to shoot at them, plus two hundred thirty caliber for the coaxial machine gun. That plus the remaining main gun shells. We'll give these Sons of Heaven something to think about."

"You could beat feet until after the fight. You have the tank and the Humvee."

"Nah. This Emperor is a psychotic bully. I hate bullies."

Mark laughed. He did have good people around him. There were even about a thousand locals hiding in the town along with Red MacBeth, Blue Baxter, and Spotted Wolf, ready to use whatever weapons they had from the rooftops. They prepared to attack any of the troops who made it past the outer defenses.

Mark went down to the foxholes containing two hundred troops overseen by large and Black Gunny Jefferson. The Marine sat with his assault weapon and two hundred rounds of ammunition. Everyone else had black powder weapons and a few bows.

"Think these people will fight?" Mark asked.

"Yes, Sir. They know how nasty Imperial soldiers can be."

"Sorry to drag you all into this."

"No dragging necessary. Freetown is my home now."

Marshal Dillon walked up to Mark. "Well, the townspeople are all primed and ready to go."

"If the soldiers make it into town, we have a severe problem."

"Well, we'll deal with it, Mayor. No matter what."

A horn sounded from the Emperor's forces. They appeared to pause about a half-mile distant. Mark watched as a single rider with a white flag rode towards Freetown.

"Well, I guess it's my turn to go talk."

The Mayor walked over to his parked motorbike, cranked it up, and went out to meet the approaching horseman. The two men met some five hundred yards in front of Freetown's defenses. Mark saw the rider was Caucasian, a bit of a surprise. He wore a nondescript set of camouflaged fatigues with a massive star on the shoulder boards.

"Where did you come from?" Mark asked when he was within hailing distance.

"The United States of America, though my people are originally from the Emerald Isle. Liam O'Grady is my name. I bet you are Mark Stone, the Mayor."

"Your intelligence is accurate. And what title do you have, Liam O'Grady?"

"Normally, I am the Emperor's Armorer and Weapon Maker. Today, I am his Senior Military Commander."

"So, now you read me the ultimatum that I

kowtow to the Emperor, right Liam? Then I refuse, and the killing begins."

Liam paused and looked around.

"That's a nice tank you have there. I'm trying to get enough metal and technology to start building motorized vehicles. Even motorbikes like yours would be cool."

"Twentieth Century refugee, right, Liam?"

"You got it. I miss my MTV."

Liam kept looking at Freetown, the tank, Mark sitting on the motorbike.

"You have electricity?"

"Working on it. We have a water wheel hooked up to a turbine we have built from spare parts. Lit up a few electric coils, hope to electrify the whole Freetown area eventually. Windmills are next."

"The Emperor would like that," said Liam.

"Okay, this is turning into one big stall. Come on, Liam O'Grady, what do you and the Emperor want? And don't say surrender as that is a non--starter."

The Irishman turned in his saddle and gestured towards the Emperor's forces.

"Use your binoculars and find a man with a highly ornamented uniform, sitting on a tall white stallion."

Mark played along with the request and found the Chinese General.

"That is the Second in Command, Zhang Li. He is here to make sure I follow orders. The Emperor is frustrated and thinks maybe a round-eyed barbarian may succeed where all the Chinese commanders can't. At the same time, he does not trust me. Thus, I have a handler."

Mark set his binoculars aside.

"So, now what?"

"Think your tanker can hit him and his entourage with a shell?"

General Zhang Li watched thru a telescope the two round-eyes talking and was becoming impatient with the non-activity. His Emperor had told him to give the barbarian a loose rein in dealing with the Freetown Rebels. However, Zhang was now becoming impatient. He watched the Freetown Barbarian drive his machine back to the metal beast machine. The man sitting on top of the metal beast conferred with the round-eye negotiator and then disappeared inside the machine. Zhang Li saw the gun on the turret shift and point towards him. Zhang Li cursed and yelled out orders.

"Gunners! Artillery to the front! Cavalry, attack formation. The barbarians prepare –"

The high explosive shell from the 90MM tank gun atomized Zhang and shredded those about him. The Emperor's forces scrambled about confused as subordinate officers tried to take control. A squadron of cavalry charged down the hill; whether to rescue Liam or enact revenge was unknown. Liam slapped his horse away towards the left flank and jumped on the back of Mark's motorbike. Mark Stone had told him about the landmines and pits if he charged ahead.

The cavalry unit commander led his horseman directly at the M-48. Several horses went down as they tripped in the punji stick holes developed for an infantry attack. Then a landmine exploded. The young commander realized the enemy suckered him into charging into a landmine field and tried to stop the headlong charge. A burst from the tank coaxial machinegun took the young officer out, plus two other mounted troops. Confusion reigned as more of the cavalry fell into tiger pits, tripped in the punji stick holes, and smashed into other horses.

Suddenly, Jefferson launched lit black powder grenades using quickly manufactured miniature catapults. Most of the grenades exploded in the air before reaching the targeted horseman, the fuse length being haphazard. However, even the air explosions hurt the attacking forces. Panicked, even more, the horseman began to flee.

Some of the surviving senior commanders managed to form five hundred infantry in a long line. With officers and NCOs out front, screaming orders, the Emperor's soldiers began a slow advance on Freetown. Concurrently, the six field pieces wheeled into position to fire on Freetown.

Sergeant Virgil and his tankers fired the black powder ball round at the nearest cannon. It was surprisingly accurate, the ball killing the crewman swabbing the cannon barrel. It then smashed into the carriage and cracked the gun mount.

"We'll have to have Chris build a few more of those," the Sergeant said to his crew. "They work pretty well."

The advancing infantry then began a more sophisticated tactic than in past combat. They began to fire their bolt action rifles and breech loaders as they advanced.

"Somebody taught them suppressive fire," said Mark as he stopped the motorbike near the lookout tower.

"I did," said Liam. "This switching of sides was a spur of the moment decision."

"Well, we have a few tricks up our sleeves." Mark reached into a motorbike saddlebag, removed a flare gun, and fired it. No sooner had the flare arched towards the advancing enemy than a sizeable flaming ball flew over the town and into the advancing infantry. When the projectile struck the ground, it exploded, sending flaming tar and oil in every direction. Infantrymen ran screaming, and the advance of the middle of the line faltered.

"Not afraid of a short catapult round setting the town on fire?" asked Liam.

"In for the penny, in for the pound. It is a calculated risk."

As a second catapult shot flew over Freetown, the Humvee, which came with the Tankers, sped into view. Special Ops troop Jesus Garcia fired a mounted M-60 machine gun while Corporal Running Dear hauled ass in her Humvee. The spreading oil and tar from the second catapult round sent many more soldiers in flaming runs to the rear. Aimed bursts from the M-60 broke the formation. Chinese troops threw down their weapons and ran.

The Humvee sped to within M-60 range of the Imperial cannon as Jesus fired short bursts. There was a sizable explosion near one field gun as the black powder cache exploded. Bullets spranged off the Humvee, and Running Deer decided it was time to return to her lines. The M-48 gun boomed, and one of the remaining Willie Pete rounds hit in the center of a mass of infantry. Soldiers ran screaming as white phosphate burnt down to the bone. Another cache of black powder exploded, sending panicked soldiers running. Surviving senior commanders tried to establish order among the troops with varied success.

A field piece fired into Freetown. There was an explosion, and the alarm bell for the fire response team began to clang. A practice round from the 90MM slammed into the cannon, cracking the barrel and killing two gun crews. Another line of semi-organized infantry began to advance on Freetown, this time at a jog. Mark fired his recovered fifty caliber breech-loader and took down an officer leading the charge. His death did not slow the assault.

"Shit," cursed Mark. "You trained them too

well, Liam."

Jefferson's militia popped out of their fox holes and began firing. The Gunny used his M-4 to pick off anyone who looked like a leader. The Sergeant showed what a traditional well trained Marine rifleman could do. Thirty rounds, thirty hits. His militia began scoring hits, then threw more grenades. The line formation broke up, but some of the infantry continued their assault into the Freetown foxholes. Soon it was hand to hand with bayonets, clubs, knives, and teeth.

Mark Stone ran forward, firing a Chinese Clone Colt revolver just as Marshal Dillon appeared with two deputies. The Marshal's double-barreled fowling-piece sent a double load of buckshot into the remaining attackers. The attack faltered, and survivors fled back to their own lines. Mark looked up and saw a third assault line forming as another cannon shell struck Freetown.

"Fuck. You trained them too well, Liam. Built too many rifles for them."

The M-48s main gun boomed, and the shell smashed the last operational cannon off its mounting. A Cavalry unit began to form behind the infantry, and Mark cursed his lack of planning and preparation even more.

"We're going to use up all the tank main gun ammo; it seems," Mark said. "And all the fifty and thirty ammunition."

He saw many of the militia were dead or wounded and watched Gunny Jefferson scramble to obtain medical help for his men. The Humvee had some M-60 ammunition left but not much. This time, the fight may continue into Freetown. At least the Emperor's forces had not trashed the C-17 Globemaster yet.

Mark looked at the enemy forces as they formed up for the next assault. He still had the Roman designed ballistae and scorpio to launch some arrows at the advancing troops. Mark thought maybe if he saved them for the cavalry as they entered Freetown, it would help block the infantry with a bunch of dead and dying horses.

"Your tank will survive, Mayor," said Liam. " but the crew will have to come out someday."

"Well, the tank and the Humvee could run for it."

"Where? They'll have to find some fuel somewhere."

"Then I guess this is the Alamo, Elsewhen version." Mark looked at Liam. "You might be able to talk the Emperor into not killing you; tell him your switching size was a ruse."

Liam laughed. "Yeah, sure. I'd be lucky if he just cut my hands off and made me a beggar. "

Only then, an odd-sounding horn blasted a note from behind the Emperor's forces. Mark used his binoculars to look over the enemy forces. Suddenly, they were scrambling to face some of their troops in the other direction. Then, Mark and Liam heard some loud firearms reports. An odd undulating high pitch cry arose from numerous throats.

"What the—" Mark's comment was cut short when the Emperor's remaining forces began to scatter ever way imaginable. Then Mark and Liam saw the reason why.

One hundred mounted armored warriors smashed into the Chinese, wielding large broadswords and equally large two barreled horse pistols. Mark saw through his binoculars limbs and heads sent flying as the leathery armor seemed to resist the penetration of the Emperor's rifles. Mark could swear he also heard some automatic fire. The remaining invasion forces fled back down the road they had traveled on.

"First time I saw an Amazon," said Liam. "I thought it was some B.S. story."

"Nope. We had one visit a few months ago. Three of our guys went to make nice with them. I guess they made it back at just the right time."

Another surprise rode up to Mark and Liam. A young brunette woman reined in her large steed and spoke to the mayor in perfect American English.

"Former U.S. Air Force Senior Airman Leslie Owens at your service. You must be the mayor that Masters, Quinn, and Franzetti mentioned."

"Guilty as charged, young lady. Is a certain woman named Chabra with you?"

"Of Course. War Leader Chabra Strangerfinder is the reason we are here."

"Is that an M-16 slung on your back, Airman?"

"Call me Dragonslayer First Class, please. I'm a True Woman, an Amazon now."

The big blonde known to Mark Stone as Chabra rode up and reined in her large mount, then slid off with ease. "Friend!" the shieldmaiden of old said as she locked Mark in a bear hug and lifted him off his feet.

Then Chabra set him down and grinned at Liam. "American?"

"Why, yes. Liam O'Grady at your service."

Chabra slapped him on his chest in greeting and said, "Friend, also." Chabra truned back to Mark. "Leslie has taught me your language. So, we can drink, wheel and deal. For my people want to be friends, allies with Freetown."

"Well, you showed up at just the right time, Chabra. So mi casa is tu casa. Come in and say hello to my wife, Susan, and all the rest."

"First, we women chase the Emperor's scum back to Beijing. Then we talk."

Chabra slapped Mark's chest again, lept onto her horse, and was off in a cloud of dust but no Hi-Ho Silver.

"I'll stay here, Mayor," said Leslie Owens. "Grease the wheels of progress, as they say."

"Is that dragon leather?" asked Liam.

"Yes, sir. It stops a lot of bullets and blades."

Mark looked around, saw townspeople coming out to help collect the dead and wounded. It seemed everyday something in Elsewh surprised him even more.

And Mark once again dodged a bullet—literally.

"Well, let's go into Freetown, Leslie, and you can tell me how you got here to Barsoom."

The young woman laughed. "I think you know that already."

Mark conferred with Leslie Owens and Liam O'Grady as he waited for Chabra to return. Under the supervision of Matt Dillon and Chris Walken, townspeople recovered useful firearms from the battlefield. They reported some thousand repeating rifles, valuable ammunition, and a few dozed handguns recovered. Red, Blue, and Spotted Wolf used their horses and mules to haul down the damaged field guns to Freetown. Soon, the townspeople were stripping the dead bodies of valuable equipment, then creating a funeral pyre. Rotting bodies were a health and sanitation problem.

One hundred militia members were dead or wounded. Three civilians died from the shelling, with three more injured. The Fire Department kept flames from spreading throughout the town. Mark knew that if the Amazons did not hit the enemy troops from the rear, they would enter into Freetown, M-48 or not. There was only one tank with limited ammunition.

Gunny Jefferson approached the trio and said, "I just heard from Major Finch on my radio. They were about to send some people to shoot up the rear of the Emperor's forces when the Amazon appeared. "

"Tell them thanks, but the C-17 cannot fall into the Emperor's greedy hands. The medical support they provide is invaluable."

Mark looked at Leslie. "So, name your price. You're in the catbird seat for saving our asses."

Leslie laughed. "Chabra already said we could give you the metal you wish, plus a few male technicians who can help construct weapon and ammunition making machines. A lot will be handloading mechanisms, but you have some citizens who will need jobs, right?"

"Yes, ma'am. What do you want in return to start with?"

"Amazons are always looking for new breeding stock. So a few young and healthy human males. Plus, we'll take medical aid as well as surplus munitions. We still have the Germans on the coast to deal with."

"Germans?"

"World War One types and technology, who are getting aggressive with trying to seize our Iron Mountain. If they can increase their numbers, we will have serious problems."

Mark shook his head. "Why are we humans so damned violent with each other? We are all transported here against our will."

"There are always people who want to be in charge, force their opinions on others," interjected Liam.

"But Hell, this is not even our world, Liam."

"Tell that to the Conquistadores."

Mark poured Leslie another glass of local wine.

"So, how did you get to this version of Barsoom."

Leslie smiled. "USAF Security Police and a few Marines at the northern firing range on Okinawa, Japan one minute, then the next minute we are here. So, Captain Milner, a Marine Lieutenant, and the firearms training staff, kept us together until we met the Amazons. That was over a year ago."

"What year did you come from?"

"1979."

"Damn. Cold War. It ended after a fashion."

"You'll have to take a trip to Iron Mountain and compare notes with the Captain."

"I look forward to that. Now, when your comrades complete chasing the Emperor's thugs back to New Beijing, you can all meet the other movers and shakers in Freetown."

Mark looked at Liam. "Other than helping disorganize the attack by telling me who to kill, what can you offer to the community."

Liam refilled his glass with wine. "I am good friends with the Assasins Guild. I think a working relationship would help before they are used to whack you."

Mark laughed. "Not the first time someone put a price on my head; what else?"

"I am a class A gunsmith. So, there is that."

Mark sipped his wine. "Okay. As the senior

Immigration Official, you are hereby granted entry. But you have to tell me why you defected."

"I am tired of looking over my shoulder, waiting for the executioner's ax to fall. The Emperor killed a predecessor in front of me." Liam sighed. "Damn. I am going to miss my concubines and all the benefits of a favorite of the Emperor. However. I think I can find a decent place here."

Mark smiled. Liam was not the first person who found a new life in Freetown. He would not be the last.

"Come on, you two. I have to check on my wife, Susan, the Chief Doctor here. She has a lot of new patients, to include a few wounded Chinese troops."

"You'll treat them?" asked Liam.

"And send them back to New Bejing to spread the good word about us barbarians. Until the Emperor kills them for subversion."

Liam O'Grady laughed. "A sly fox after my own heart. I think this is the beginning of a beautiful friendship."

"Casablanca. 1942. So who is Claude Rains, and who is Humphry Bogart?"

"We can work that out later, Mark."

Leslie Owens laughed. This was becoming interesting.

# 13
# A TRIP TO THE DUMP

**N**ow I know why the Emperor was never in a hurry to make this trip," said Liam O'Grady as he shifted in his saddle.

"I'm surprised he did not send a small army of soldiers with some impressed merchants and all their pack animals," replied Mark Stone, President Pro tem and Mayor of the city-state of Freetown.

"Because once out of the Emperor's area of control, the merchants would try to sneak off either west or east, and half of the soldiers would desert to Camelot, or New Rome, or disappear to become bandits on the various trade routes."

"Then how did he stay in control?" Mark asked.

"Keep people near enough so he could scare the crap out of them with an occasional beheading."

Mark grunted as he controlled the mules' reins pulling his wagon. Behind him were two more wagons drove by Red MacBeth and Blue Baxter. The two Mountain men were excellent muleskinners and had taught Mark how to handle the demanding and temperamental beasts. Bringing up the rear on a pinto pony was Spotted Wolf, a former Comanche Warrior with a Russian Wife in Freetown, in the world of Elsewhen. People had asked Mark why such a small group, why not bring some fifty of the Militia with him? His answer was simple.

"We need people to defend Freetown until we get back. And a large force draws too much attention."

With the help of Sergeant Virgil's M-48 Tank crew and the personnel from the C-17 cargo plane, Freetown had beat off an attempt by the Emperor in New Beijing to subjugate the city-state. The timely arrival of a force of Amazonian Warriors from the Far West helped decimate the attackers before they reached the city center. Out of just over three thousand New Beijing troops, primarily Asians, half were killed in combat or died during their retreat. Of course, the defection of Liam O'Grady, the former Senior Armorer for New Beijing and the Commander of the attacking force helped.

"How far away do you estimate is the so-called Smash Dump?" asked Mark.

Liam stood up in his stirrups and looked at the hazy, low mountain/large hill in the distance.

"At this pace, about two to three days. It's hard to tell as I have no first-hand knowledge as to the actual size.

Right now, it's a shape on the horizon."

"But we do know that mound is full of metal and machinery which someone or something dumped there."

"Yes. President Pro tempore."

"Hey, I'm only elected as Mayor, nothing else."

"But you are recognized as the leader of Freetown, so the election is perfunctory ."

"Why don't you run for the position, Liam?"

The Irishman laughed. "Hey, I'm Irish. Once in the barrel of leadership is enough for me. I may be Irish and drink, but I am not feeble-minded."

Three days later, the small wagon train was at the foothills of the Smash Dump. The men from Freetown stopped and stared.

"I don't ken a half of the things I see," said Red.

"Well, my good friend," said Mark, "I recognize a lot of metal machines and pieces of weapons from at least the 20th Century."

"Much metal," said Spotted Wolf from his horse. "We are rich."

Liam laughed. "We can fill our wagons, nothing more. And if you look closer, someone has built a small stockade up ahead. They may claim previous ownership."

Some three hundred yards ahead, a figure exited the mentioned stockade. Mark Stone looked through his well-used binoculars at the slowly approaching figure.

"That man looks like he has paratrooper boots and

a Thompson Submachine gun. I will wager he is from World War Two."

"Another lost soul?" asked Blue Bailey.

"No more lost than we are. You people cover me while I parley."

Mark reached into the back of his wagon for the copy of a PPS-43 submachine gun. The Russian sisters Ivana and Marianna manufactured the weapon, and others like it since the last attempted invasion. Mark once again thanked whatever gods ruled Elsewhen that the sisters fell down the Rabbithole. The two former students of physics and mechanics with some study of traditional weapons were a godsend.

He slung the weapon and hitched his belt holding the cross-draw Colt Navy Clone manufactured in New Bejing. Concealed in his deep pants pocket was his Ruger SP-101 in .357 Magnum, which came with him down the slide into another reality. Mark ambled towards the advancing soldier, palms up to show he was not looking for a fight. Blue, Red, and Spotted Wolf would cover him with Sharps 45-70 new manufactured rifles and a wicked compound bow. Liam had a Mauser Box Cannon from his New Bejing days, shoulder stock and all.

"Hi there," Mark called out. "You look like Airborne."

"You an American?" the man in the faded uniform called back.

"Yes, Sir. Born and raised. Mark Stone, Mayor of

Freetown at your service."

"Private First Class Mike Emerson, 82nd Airborne, last jump in Normandy."

"Let me guess. You popped out here in Elsewhen."

The stocky young man with light brown hair grinned as he neared but still had his Thompson ready for action.

"I take it you have had problems with friendly strangers before," Mark stated.

"You got it. I have been here just shy of two years. In that time, I have had people of every kind and color pass by here. Too many were ready to kill me."

Mark stopped some twenty-five feet from the former paratrooper.

"Ever heard of Freetown?" Mark asked.

"Yessir. From a Chinese merchant who spoke excellent English. One of his sons tried to slit my throat. Now I have friends watching over me, including some dogs."

Mark surveyed the metal enclosure and thought he saw a rifle barrel pointed at him.

"Well, Private, I can offer you an honest conversation with some Freetown beer and moonshine. We think it's high quality."

"Beer? I have a working icebox. I would almost kill for a cold beer."

"Well, killing is the last thing on my mind; trade is

the first. Bring some chairs out, and we can meet here while we still have sunlight."

Within a half-hour, six more people came out of concealment. They were a mixed lot, from various times and countries. One was a ten-year-old African American boy who had come down the Rabbit Hole by himself. The others included two Civil War Southerners, a World War One veteran, a young woman attending the Woodstock music festival, and a couple with their teenage daughter sailing in the so-called Bermuda Triangle. Their sailboat was on the far side of the Smash Dump with a busted keel. But they had survived the drop of a couple of stories with just bumps and bruises. The sailing family was the most recent arrivals, dropping in only three months prior.

"So you came from the 21st Century like us?" Stan Dawson, the husband of the sailing couple, asked Mark.

"Yes, Sir."

"And you have no idea either how you got here?" asked Stan's wife, Carol.

"No, Ma'am. A lot of people have a lot of theories, but none that fit. Someone or thing seems to have a thing about yanking us Earthlings here to Elsewhen."

"Not just people from Earth," said the couple's teenage daughter, Debra.

"What do you mean?" Liam asked. The Dawsons exchanged glances as if deciding how far to go with their story.

Mike Emerson derailed any debate. "They ran into

a Spaceman, a Martian, or some such."

"You mean some creature from another planet?" asked Blue. He and Red looked like ignorant backwoods hillbillies, but they were far from stupid. They had been in Elsewhen longer than most in Freetown and were known for the knowledge they obtained from other travelers.

"I guess," replied Stan.

"What happened?" asked Mark Stone.

"Dad shot him—or her," replied Debra. "The—being pointed a weapon at us, and Dad shot him with a spear gun we used for scuba fishing."

"How do you know it was a weapon?"

"We have it stashed," said the former paratrooper. "It's a regular raygun from some science fiction story or Flash Gordon."

Liam whistled. "When you get a chance, I'd like to see that."

"What did you do with the body of—It."

"We left it where it fell," said Stan. "I grabbed the weapon but was worried about alien bacteria. The Corona Virus back home scared us all enough."

"I took a photo with my cell phone," said Debra. "I turned it off as we were afraid of losing all the charge."

"That one of the pictures taking machines?" asked Red Macbeth. Debra nodded, and Red laughed. "I doubt I would have lived to see all that on Earth. But here on Elsewhen? I seen things people claim are just dreams and phantoms."

"Well, when you get the chance, I'd like to see the photo," said Mark. "It might help explain more about Elsewhen."

"I take it you want to fill those wagons full of salvage?" Mike Emerson asked.

"Yes, Sir. So, do we dicker or—"

"We don't own this. We are just caretakers."

"So, we can load up?"

"Yes, you can. I decided a long time ago that this belongs to those of us dumped here," replied Mike. "I mean, I won't let one group or another take control and deny others access."

Then the man grinned. "But we have gleaned some beneficial items that we claim as ours and are using for trade."

Mark laughed. "So now we dicker!"

The Freetown group spent two days exploring as much of the Smash Dump as they could. Mike haggled with them over some clean small fuel-powered generators. The Dawsons also produced some state-of-the-art solar panels, of which the former paratrooper had little knowledge. The stockade group used similar solar panels to create a limited power grid. Mike traded some relatively fresh fruit from packed coolers, newly canned vegetables, meat, and fruit, with some added medical supplies.

"These antibiotics will help," said Carol Dawson, a former Registered Nurse. Her husband was a structural engineer. Mark asked them both if they wanted to relocate to Freetown.

"I think we need to stay here and help Mike," replied Stan. "He needs us, especially to deal with new arrivals."

"He saved us," added Carol. "We were wandering all over the place when Mike brought us here to the stockade. It's home, now."

The Dawson's daughter Debra walked up, the former Woodstock flower child Tanya in tow. "Tanya wants to go to Freetown, Mister Stone," said Debra.

"How about you, Debra?" Mark asked.

The blonde young lady looked at her parents before answering. "Next year, I think. Have you set up some schools in Freetown?"

"My wife, the senior doctor, has organized a medical school. We have some military personnel teaching some skilled trades. As Freetown grows, so does the education system."

Light brown-haired Tanya went to gather her things. Mike thought she looked about eighteen. One minute she enjoyed the Woodstock Music Festival; the next, something or someone yanked Tanya to Elsewhen. Mark had a previous life; Tanya's life was barely starting.

Debra showed Mark Stone the photo of the dead Alien she had saved on her cell phone. The Mayor/President Pro tem looked at the photograph and exclaimed, "That is a stereotypical Grey. I thought they were a myth."

"I had a friend at school," replied Debra, "who was really into all the UFO stuff. I guess he wasn't as nuts as I thought he was at the time."

"Well, this gives me something to consider. Thanks for showing it to me, young lady."

Mark walked over and examined the filled wagons. In addition to scrap metal and other raw materials for construction, the group had located machinery and electronics to bring Freetown into at least the early 20th Century. A set of encyclopedias from the latter half of that century would help with the rapidly increasing young population's education. Plus, they returned with a rare find; two puppies, a male, and a female. Too many dogs were used as food or killed by the native predators.

As Mark stood and smiled with satisfaction at the haul of goods, he heard a voice behind him. "Mister, can I leave with you? I heard Tanya is going."

Mark turned to see the young Black boy introduced as William Adams standing behind him.

"How long have you been here, William?"

"Too long. The people here are friendly, even the two crack- I mean Southern men. But I have no family here, nobody who looks like me."

Mark tried to imagine showing up in Elsewhere at William's age with *no* support, friends, or family. He was lucky no Chinese merchant had grabbed him for sale as a slave.

"If you come with us, young man, when you get to Freetown, you'll have to stay with a family. Okay?"

"Yessir. "

"Your family on Earth, who were they?"

"We were sharecroppers in Mississippi, 1920."

Mark knew that life there sucked for a young Black male. "Any school?"

"Fourth grade. I read real good."

"That'll help. Get your stuff packed. We leave at sunrise in the morning."

Mark was up before dawn and shared coffee with Mike and Liam around a campfire. Mike relayed the story of watching a semi-tractor trailer appear above the edge of the Smash Dump and then crash downward. The paratrooper reached it a half-hour later to discover it abandoned by its driver. However, it was full of supplies for a well-known (over fifty years after Normandy) coffee shop chain. Coffee from the truck supplied the morning beverage as the three swapped stories.

"I'm coming up on my second anniversary since I dropped through the Rabbit Hole," said Mark.

"You left people behind?" asked Mike.

"A wife, sisters, no children, thank God. How about you. Mike?"

"Just my parents, a brother and a sister. I was waiting for the War to end before looking for a wife." He sighed. "I guess I'll have to visit Freetown to find a candidate."

"Well, I came here single also," said Liam. "I had a string of concubines with the Emperor. That is the one thing I miss from my days of service in New Bejing. I always had some bed warmers."

The three men laughed, and then Mike asked. "Mark, you have an Elsewhen wife now, yes?"

"Yep. Two sons." Mark slurped his coffee before continuing. "I am hoping the trip to Elsewhen gave me a shot of the Fountain of Youth from Ponce De Leon. Otherwise, I'll be old and decrepit when my sons get to the marrying age."

"You miss your Earth wife?"

"Hell, yeah. I love Cheri still as I love Susan here. If I somehow could make it back …" A frown formed on his face.

"You'll need to find a place that accepts polygamy," interjected Liam.

"Huh. I don't think either woman wants to share. However, the chances are remote the Rabbit Hole is a two-way street."

"You don't think the dead spaceman might have friends who can travel both ways?" Liam asked.

Mark finished off his cup of coffee in one gulp.

"Who knows? And since they shot some raygun at the Dawson family, they may not be friendly."

Mark Stone stood up and stretched. "Much as I

enjoy the company, it is time to leave.”

Mike stood up and stepped over to shake hands with Mark and Liam.

“Don't be a stranger, Mister Stone. Bring us more business. And people who want to help with the Smash Dump.”

“Maybe we can convince some people who are unhappy how things in Freetown,” said Liam, “and convince them to relocate.”

“No, Sir. I will not be transporting my problems to Mike. We are not Britain, and this is not Australia.”

Tanya and William approached the campfire with smiles on their faces. Just as they were about to voice a greeting, Tanya's eyes widened, and she screamed. Mark spun around in the direction Tanya looked, his Colt revolver out. Traveling on what looked like large platformed Earth drones were four Alien Greys. As Mike yelled a warning and Mark aimed his cocked pistol, soccerball-sized spheres exploded over the human's heads. Nets spread and fell over the five figures.

Mark fanned three rounds off before the net entangled him. He must have scored hits as one of the Greys fell off its flying platform. No one else could bring a gun to bear as the nets began to tighten around the five captives. Liam tried to free his Bowie knife but failed. Then the four Greys stood over them, one of them holding a damaged four-digit hand. The beings talked in some lisping and hissing language as the humans struggled to free themselves.

A loud booming report told Mark someone had a Sharps rifle out and working. One Grey's head snapped back on a long neck, and it fell to the ground. Another shot and what must be a weapon flew from the hand of one of the Greys. Three arrows plunged downward into one of the Greys in rapid succession as it fired an energy weapon. A bolt of energy went wide around the stockade. Another Sharps rifle spoke, and a struck Grey stumbled backward.

"Goddamned things have an armor of some such," Mark called out. "Aim for the heads."

Mark knew at any moment; Alien reinforcements would appear. He struggled to free his arms and reach his concealed .357 Magnum as three large-caliber rifles fired in unison. A flying platform was sent spinning throwing off into the sky as a Grey toppled to the sandy dirt. Another Grey shook off the effects of a 45-70 Sharps rifle shot and aimed a beam weapon at the projectiles' sources.

A blue beam flashed from the enclosure and sliced the armed Grey nearly in half. The three remaining aliens seemed stunned for a moment as they watched the smoldering body of their companion.

Young William used his less than adult size to wiggle free from under the capture netting. He lunged and recovered Mark's dropped Chinese clone Colt revolver. In one smooth motion, he fired a bullet into the face of the nearest Grey. This new attack spurred the remaining creatures into action despite its weak effect. One creature drew a bladed weapon and strode towards Willian. Mark was about to yell when a blue flash took the weapon arm off at the elbow. The Grey let loose with a scream none of the Earthlings would ever forget.

A barrage of forty-five and fifty caliber rifle bullets slammed into the Greys. They all stumbled and fell. The nets around the adults suddenly loosened as some control feature failed from damage. Mark scrambled to his feet and pulled his .357. Spotted Wolf appeared as if from thin air and fired arrow after arrow into the Greys' heads and faces before he could bring a weapon into action. Mike then used his paratrooper combat knife to slice the throats of any moving Grey.

All was quiet except for the whirring of two orbiting flying platforms. It took a few moments to ensure there were no more aliens and check the humans for injuries.

"They had some form of electricity-backed armor," said Mike.

"Star Trek," said Stan Dawson as he approached with a Grey raygun in his hands. Mike gave him a quizzical look at the mention of the old television program. Mark walked over to the Dawsons and hugged them all.

"Thanks for saving our butts."

"Any time, Mark Stone. We need to keep you all in business so we can visit a city someday."

Blue and Red managed to get the mules calmed

down and hooked up to the wagons. Liam produced a bottle of Scotch, and everyone had a calming drink, including William. Mark recovered one of the energy pistols from the Greys and stashed it under his conveyance's seat.

"Where'd they come from?" asked Mike Emerson.

"Good question," replied Mark. "I think you all need to hunker down in the stockade while we beat feet to Freetown for some reinforcements."

"I will ride ahead," stated Spotted Wolf. "I will warn Freetown, then bring some militia back."

"Good idea. Take off, friend."

The Comanche was off in a flash. The three wagons followed in five minutes. William rode with Mark, and Tanya rode with Blue. The loaded wagons would be slower than when they were empty, but it could not be helped. The three wagon loads were the reason they were here.

"Think they'll be back?" William asked.

"Hard to say, William. Grey Aliens in my time are part of fantasy and conspiracy theory. I guess at least here they are real."

"Think Mike and the others can fight them off?"

"Yep. Those two former Confederates are tough; their shooting helped to save us. The Dawsons have that energy weapon also."

The two humans rode in silence. Then William asked, "Who will I live with?"

"We have some Black families in Freetown. Or maybe an Asian or Caucasian family. We'll work it out."

A few moments later, William spoke again. "Could I live with you?"

"Yeah. But I'm not Black."

"So? At least you're not Grey."

Mark Stone, Mayor and President Pro Tem of Freetown's city-state, looked at the Black youth and began to laugh. William soon joined in. The mules added their brays to the joyful sound.

At that moment, life was good, as it could and should be, even in Elsewhen.

# 14
# PANZER

Mark Stone, President ProTem of the city-state of Freetown, sat on his front porch sipping a glass of local bourbon and branch water. His Elsewhen wife and local senior doctor, Susan Von Braun, was nursing their two healthy twins, one boy, and one girl, in a padded chair next to him. Mark rested his feet on a locally produced settee well padded with hair from a llama-like creature and leather-like skin from a Standing Dragon, a local cross between a man-tall Godzilla and a T-rex. He sipped his drink once again and sighed in satisfaction.

"Nothing like a not-too-hot sunny day in Freetown," he said, "sitting on my veranda and watching the world go by."

Susan grinned at him.

"It does not take much to keep men such as you happy, my husband," said the buxom brunette lady.

"Compared to what, almost two years ago? This is

paradise, Susan."

After falling through the rabbit hole to Elsewhen, he'd met Susan on this planet with two moons and numerous people and things from multiple places and times. Not too long ago, Mark had encountered some ET Aliens from God knew where. So, Elsewhen was a dumping ground for someone or something. There was even a Smash Dump Mountain, a pile of machines, metal, and salvage from who knew where.

The one point of contention was that Mark had left a wife he loved, Cheri, behind on 21st Century Earth. As the chances of finding a reverse rabbit hole were remote, Mark made the best of it.

Mark had saved Susan from the deprivations of the other significant pain in the butt, the Emperor of New Beijing and his minions. He and the citizens of Freetown had been fighting with them ever since. The personnel aboard a C-17 Globemaster medivac aircraft, an M-48 tank crew, a real-life Marshal Dillion, and transported frontiersmen (and a Comanche warrior) helped keep Freetown from the clutches of the Emperor. Thus. Mark could sit and enjoy local libations with his local wife and two children.

"Time to change your children," said Susan.

"Want some help with Sam and Samantha?"

"No, you sit there and enjoy the simple pleasures. Quiet is a valuable commodity, between sewing head stitches and settling disputes between merchants."

"Thank you, my dear."

Susan blew him a kiss as she carried the twins into their four-bedroom house. Mark had added onto an existing cabin at the Westend of Freetown, set back some twenty-five yards off Mainstreet. Thus, Mark could sit and watch while dodging most of the dust and bad smells of what looked like a late 19th Century-Old West Town. In some respects, it was now a town in the 20th Century with hydro-powered electricity from a dammed river, a modern hospital, and staff (the Medivac personnel helped with that), plus an organized militia and arms manufacturing. Many claimed it was the coming of Mark and Susan that started it all. Mark did not care why; he was just glad things were better.

Mark sipped his drink with the melting ice cubes thanks to electricity and mused. "Not bad, bourbon," he mumbled. "Next, we try scotch. "

The town klaxon went off, and Mark almost dumped his drink.

"Damnit," he exclaimed as he stood up and grabbed the hardline telephone near the front door. Freetown had a primitive two-wire party line system with a switchboard at the Grand Hotel. Electricity for the soon-to-be 20,000 citizens in Freetown city-state limits had been the primary project. A crude crystal radio system with one broadcast channel worked, with a comprehensive telephone system the next priority. He had a portable military radio in his front room to contact the C-17 and the M-48 tank, but that was it. When they could start manufacturing transistors and tubes-he delayed that thought as he cranked a bell ringing device to alert the switchboard.

"Mary? Connect me with the lookouts, please."

Young Hans Gruber on the Eastside lookout tower began rambling in German when he picked up the phone in his station. Wang Lin was at the Eastside lookout and yelled in the phone line, "English!"

"Tank! Like the M-48!"

"Where?"

"Two miles away, coming slow."

"Okay. Keep watch."

Mark scrambled into the front room and grabbed the handheld radio. "Virgil, or whoever is on duty. You have armored company headed your way!"

"Roger, Mister President." It was Tank Jefferson to differentiate Gunny Sergeant Jefferson on the C-17. It was found that, in the Earth timeline, Tank Jefferson was a long-lost uncle of C-17 Jefferson. Thus, Mark knew that humans seem to come from the same Earth, just at different times. Or was that always the case?

"What do you have loaded?"

"One of the reload training rounds." With armorer Chris Walker's help and some several hundred pounds of iron ore received as trade from the Amazon's at Iron Mountain, they replaced the easily fragmented light pot metal shell with heat hardened capped armor-piercing shell on several of the remaining practice 90MM rounds. They reloaded two shell casings from fired rounds as a combination of beehive/canister rounds. The tankers also still had the two issued armor-piercing rounds, one High Explosive and one Willie Pete round.

Mark grabbed his lever action .44 rifle and scrambled out to his motorbike in the attached garage/stable. Susan stood on the porch as he pushed the vehicle out to the street.

"You be careful, husband."

"Always, my dear. But the work of a President and Commander in Chief is never done." Mark cranked the engine, revved it, jumped on the bike, and took off to the West.

He met Mike Virgil and the other Tankers at the M-48. The Sergeant First Class used binoculars to examine the now stopped possible threat.

"What do we have?" asked Mark.

"Believe it or not, it looks like an old Africa Corps Mark-IV tank, with a half-track mounted anti-aircraft gun behind it. The vehicles halted, and an officer is conversing with two men on a motorcycle and sidecar."

"World War Two Germans, maybe Nazis?"

"Yes. But nothing our main gun can't handle."

James Chou, the current Militia Commander, came jogging up with two dozen rifle-armed militia.

"Are those armored vehicles I see?" James asked.

"Yep," answered Mark. "Germans, maybe a

few Nazis."

"Want me to call out the reserves and the gun crews?"

"Let me go talk first. The tank crew can blow our new visitors to kingdom come if they don't want to talk friendly-like."

Liam O'Grady, the new Secretary of State for Freetown, due to his gift of gab and past dealing with Emperor of New Bejing, walked up to the group.

"Anything I can do?" Liam asked.

"Want to take a stroll and greet the potential new immigrants to Freetown?"

Liam shrugged. "Sure, Mark, why not?"

The panzer and the half-track had remained motionless since coming within a mile of Freetown. Liam hopped on the back of Mark's motorbike, and they slowly wheeled out towards the vehicles. Mark stopped the motorbike and fifty yards from the actual German machines, Maltese Crosses and all.

"I hope someone speaks English, as my German is limited," Mark called out.

A man who walked with the air of authority slowly walked towards the Freetown officials as several soldiers with small arms covered him.

"Lieutenant Paul Hauser, commander of this small unit," the light brown-haired officer called out in accentless English. "May I ask with whom I am speaking? "

"President Pro Tem Mark Stone, of Freetown city-state. Liam O'Grady, next to me, is our Secretary of State. I think I recognize some Afrika Corps markings on your tank."

The Lieutenant smiled and walked closer. "You have me at a disadvantage, Mein Herr. You know something about me; I know next to nothing about you."

Mark smiled back and reached into a saddlebag he removed from his motorbike. "How about you share some local bourbon whiskey with me while I tell you the truth of Freetown. You and your men will need some alcohol to understand what I am about to say."

The half-track crew produced folding chairs, and Paul Hauser introduced an Italian Lieutenant from the motorcycle sidecar.

"May I present Nico Sgarlato, Lieutenant from the Italian forces here in North Africa."

"El Presidente," the Italian officer said as he saluted Mark. The former special agent grinned.

"If you could produce some cups and glasses to share this alcohol, I will explain why this is *not* North Africa."

"Before that conversation," said Paul Hauser, "do you have a doctor? We have a wounded man who needs attention."

"My wife is the senior doctor here. Excuse me while I radio for an ambulance."

After a rebuilt SUV from the Smash Dump picked the wounded soldier up and hauled ass to the Freetown Hospital, Mark sat down and began pouring drinks. Only the officers drank with him.

"Our soldiers have limited English, Mister President," explained the German Lieutenant. "Nico and I will explain the situation after we understand it."

"How long have you been here?" asked Liam.

"Two days," answered Paul.

"You saw the two moons and the bright star at night people call Night Sun?"

"We thought it might be a-mirage?" said Nico.

Mark explained it as quickly and as thoroughly as possible. There was no good reason to sugarcoat the reality, especially to armed soldiers who were in a shooting war days before.

"So, Elsewhen is a… planet?" asked Paul.

"Seems to be," said Mark as he poured them all another drink. When the President of Freetown had produced ice cubes from a thermos, the two officers' eyes widened slightly.

"And you are in charge," said Paul as he sipped his drink.

"Duly elected as Mayor in Freetown, and trying to set up an election for President."

"Which I tell him is a waste of time as the people will elect him in a landslide," said Liam.

"Having a President by a board is not suitable for a true Republic, Liam."

"So, you have Americans, Chinese, Germans, English, and Japanese here—how about Italians?" asked Nico

"A few here. On the Great Eastern Sea, there is a New Rome, formed by some Romans and Italians from the time of the Roman Empire and beyond."

"The passage of time here is not normal," said Paul. "Plus, there is no rhyme nor reason who arrives here. Nor do you know who and why does this—populating of Elsewhen."

"You got it, Paul," Mark said. "People who show up either adapt or go nuts and die. Sometimes it's by suicide."

Paul and Nico sipped their drinks in silence. Then the Italian spoke. "I have just Sergeant Argento Salvatore. We stumbled upon Paul Hauser while reforming after Kasserine Pass."

"You kicked some American ass there," replied Mark.

"So, our time is your history," said Paul.

"A history, maybe a slightly different timeline. We can't tell as we don't know how this all happens. It just does."

"Then, my new drinking partner Mark Stone, how does a German Officer with thirteen soldiers plus a tank and a half-track figure into this reality?"

"That is up to you and Nico. We accept all peaceful people, or not so gentle, as long as they fight on our side."

"We shot four Chinese horsemen on our way here," Nico interjected. "They tried to stop us as if we belonged to them."

"The Emperor's men, snooping around. We are in an ongoing conflict with him. Liam used to work for the guy before he saw the light."

Paul looked at the Irish-American. "Some Irish helped Germany against England."

"Well, Lieutenant, that is a different time and place. I'm with Freetown now."

"We could offer our services to the Chinese if we wished," replied the German officer.

"You could," answered Mark Stone. "How much fuel do you have? He is a good week or two travel east, depending on your speed."

"So, what do you want?" asked Nico.

"Peace. Expansion of our standard of living. We have electricity, are trying to refine petroleum ooze into decent fuel. You could help us in our endeavors or can leave. We don't accept Nazis, Marxist Revolutionaries, nor Fascists here if they try to force their ideas onto others." Mark threw back the remains of his drink. "I did not want to, but I had to start training people for war, create an alliance with the Amazons from the West. We have killed thousands. If you try to take what is ours, we will kill you."

The German Officer finished his drink and

stood up.

"I will have to discuss this with my men. I am a Party member for career advancement. I have no problems with Jews or Gypsies. Some of my men are not so understanding."

"I will want to stay with you, Mark Stone," said Nico. "At least until I can find a way home. Sgt. Salvatore will stay with me."

"Okay. You'll have to find a trade to support yourself."

Mark stood up and shook the German's and Italian's hand. "Time for me to return to Freetown and wait for your answer. It was nice talking to you, Lieutenant Hauser."

"Likewise, as you say in America. I will give you an answer in the hour."

Mike and Liam rode the motorbike back to the edge of town.

"What's the status?" asked Sgt. Virgil.

"We will find out in an hour. Get ready for trouble if the Panzerwaffen Officer decides he wants to try and take the town. However, as one of his men used a captured BAR to cover us, I think they are short of fuel and ammunition. Liam, you want to brief the Globemaster people? Just in case the Germans decide to go all Nazi on us."

"Will do."

"And get ahold of our Amazon Representative

Leslie Owens. They have their own German problems. If Paul Hauser decides to hook up with his brethren from Imperial Germany, we may have a big problem."

An hour passed. Then Mark noticed Paul Hauser walking towards them. The President of Freetown drove his motorbike out to meet him.

"Well, Lieutenant, what's the decision?"

"We will bring our equipment up to the edge of your Freetown. We will post a guard to keep it from being damaged or stolen. The men want to keep their sidearms as they examine your town."

"Okay. We are what came to mean in my time an 'open carry' city. I'll introduce you to Marshal Dillon, and he'll tell you what will get you in trouble. We have two legal houses of prostitution, a bunch of drinking establishments, and restaurants, not to mention many family-owned businesses. Treat everyone with respect, and you should not have any problems."

"Most of the soldiers want to see if this might be a new home. Most have realized the chances of us seeing our own Moon and not the two moons are minute."

Mark Stone arranged to park the half-track and tank near the lookout tower. The two Italians drove their motorcycle downtown and parked in front of an Italian Pizza restaurant. The two Italian soldiers were soon having an old home week with the family who owned the eatery. The dozen Germans were much more reserved.

The people in Europe and Russia saw the German as an aggressive occupying army and did not welcome them. Thus, the Germans watched their backs and throats. Plus, a couple might be hardened Nazis. Mark had no way to interview everyone who came to Elsewhen and Freetown to see if they were stone-cold bigots who wanted to build a new Dachau.

Marshall Dillon gave a short "Come to Jesus" lecture to the Germans.

"We have people of all beliefs and skin color here," the Marshal said. "Don't start fights with them, or you may wind up with your throat slit unless I get to you first. We have a nice new jail here and lots of community projects that could use some prison labor."

Mark went to the hospital and talked to his wife, Susan. She made it a point to treat the injured German soldier, bringing their Twins with her to the hospital. Susan pigeon-holed him and demanded all the details. At the end of the explanation, Susan stated, "We will invite Lieutenant Hauser over for dinner. He will be as lonely as we were coming to Elsewhen."

"What if he turns out to be a closet Nazi?" Mark asked.

"That is before my time, remember? From what you said, Hitler was recovering from World War One when I was in China."

Mark knew that a happy wife means a happy life, so he searched for Paul Hauser the next day. He found the panzer commander still riding heard on his men.

"Hello, Herr Hauser. My German wife Susan states I must invite you for dinner."

Paul smiled and nodded. "I will gladly come if it helps you have a good life here."

"How are your men holding up?"

"The ones with families, children are the ones having the most difficult. Six of the twelve are in that category."

"I forgot to ask. Do you have a family in Germany?"

"No. My military career interfered with me settling down, as people say." The Lieutenant looked around. "I see a vibrant city more than just a town here. There are many former Europeans and Americans in Freetown. What is your population?"

"Good question. I need to take an official census. I think within five miles of Freetown itself and downtown added in, we are now close to twenty thousand. Hard to remember that when I showed up about two years ago, there were less than five thousand residents."

"Under your leadership, it has grown."

Mark laughed. "There was a lot of chance and luck involved, like having the C-17 Medivac aircraft show up, then a tank, plus two young Russian engineering students. Everything came together to keep us free from the Emperor and create niceties like electric power and indoor plumbing. By the way, any German soldiers with mechanical and technical skills will have a job if they ask for one."

"I will double-check, Mark Stone. I know my large panzer gunner, Helmut Ritgen, comes from a long line of butchers. So, if you have a slaughterhouse, he will be at home."

"That may be next, Paul, as we expand our beef herd. A bunch of longhorn cattle appeared on the edge of town last month."

"What time do you wish me to arrive?"

"Come on by our house at six tomorrow evening. Everyone knows where we live, so ask someone to point it out."

"Thank you. Tell your wife I look forward to meeting her."

The following day, Mark was doing his regular POF (President of Freetown) when a Deputy contacted him in his office on Mainstreet.

"Sir, Marshall Dillon asks you to meet him at the Grand Hotel. There is a problem, and he needs to talk with you."

"I'm on my way, Lad."

Mark locked his office door and left the office he shared with Liam O'Grady and a local lawyer. Mark had decided a long time ago that he did not need any pomp or circumstance, to include private offices. The POF quickly walked over to the Grand with the military radio in his hand. He kept it close at hand these days as more and more people and things were dropping into Elsewhere at the damndest time.

Matt Dillon met him at the front, talking to the Grand Hotel Manager. It was next to Ma Bell's Saloon and Bawdy House, Ma Bell being the hotel owner. She supported Mark Stone for Mayor and had grown in property and influence, helped by she ran well-kept establishments and provided clean ladies of the evening. Now, something terrible had happened.

"Hey, Marshal," Mark said in greeting.

"Mister President," Matt said with a tip of his cowboy hat.

"I'd wish you'd call me Mark. I still look around for someone else when they say, President."

Matt Dillon chuckled, then motioned towards Bob Smyth, the hotel manager. "Bob has a problem we are trying to keep under wraps right now. Bob, lead on, please."

The slender mixed-race man led the two officials to a back hotel room and unlocked the door. Inside the room was a bathtub containing the body of a man. Mark saw the blood-tainted water.

"Killed himself?" asked Mark as he looked at the German uniform item piled on the nearby chair.

"Yes. Sir, it appears that way. I guess we could ask your wife or one of the other doctors to act as a coroner, but I think it's pretty evident."

"Yes, Matt, it is. We'll need to contact Lt. Hauser.

He's coming over to my place for dinner, so I can probably get him to open up about the man later tonight, get the details about him.”

"Sounds good to me. I'll locate Hauser and tell him what happened. I hope this doesn't upset the apple cart. So far, everyone's been friendly.”

"You and me both, Matt. I'll feel Hauser out, see if any of the other Germans may have problems.” Mark looked at the hotel manager.

"Quiet about this, okay?”

"You got it, Boss,” replied Bob.

Paul Hauser arrived at Matt and Susan's house promptly at Six PM. Susan met him at the door, rattled a German greeting to him, then slipped into English.

"My husband speaks Spanish but is slow on the uptake with German.”

"No problem, Mrs. Stone. These flowers and bottle of German Schnapps are for you.” Paul turned towards Mark, clicked his heels, and spoke.

"President Stone, it is an honor to be invited into your home.”

Mark stepped forward and shook the German's hand.

"Please accept my condolences on the death of your countryman. Both Susan and I can attest the trip to Elsewhen is not pleasant for many.”

"I thank you for your caring," replied Paul. "I also thank you for helping my men transcend into this new—life."

"Was the young man married back on Earth?" asked Susan.

"Yes, with a newborn. The thought of Fritz Bayerling's inability to return to his family was too much. So he took a Roman Death."

Paul Hauser smiled. "But let us not dwell on the sad. I smell some German cooking. May we enjoy it together?"

Susan's cooking was the hit of the evening, Paul having existed on field rations for months. The food in town was good, but it lacked the homecooked taste. His tale was an up-and-coming Africa Corps panzer leader who received a Mark IV Special tank command with the longer high-velocity gun. He and his crew had five kills with the newer tank to add to several former hits and destroyed vehicles. What looked like a sand storm separated the tank from his unit, and then they were in Elsewhen.

"We found the half-track under the command of Senior Sergeant Hans Gruber; Fritz was one of his crew. Then, Nico rode upon us on his motorcycle. The rest is now—Elsewhen history."

"So, what is the feedback, the opinions on the future from your men?" asked Mark.

"My tank crew wants to stay together, The anti-aircraft gun crew, less so. I think Fritz's death points to confusion as to what they want."

Paul took the final bite of some arcane potato and sausage dish from Susan, laughed, and then patted his stomach. "If I were married to you, Frau Stone, I would soon be fat and lazy. Your husband has a stronger will than I when it comes to homecooked German food."

Susan laughed, stood up, and retrieved a bottle of local aperitif. "I think you will enjoy this after-dinner drink made from local plums. There is a kick to it, as the Americans say."

"I believe there are some young European maidens in and around Freetown," said Mark. "One of them probably has cooking skills and would love to find a young military officer."

The cries from the Twins in the adjoining room interrupted the conversation.

"Excuse me, Gentlemen. Duty and feeding time intrudes."

Mark and Paul stood as Susan smiled and went to feed Samuel and Samantha.

The men sat back down, and Mark topped off their drinks.

"Speaking of attractive young women, Mark, I had a pleasant conversation with Leslie Owens, the Amazon representative."

"Let me guess. Leslie mentioned some Germans on the eastern Other Sea."

"Yes. She warned me about investing any loyalty with these Imperial Germans from a time just before the First World War."

*Good old Leslie,* thought Mark. *I wonder if she was this blunt before becoming an Amazon in Elsewhen.*

"Well, those Germans and some coastal people want Iron Mountain. The Amazons control it since about two hundred years ago, based on my information. And, since the Amazons and Freetown have a treaty, well, if the Germans there attack..." Mark spread his hands in supplication.

"You would supply military aid," Paul said as he sipped his drink.

"Yep. I gave my word thus I would honor the treaty."Mark sipped his drink. "They trade us iron ore, some warriors when needed to push back the Chinese; we supply them with ammunition, a form of wool, and soon some beef cattle. I hope to start a herd there. Oh, and stud services to selected females."

Paul frowned. "I am a bit confused. Am I missing something in translation?"

Mark laughed. "I guess Leslie failed to mention the Amazons need fresh blood, in a genetic sense. They understand the dangers of inbreeding and have limited males in their society?'

"They are not followers of Lesbos?"

"Some are, Paul. But you need man spunk to make babies. So, we are not yet obsolete."

Paul paused in thought, then spoke. "Leslie is, or was, an American, yes?"

"American military. There is a small unit of armed Americans living with and helping the Amazons. They have some medical knowledge that we add to and support the Amazons."

"So, Fraulein Owens is not betrothed to anyone?"

Mark laughed again. "No, and she seems to prefer men. Good luck in courting her, though. This thing with the Germans on the coast is a big sticky point."

The German panzer commander smiled. "She is attractive, strong, and intelligent. And, I am now out of Hitler's war. What better pastime but to court the unattainable?"

"I'll toast to that, Herr Hauser. But do not let frustration get the best of you."

Paul's mouth formed into a sly smile. "You have two bawdy houses, as some people call them. I do not think I will be frustrated."

After a pleasant night of drinking and picking Paul Hauser's brain, the next day, Mark Stone went looking for the Amazon Ambassador, former Senior Airman Leslie Owens. He found her at the main stables, currying her horse.

"So, you mentioned the Germans who are giving you Amazons grief."

"Might as well. Paul Hauser and the others will

find out soon enough from the locals. They know the story since Chabra first came here hunting the giant monitor lizards. What Amazons call Dragons."

"Well, I was hoping to break it to them slowly, not tell them there are former Imperial Germans with desires of an imperial empire."

"This way, these possible Nazis know they will have to pick sides and face the consequences."

"Again, I am trying to integrate a group of soldiers who just came from a warzone into normal society. Or at least, normal for Elsewhen."

Leslie Owens laughed. "I like your optimism. But since my fellow Security Police and I popped into existence here, all I have seen is war and strife."

"Well, my hard-headed young lady, I, for one, still try to have less war and strife."

Leslie smiled at him. "The Captain said I was hard-headed also. So do the Amazons. That is why they accepted me over the rest of the women in the group."

Mark shook his head in frustration. Circumstances had delayed a planned trip of his to Amazonia to deal with the Queen face to face and meet Captain Milner, who held the remaining USAF personnel from 1979 together as a cohesive unit. Leslie told him the Amazons respected her fellow military men and women, especially since they brought weapons and used them to fight off the Imperials. Some Marksman Training Unit personnel's technical ability with the Cops helped the existing scientific bent local males produce weapons. Freetown's trade agreements to provide ammunition and other usable trade goods cemented a friendly relationship Mark did not want to see stressed because some German soldiers appeared."

"Well, my hard-headed ambassador, please don't start any fights."

"Amazons don't start fights. We just finish them and then ride away."

President Pro-tem walked the streets of Freetown, which took longer and longer as the small town turned into a city. Mark called it a city-state, with the C-17 aircraft and its personnel referred to as the separate independent community of Globemaster. The separation of powers meant the Medivac personnel kept distinct decision-making abilities. Mark saw people in Elsewhere seemed to screw things up when they had too much centralized control.

The streets hustled and bustled with activity as Mark walked. Since the last kerfuffle with the Emperor's minions and the butt-kicking they took thanks to the timely arrival of Amazon Calvary, there had been a distinct increase in merchant caravans. The word was out there was a people who resisted the Emperor's chains and provided strange new products, like electricity, high-end medical treatments, and modern smokeless powder firearms. People with money used merchant caravans as cover and took various routes into Freetown to not face the ruler's wrath. They bought clothes made from a local form of cotton, sampled the steel from the small forges, which popped up thanks to Amazon iron ore and began eating beef venison and beef steaks. With a large herd of temperamental longhorns as a new resource, Mark thought he would have a thousand head of beef cattle by the end of the Elsewhen year. The next step would be enough cattle for animal drives to New Rome and Camelot on the coast of the Great Eastern Sea as a way of introduction. Information Mark gleaned from new immigrants and merchants stated other than milk cows, people in Elsewhen never saw the occasional wild beeves as a herdable resource. The Chinese raised many chickens and pigs, there were goats, oversized llamas, and sheeplike creatures kept by various peoples in the Northern Mountains. Elsewhen residents hunted beef cattle and occasional bison more as pests than as a renewable resource. Small antelope seemed to be the preferred venison.

A single Mexican Vaquero showed up some six months ago, trying to find a priest to absolve his sins. Juan Garcia thought he was in Purgatory at least, and it took some convincing by Mark and a couple of other Spanish speakers that he was not in some level of Hell. After accepting that he was stuck here, the young man offered his services to help bring in a few while cattle into Freetown before one of the Great Dragons he saw sunning itself ate them. Thus, Cowboying grew in Freetown.

Mark smiled as people greeted him during his walk, forced food and drinks on him. When he walked by the bawdy houses and the evening ladies came out to greet him, they knew better than expected him to sample their wares. Susan was their primary gynecologist, and they would not risk her wrath. He would have to visit the new veterinarian in town, an old horse doctor named Evan Cable. The two dogs he had obtained from Mike Emerson at the Smash Dump produced pups now under the close care of Doctor Cable. Trying to get the Chinese to stop the traditional habit of eating dogs was not easy. Mark wanted as many working dogs as possible in the years to come. Leslie told him that among the personnel in her USAF group were some military working dog handlers. That was a resource he wanted to tap as soon as he could visit the Amazons.

A loud cry, followed by the sounds of arguing, caused Mark to speed his walk to a slow jog. A small crowd was forming around a couple of figures, one male and one female. Mark quickly saw the young lady Ivana Klimenko, a resident technician, entrepreneur, and Spotted Wolf, the Comanche's wife. The man Mark recognized as Helmut Ritgen, the tank gunner for the Mark IV.

Helmut was yelling and cursing at Ivana as Mark approached.

"Hey, Sergeant. Cool it." Mark's loud voice got Helmut's attention. The giant German sneered and spit.

"Filthy Russians. My brother dead on the Eastern Front," the man said in passable English.

"Well, that was then; this is now. How about I buy you a drink—"

The German cursed loudly using words Susan did when she was angry.

"Now, Helmut—" Mark stepped forward and was rewarded with a fist aimed at his face. Mark half blocked it and stumbled back. The redfaced soldier pulled a slab-sided pistol from under his shirt, which Mark recognized as a liberated Colt 1911 .45.

"Shit—" said the retired special agent as he went for his Ruger revolver.

Marshal Dillon moved fast for a large man. One swing of his long-barreled Colt Peacemaker and he buffaloed Helmut to the ground. Two of his deputies appeared and slapped irons on the large and now stunned panzer Soldaten.

"How many times must I tell our President and Mayor to leave enforcing the law to me and mine?" Matt asked gruffly.

"Sorry, Marshal. I was trying to talk him down and failed."

"We'll let this German spend the night in our lockup. I'll see if the Judge wants to see him in the morning."

"I'll have Paul Hauser visit him, see if he can soothe his anger."

"I was just speaking Russian to a store clerk, and this German started yelling at us," interjected Ivana. "I think I smell vodka on his breath."

"Sorry about this, Ivana. Speaking Russian is not a crime in Freetown."

Seemingly out of nowhere, Spotted Wolf appeared with murder in his eyes. Some bad news traveled fast in Freetown. Mark stepped in his way.

"It's over, my friend. No one laid a hand on your wife."

"I will kill him if he tries again," said Spotted Wolf.

"Please let us handle it, okay?"

"Since you ask me, yes." The Comanche then took Ivana by her arm and led her away. Mark and the Comanche had been through a lot, and Mark was Ivana's adopted Uncle. Thus, Spotted Wolf trusted him.

As Marshal Dillon made sure Helmut reached the hoosegow, Mark Stone went looking for Paul. He was surprised when he found him at the stables with Leslie Owens as she fed and brushed her horse.

"The President seeks me out, so there must be a problem," said the German officer with a bit of a smile. Mark gave him a quick and dirty description of what happened.

"So, I will see Helmut in jail in the morning," said

Paul Hauser. "I was just discussing with Leslie the concept of keeping a military unit together when the home military no longer exists, at least in this reality."

"I was just explaining to the Lieutenant what happened in 1945," Leslie said with a bit of a mischievous grin.

*I'm going to have to have a talk with her about appropriate timing,* thought Mark.

"No real shock to you, Paul?" asked Mark Stone.

The German officer shrugged. "We knew things were not going well by 1943," replied Paul. "I am surprised Adolf Hitler killed himself. But, I have no reason not to believe our Amazon here." Paul smiled at the lithe young lady. "And please, Leslie, call me Paul. I think military rank will disappear soon as not being important."

Leslie smiled at the handsome German, which surprised the President of Freetown. Leslie was compartmentalizing the Imperial Germans' problems with the Amazons while she was friendly with at least one of the 'new' Germans. At least, that would reduce future strife between the groups in Freetown. At least, that was Mark's hope.

"Well, after Leslie's time, East and West Germany reunited and became a One Germany European powerhouse. "

"You can't keep us down, Mark. The German spirit is tough."

"Think that will enable you and the other soldiers

to make a new home in Elsewhen?"

"I think so. Whether in Freetown is a question." Paul frowned. "Helmut shows underlying frustration as we realize the chance of returning to Germany is nil."

"Well, those with skills or a desire to work are welcome here. We have a lot of projects as we approach twenty thousand population in our city-state."

"I will have to arrange a meeting of us Germans. I do not want to lose any more comrades in arms." Paul Hauser turned towards Leslie, smiled, bowed slightly, and clicked his heels.

"Until next time Fraulein."

"Of course- Paul."

Mark watched as the German officer went on a mission to round up the other Germans. It was difficult enough for an individual who 'fell' into Elsewhen to adapt. A military unit amid a war? That was something else. Mark smiled at Leslie.

"So, what will Chabra saw if the Ambassador is playing footsies with some Germans?"

"How can I play footsie in a stable?" replied Leslie as she tried not to smile.

"Hey, you're talking to an old Cop here. I've seen it all or did it at least once myself. "

"Paul is friendly, intelligent, is not a Nazi—"

"Hansome, debonair—"

"Oh, stop it. I'm of age to make my own decisions. Amazons are allowed to pair-bond. They just don't do it very often. When you have a guy and home, kids usually follow. That interferes with your responsibility as a warrior."

"Which is why you have a small population of traditional mothers who become pregnant and raise babies."

"They also raise the occasional 'accident' when someone's birth control fails. Amazons do not believe in abortion. They need all the warriors they can find."

"What about boy babies?"

"They're raised to become our technicians, craftsmen, medical people. However, the Amazon's try to use as studs those men who seem to produce the right sperm for girl babies. If we offer a man a position as a Sire, if the first child is male, rarely are they used for procreation again."

"Well, we men do determine the gender of the baby. So that seems logical."

"Amazon's have a rich and long history. We currently have just over a thousand female children. And a dozen males."

"But your nation still looks for new blood?"

"Inbreeding is a problem Amazons had in the more ancient past. It led to some genetic weaknesses and many deaths due to disease. It has not been a problem for over two Elsewhen centuries."

"Do you want kids?" Mark asked.

"I have not decided yet. Were your

twins planned?"

"Honestly, no. I had no children on Earth with my wife. With Susan—" Mark paused for a moment. It had been both a joy and a terror when Susan become pregnant. A father in his fifties when he should be a grandfather was a shock at first. Now, he had two young ones to help carry on Freetown.

"Well, since I don't see a way back, I'll have to plan on growing old here," Leslie said. "So, I'll have to decide if I want to be pregnant."

"That is the one advantage men have. We don't have to worry about carrying a baby for nine months, then care for it and all the rest."

"Yeah, you can be deadbeats and disappear. At least as an Amazon, we have lots of sisters to help."

Mark could see the pluses of such a sisterhood, especially in a world like Elsewhen. People needed to band together in a place where people and things could just drop in from the sky.

Mark bid farewell to Leslie and continued on his rounds. He talked with various business owners and merchants, eliciting information on how the Germans fitted in. For the most part, things seemed going well with few complaints. Mark hoped that reality would continue. The Day Sun was setting as Mark walked home and met Susan. Marianna Klimenko still lived with them as she had not found a mate like her sister Ivana. Which was just fine with Mark as Marianna helped care for the Twins.

"I heard my sister had a problem today with a drunk German."

"Marshal Dillon took care of it. The miscreant is spending a night in jail. Which prevented Spotted Wolf from slicing his throat."

"He is very protective of her," replied Marianna.

"The Comanche have a reputation in the Old West of being hard on their women, working them to a frazzle."

Marianna grinned. "Ivana set the rules before the wedding. No male chauvinist crap or she walks. We have our own income."

Mark laughed. Parts of Elsewhen seemed downright progressive compared to more primitive areas. Suppose there some rhyme or reason to who arrived here and how things would be more comfortable. Mark relaxed with Susan and the Twins after dinner. The one thing he missed sometimes was being able to zone out in front of the television. Someday, maybe, he'd bring television entertainment to Freetown. Then, people from all periods in history could rot their brains.

Mark was sleeping soundly when the hardline former military field phone rang. The Freetown administration salvaged an old field network from the Smash Dump and installed it in various strategic spots in the soon-to-be small city. The President's home was one spot.

"Yeah? What! I'll be right there."

A sleepy Susan looked at him. "What happened?"

"The damned Soldatans are using the anti-aircraft halftrack to break Helmut out of jail."

"I'll come with you. Marianna will watch the Twins. You will need a good German speaker."

Susan and Mark threw some clothes on, and she rode on the back of the motorbike. Within minutes they were at the jail. Matt Dillonstood out front, facing down a 37MM Anti Aircraft Gun while holding an 1897 Winchester pump twelve gauge. He was not one to be pushed away from his duty, no matter what the odds. Mark and Susan clambered off the motorbike, with Mark stepping towards the Germans with hands upraised.

"How about we all calm down?"

"Go away!" snapped back one soldier standing next to the half-track holding a Luger pointed towards the jailhouse.

Susan broke into a stream of Deutsch at the five soldiers, chewing ass based on her tone. The Luger-holder snapped back with abuses and curse words even Mark recognized. The President began to step forward with violence in his eyes.

"Halten Sie!" The voice of Paul Hauser reverberated down the street as he strode up. The officer strode directly towards the pistol holder. When the man started to talk back, Paul stopped his comments with a fist to the jaw. The German collapsed to the street, and Paul scooped up the dropped pistol. He yelled commands in German as he fired a round inches above the gun crew's heads. In seconds, the four soldiers were standing at attention on the street. Paul proceeded to walk up to each soldier and scream in his face. After a five-minute diatribe, Paul walked up to Susan and Mark.

"I apologize for this unprofessional and rude behavior. If we were still in North Africa, they would be in chains or possibly shot. Using Army equipment for a personal dispute? Never!"

"I appreciate their anger," interjected Marshal Dillon. "However, I can't release my prisoner while there is a complaint pending."

"If I withdraw the complaint?" asked Mark. "He tried to hit me, and you flattened him."

"May you release Helmet to my custody?"Asked Paul.

"No complaint, he is sober now. I don't see why not."

"Thank you." Paul turned towards the chastised soldiers and yelled what he was doing. In a heartbeat, the men clicked heals, picked up the unconscious comrade, and the five Germans disappeared into the night.

"Now, could someone remove this metal beast?" asked the Marshall. "The cannon aimed at the jailhouse makes me nervous."

Back at home, Susan said to Mark, "Paul may have made some enemies this night. The gun crew is not his tank crew and did this out of drink and frustration. They are no longer in the German Army. Paul hurt their pride in public even if he was the senior officer."

"Well, we have his back, my dear. The Germans will have to learn how we do things or suffer the consequences. We are trying to civilize stuff around here. They do not realize what would happen if the Emperor was in charge."

The next day, Mark was tired as he was no longer a twenty or thirty-something who could bounce back after having a night of sleep interrupted.      He went to work in his downtown office anyways. A couple of cups of Freetown coffee (beans are grown in a local plant hothouse) with sweetener from a local unique 'candyplant' and added fresh cream helped make the morning survivable. Mark sighed. The more 'civilization' came to Freetown, the more paperwork and politics. Leslie Owens had provided him with telegraph cable from the Amazons again, asking when he would visit. The telegraph wire system had been an early major project. The telegraph and the holograph system from mountain tops beat the Hell out of the Emperor's carrier pigeons for distant communication. However, it also increased paperwork as now he must write replies.

Several petitions for new community improvement programs from local businesses, an application, and a fee for a merchant's license authorizing legal trade through Freetown ( transit control generated revenue), sat on his desk. Add a report from the three

Official Scouts Blue, Red, and Spotted Wolf, probably completed by Ivana, also demanded Mark's attention. Blue Baxter and Red MacBeth could read and write after a fashion. Spotted Wolf could read a bit, but his wife, Ivana, was the educated one; Blue said it was the best thing that happened when Ivana hitched up with the Wolf.

"Now we can have someone keep our accounts and papers, so we don't get cheated."

Also, the Freetown Scouts provided fresh meat for all the merchants and many other townspeople. The creation of a slaughterhouse and cattle herd would cut into the hunting industry, although dragon skin was always welcome.

There was a knock on his office door, and Mark called out, "Come in!" without looking up. Someone cleared their throat, and Mark looked up to see Helmut Ritgen, standing hat in hand.

"The Lieutenant said you freed me."

"I withdrew my complaint about taking a swipe at me, yes."

"I thank you, Sir."

"Aren't you glad you didn't shoot me?"

"Ja, naturlich. I—was angry. I heard the Russian, remembered enemies, lost my temper. I apologize." The giant German stuck his hand out, and Mark stood to shake it.

"You have a good grip there, Helmut. I understand you come from a long line of butchers."

"Yes. I know my meat and cut it well."

Mark picked up a proposal from his desk. "I have a couple of merchants who want to build a meat locker here. We can start with ice from the Great Mountains until I can have some large refrigeration units built or recovered from the Smash Dump if they exist. A good butcher makes a meat locker work. Farmers and hunters can bring their animals in, even ask for help with the butchering, and their meat is kept from rotting until they use it. Think you can do that?"

Helmut stood tall. "Ja. I was the best butcher in my family when I went to war. Bring me meat; I show you."

"Well, if you plan on staying and can learn to live with Russians, once we build this locker, you'll have a job. Until then, we have a growing cattle yard out west of town that slaughters an animal about every other day. Think you can help them? The steaks I've seen look raggedy."

"Yes. Thank you, Sir. I go."

"Tell the stockyard people them I sent you. They'll listen."

Helmut nodded and turned to go, then stopped. "May I ask a question?"

"Sure, my large friend."

"I heard you are a duelist; they call you a pistol man. Is that true?"

"I have had to shoot a few people, yes. That is

how I met my wife, shooting some Chinese soldiers who were molesting her."

"You would have shot me?"

"If you pulled that Colt before the Marshal hit you, yes."

"Then I guess God was with us that day, Herr President."

"Yes, he was."

Helmut met the rest of the tank crew minus the Lieutenant for a beer at a local tavern. An old German brewmaster who had somehow fallen through the rabbit hole owned the place. It became the official meeting place for anyone who spoke German.

As the four crewmembers drank their beers, Helmut told them of his meeting with the President.

"*So, he is as they say?*" asked the tank driver Deitrich Baum. "*He is tough but fair?*"

"*Ja. And I checked with others in town. He has killed men in gunfights. He also said so when I asked.*"

"*So he would have shot you?*"

"*He said he would, and in his eyes, I saw he spoke the truth. My mouth almost put me in a coffin.*"

"*A coffin?*" Interjected the loader, Wolfgang Zimmerman. "*We would find someone to cut up our butcher and feed you to the local dragons. See if they could stomach your tough ass!*"

Helmut kicked Wolfgang and his chair over, and the crew laughed. They had decided to stay with their

Lieutenant as he kept them alive in many deadly situations. If Paul Hauser stayed in Freetown, they would stay. The War was over—for them.

The nasty ring of the old field phone woke up Mark and Susan once again. Mark cursed and swore as he fumbled for the phone.

"Yeah? What? I'll be right there."

"Who was that?" asked Susan.

"The Hospital. Someone shot Paul Hauser."

Mark and Susan left the Twins with the understanding Marianna and hustled to the Freetown Hospital. The on-duty medical personnel included former C-17 military personnel well versed in gunshot wounds from the Mid-East wars. Thus, Paul was comfortably resting when they arrived. A surprise was Leslie Owens standing outside Paul's hospital room talking with Marshal Dillon. Susan contacted the medical staff and reviewed the treatment record as Mark walked up to Leslie.

"Fancy meeting you here, my Amazon friend."

"Well, since I killed the shooters and brought Paul here. that should explain it."

Mark's mouth fell open a bit as he looked at Matt Dillon. "Two of the Germans from the other night at the jail had some liquid courage and went looking for Paul. He wasn't alone."

Mark looked at Leslie.

"I always have my sword," she said. "They burst

into my hotel room, started shooting, and I started cutting. I was a bit slow on the cutting, so Paul was hit."

Mark gave Leslie a once-over. "Where're all the bloody clothes?"

"I wasn't wearing any."

The Marshal tried not to smile and only partly succeeded. Mark looked at the Marshal.

"Open and shut case of self-defense, I reckon as they said in the Old West."

"And that applies to Freetown. But I had better put a guard on Paul Hauser—"

"No need. Paul has an Amazon guard."

Neither the Marshal nor Mark argued with her.

The next day, Mark and Matt, with Susan as an interpreter, made it a point to track down the rest of the Germans. Helmut was ready to bust heads until the late attempted assassins' comrades convinced the rest they did not know about the planned shooting.

"Y'all have a choice. Shape up or leave," said Matt Dillon.

"And you will leave without the half-track or the tank. Your choice, make decisions."

The remaining soldiers consulted in private, and Helmut stepped forward as spokesmen.

"We will stay with the Lieutenant. We promise to follow orders."

"And you'll all find some jobs, plus be part of our Militia."

The Germans agreed, shook hands with Mark as President, and then went on their way.

"Think we can trust them?" asked the Marshal.

"Yes, I do. How about you, Susan?"

"They are German soldiers and are used to orders. I think they will toe the mark as you say."

"I hope. Otherwise, I think a certain Amazon will be on their asses."

Paul Hauser left the hospital a week later. He had two new scars from the bullets and a fiancé. Leslie had moved quickly and asked him if he wanted to have a pair bond, be married. Amazons asked their desired mates, not the other way around. Thus, Leslie did it the way of Elsewhen, not Earth. Mark gave Paul a job as a Militia Commander to help James Chou keep things on an even keel. Plus, the position meant he could ensure the tank and half-track were in working order.

Leslie pulled a sly move and had Paul hired as an official German Interpreter. The Amazons were not giant German speakers, nor had any desire to be very friendly in their contacts with the Imperials, also known as the Eastcoast Germans. There were no further incidents involving violence and the new arrivals. Freetown settled into a calmer day-to-day existence.

Mark Stone, President Pro Tem, sat on the porch sipping his drink once again. He watched as Leslie and Paul walked past on Main Street, hand in hand, with Leslie having her large sword sheathed across her back. He chuckled.

"What is funny, my husband?" Susan asked as she gently rocked the Twins in matching bassinets.

"Fate. Karma. Whatever you call it. As they say, Love wills out. Love will find a way. Even in Elsewhen."

"I believe February approaches in our modified calendar, Mark."

"Hmmm. So, Valentine's Day if we so chose? After all, I am President of all I survey."

"You sound like the Emperor."

"Hey, no need to be insulting. But do you think Valentine's Day would be a good day for a wedding?"

"Don't you think the bride and groom should be consulted?"

"I would not be surprised if Leslie has considered the date. That is unless the Amazons have a different calendar they impress on the new arrivals."

"Which then brings up the point of, what will her superiors think of her marrying or pair-bonding with a member of a group they are fighting?"

"Hmmm. I bet you, Susan, we will find the answer soon enough."

Mark Stone must have been clairvoyant as two days later, Commander Chabra Strangerfinder rode into town on the proverbial coal-black charger, flanked by four other Amazons. The group led two young white horses from a great lineage of horseflesh. Trailing behind was an oversized mule packed high. Mark and Liam hurried to meet the small entourage on Main Street.

"Commander Strangerfinder. What a pleasant surprise," Liam greeted the Amazon as the Secretary of State. Chabra slid from her horse with ease and wrapped a bearhug around Liam, then Mark.

"Friends. It is always pleasant to see you."

"What brings you here, Chabra?"asked Mark.

"Where is Leslie Dragonslayer? I must speak with her."

Mark noticed Chabra's smile seemed a bit strained as if painted on her mouth.

"I will find her for you, although news travels fast in Freetown."

As if to put truth to his statement, Leslie Owens ne Dragonslayer came striding up Main Street with Paul Hauser in tow. Leslie stopped two yards from Chabra and half bowed.

"Commander. I am glad you are well."

Chabra frowned at Paul Hauser. She then canted her head towards Mark and said, "President Stone, Is this—German a good man?"

*God, always so damned blunt*, thought Mark.

"I think so. Lieutenant Hauser is also a warrior and a commander of a war machine."

"I understand he was recently shot," the blonde female warrior said.

"Yes. An assassination attempt because Paul

stood up for what was right."

Chabra stepped up the Paul. "Show me your scars, warrior."

Paul Hauser's jaws tightened, and then Leslie stepped up to him.

"I will show you his scars if he wants. You are my commander, not his."

Chabra and Leslie then had a staredown as tension built. Paul cleared his throat.

"I would be happy to show you the scars on my chest. Will the Commander show me hers?"

Chabra stared at Paul. Mark was about to step in between them when the Amazon began to shuck her chest plate. Two of her aides stepped up and assisted her. Next came her Dragon leather vest, then her blouse, then her version of a sports bra.

"There. See my scars. This one on my breast is from the teeth of a rival for a promotion."

"You fight for advancement?" asked Mark.

"Sometimes. Now, German, your scars."

A small crowd was forming, and Marshall Dillon approached with his deputies. Liam waved him back with an 'okay' sign. The lawman stood and watched as he and his deputies stood between the Amazons and the public. Paul Hauser undid his uniform blouse and displayed the recent bullet holes and some other shrapnel scars.

"I have no dueling scars from Heidelburg as I never attended that university," Paul said with a hint of sarcasm. "I did study the saber."

Everyone seemed to be frozen. Then the zaftig Amazon grabbed Paul and crushed him to her bare bosom as she laughed. "I think you will do, even if you are a German."

Chabra then grabbed Leslie and hugged her. "I believe you must love this man to kill his attackers while nude."

"You heard of that?" said, Leslie.

"There are no secrets among Amazons. And we have brought wedding gifts."

"Your English has improved."

"I have been practicing with your Earth comrades. They miss you." As Chabra put her bra back on, she turned towards Mark. He did not look away when Chabra had displayed her lovely breasts and knew he would catch Hell when Susan found out.

"Our Queen and Captain Milner still request a meeting at Iron Mountain, President Stone."

"We've been kind of busy, Chabra. But I promise I will make time to get there."

"So, Hauser," Chabra said as she fastened her Dragon vest, "show me your war machine."

The Amazons crawled all over the tank and half-track as Paul explained the vehicle functions. Afterward, the Amazons and Freetown citizens went to the German Tavern and shared great mugs of beer. Chabra drank Paul under the table, which led to a giggle fit from Leslie and the other Amazons. Susan joined her husband and whispered in his ear that the next time she caught him looking at another woman's bare breasts, there would be Hell to pay.

"We have brought you two mounts to ride on your wedding day," said Chabra. "They are breedable so that you will have a new line of warhorses."

"How can I repay you?" Leslie asked her as Paul rested his head on the table.

"We are Sisters. He is your great love. I can tell. So, you may pay me by being happy."

"So, when can we expect a wedding or pair bonding for you, Chabra?" asked Liam.

She laughed. "I am too strong-willed and wear men out. I do not like women well enough to mate with a fellow female."

"You will be surprised, I predict. Just keep your options open."

They held the wedding on the alleged February 14th of Earth. Many people attended, and the gifts were legendary. That night, Susan and Mark snuggled together in bed.

"Do you want a wedding someday?" asked Mark Stone.

"Maybe. We are married in an official ceremony. Everyone knows we are husband and wife. A party would be nice."

"A wedding gets you gifts."

"We have gifts. Two beautiful children in a world not of our choosing."

"Once again, my wife is right. Come here, you; let's pretend it's our honeymoon."

"I thought you would never ask."

Later the President of Freetown lay awake. He remembered a life on Earth where he had a wedding and another wife. Was Cheri still worried about him? Had the years passed on Earth as they had on Elsewhen? The newly married couple had it more comfortable. They had no past marriages, children, or such complications pulling them back. Paul and Leslie could start anew.

Mark shifted and spooned his Elsewhen wife. No use worrying now. As they said, love conquers all.

He hoped.